DRAGONFLY MAID

THE QUEEN'S FAYTE
BOOK ONE

THE QUEEN'S FAYTE SERIES

Memory Thief (prequel story)
Dragonfly Maid
Slivering Curse
Shadow Rite
Guardian of the Realm

DRAGONFLY MAID

THE QUEEN'S FAYTE
BOOK ONE

D.D. CROIX

Fine Skylark Media
California

Fine Skylark Media
P.O. Box 1505
Lake Forest, California 92609-1505

Cover provided by Karri Klawiter
Editing services provided by Katrina Roets

D.D Croix
Dragonfly Maid: The Queen's Fayte Book One:
by D.D. Croix — 1st ed.
[1. Teen and Young Adult, Science Fiction and Fantasy, Historical — Fiction. 2. Teen and Young Adult, Mysteries and Thrillers, Fantasy and Supernatural — Fiction. 3. Science Fiction and Fantasy, Fantasy, Coming of Age — Fiction. 4. Science Fiction and Fantasy, Fantasy, Dark Fantasy — Fiction. 5. Science Fiction and Fantasy, Fantasy, Myths and Legends — Fiction.]

DEDICATION

To Persnickety the House Dragon for always reminding me to ask,
What if…?

CHAPTER ONE

I WAITED FOR my dragonfly beneath the low, morning clouds. I knew she would come. She always did when I ventured outdoors while the sun was up. I knew she would find me, even here, as I sat along the north wall with only my wool dress, petticoats, and maid's apron to protect me from the cold stone bench—embellished simply, as so many things at Windsor Castle were, with the VR insignia of Her Majesty Queen Victoria.

So, where was she? Where was the friend who could make me see reason? I needed to find her. I needed her comfort because right now I had none.

Back inside, every servant scurried to prepare for Queen Victoria's return from her Scottish retreat. I should be in there, too, peeling potatoes for Mrs. Crossey, the cook I assisted most days, but the summons from the House Steward had sent me into a panic.

The young page who delivered the order didn't tell me why I was being called in, but I excused myself just the same and told Mrs. Crossey I'd see to it immediately. Instead I'd come here, to the kitchen garden—an unauthorized detour, to be sure—but I needed time to compose myself. Experience had already taught me that nothing good ever came from being summoned to that dull, dank office.

But what was it this time?

Had a new complaint been lodged against me? I'd tried to be careful. I'd reported to the kitchen on time every morning this week and stayed until properly dismissed. I hadn't even palmed a single new trinket for my memory box. Not in several days anyway.

The more likely reason was the one twisting knots in my stomach and making my hands slick beneath my lambskin gloves. In the past month, two dozen members of the staff had been dismissed. Some of them maids in good standing with far better credentials than I. That I was next on the House Steward's dreaded list seemed not only possible but rather overdue.

The others, I'd heard, had their years in royal service to help them secure positions with prominent families. With only six months of experience, I couldn't hope to be so lucky. Girls like me usually ended up on street corners begging for coins, not employed in a royal castle. If I'd come into this world with any luck at all, I was sure it was used up the day I was delivered to the servants' door and handed a scullery maid's apron, even if it hadn't seemed so at the time.

If I was turned out now, I'd end up in a workhouse or worse. Probably worse.

What was I going to do?

"Dragonfly! Where are you?" I hissed the words through clenched teeth, my fists balled at my sides. I needed my friend. I needed her to tell me again all would be well.

Then I spied a shiver in the air; that small, silvery dart with the glittering wings.

Had she soared over the castle wall? Had she slipped through an oak tree's canopy? I hardly knew, but I was relieved beyond measure to see her hovering in front of me now, fixing me with her wide, violet eyes.

"Finally, you've come. Where have you been?"

Behind me, the creak of a door hinge told me we were no longer alone. At the intrusion, my dragonfly flew away.

No! I screamed the word without a sound, but she didn't turn back. She was already gone.

I steeled myself to face the House Steward's ire until a squeal of laughter filled the air. The intruders were only two maids, like myself. One of them was my roommate, Marlene Carlisle, who everyone called Marlie. She was a willowy girl with hair the color of wheat and a smear of freckles on her nose, and I recognized her happy Highland lilt at once.

I strode away along the gray pebble path, hoping she'd ignore me, as she usually did.

"Jane, is that you? What are you doing out here?"

I cringed and debated whether to keep walking.

"Mrs. Crossey is searching for you. She's beside herself. I'd get back inside if I were you."

As if she cared a whit about me. We shared a room in the maids' quarters, but little else. Most days we hardly spoke at all, which suited me just fine. If only this were one of those days.

Since she wouldn't let me be, I tucked a loose, dark curl behind my ear and muttered something about needing air. It wasn't convincing, not even a little. It certainly wasn't to Marlie's companion, a pretty but bossy girl named Abigail, who was tugging Marlie away.

And even now that girl glared at me.

I suppose I deserved it, but there wasn't time to regret those past mistakes now.

Marlie held her ground.

"Then come with us," she said.

I turned, startled by the invitation. She'd never invited me anywhere before. Was it pity? Did she know something I didn't? Did she already know my fate?

"Why?" I braced, fearing the answer.

"You spend too much time alone, silly. It isn't right. It

isn't normal."

Abigail laughed, but there was no joy in it. She leaned closer to Marlie and whispered, though loudly enough for me to hear, "Of course it's not normal. *She's* not normal."

Marlie nudged her away, but the words hit their mark. I swallowed hard. I didn't care what they thought of me. I'd stopped caring what anyone thought a long time ago.

I was almost relieved when the kitchen door flew open again.

But my rage spiked when I saw it was only the new stable hand on his way back to the mews with a sandwich in hand. Not surprising. That young man ate more than any three men combined, though you'd never know it by the lanky look of him.

"Good morning, Mr. Wyck," Abigail called out in a singsong voice. "The farmer's girl didn't deliver the cream this morning, so we're off to collect it. Care to join us?"

It had become a game among the maids to try to win Mr. Wyck's favor, or at least get closer to that flop of chestnut hair and those scowling nutmeg eyes.

I don't know what they saw in him. There was nothing charming in the way he strutted through the kitchen whenever he pleased, pretending to be oblivious to the fuss and fluster he created among the young women. He was a nuisance, and a smug one at that.

"Jane Shackle! There you are. What in the world are you doing out here? Mr. MacDougall won't wait all day."

Mrs. Crossey leaned out the door and waved me in with a sweep of her thick, fleshy hand.

I resisted the urge to glance at Marlie, Abigail, or Mr. Wyck. If they observed this humiliation, I didn't want to know. It was better to think they were on their way to wherever they were going and that they weren't taking the slightest interest in me.

It was wishful thinking, to be sure. If my dragonfly were here, she'd laugh and tell me to expect a thorough account to be conveyed in whispers from maid to page, footman to cook, and underbutler to valet before the evening meal.

And she'd be right, of course, because that's how things worked around here. Servants know everything.

~ ~ ~

I stood at Mr. MacDougall's closed office door, staring into the whorls of the wood grain. There was nothing exceptional about them. The door was as plain as any along this narrow hallway.

It was just far too familiar. Every disagreement, every complaint lodged against me—they all led me here. I'd lost count of the times I'd faced this door and the man within.

"Go on, then," Mrs. Crossey whispered, her wide, ruddy face appearing at my shoulder.

Though we stood eye to eye, she still treated me like a child instead of a young woman nearly eighteen years old. I shook her off, tugged at my gloves, and knocked twice.

"Enter!"

The baritone command carried the man's typical rise at the end of the word that always set my nerves on edge.

"Don't just stand there," Mrs. Crossey prodded.

"I know." I didn't mean to be curt, but fear was getting the better of me. I didn't want to lose my job. I didn't want to end up in a workhouse. I'd already endured Chadwick Hollow School for Orphaned Girls, a dumping ground for unwanted daughters with nowhere else to go. I'd received adequate food and lodging, and a serviceable education, but it was no place for a girl with secrets to hide. I learned that early enough, and I imagined a workhouse would be much the same.

I wouldn't survive it again.

"Go!" Mrs. Crossey reached around, turned the brass knob herself, and gestured forward.

I had no choice. I smoothed my apron, steeled my nerves, and slipped in with my head held high.

Mr. MacDougall sat behind his desk, scratching something into a leather-bound ledger. He dipped his nib in the inkwell and scribbled again before looking up at me through those ruthlessly tangled brows.

I dropped my gaze to the worn toes of my black boots, but every muscle, every nerve remained riveted on the skeleton of a man before me. "Can I just say again," I said, grasping for a thread of hope, "how sorry I am about the trouble with Abigail's locket? It was a misunderstanding, truly. I don't know why she would accuse me."

"This has nothing to do with Abigail's locket."

The voice was behind me. I whipped around to see Mrs. Crossey standing in front of the closed door, fussing and fidgeting like the time the oven's firewood refused to light or when I'd added sugar instead of salt to her soup.

Why was she still here? She'd never stayed for my interrogations before. I wanted her to leave.

But she intended to stay. I could see it in the soft crease of her forehead and the distress tugging at her hazel eyes. She looked from me to Mr. MacDougall and said, "Shall we begin?"

She was part of this? My stomach churned.

Mr. MacDougall leaned back into the embrace of his wingback chair with nothing but contempt in his dark eyes. Then he rose from his desk and settled his arctic glare on Mrs. Crossey. "Madam, I must caution against it."

She straightened to her full height and jutted her chin, which was usually lost in the soft folds of her jaw. "I understand your hesitation, but I must insist."

I stared at her, too perplexed to speak. Within the castle—among the kitchen servants, at least—Mr. MacDougall's word was law.

My fear for myself became fear for her. Had she lost her mind?

Yet I saw no outrage in his cavernous eyes, only a flicker of something I didn't recognize. As I watched, he seemed to shrink where he stood, like a wild dog suddenly, inexplicably tamed. He pivoted and considered his reflection in the mirror above the mantelpiece behind his desk. Licking one finger, he ran it across his brows, straightening the wiry hairs, then laid a hand on one of the two protruding dragon heads carved into the corners of the mantel's shelf and stroked it between the ears like a pet before turning back to us.

His grimace landed on me, making it clear that Mrs. Crossey had nothing to fear. I did.

My fingers hid in the folds of my skirt.

Mrs. Crossey gestured to the pair of wooden chairs in front of the desk. "Take a seat, dear."

Motherly concern laced her voice, but there was pity there as well. I pulled back. My fears had been right after all. The emotion passed through me in a wave before calm resignation took hold. I swallowed and straightened to my full height. "It won't be necessary. I'll clear out my room and be gone before afternoon tea."

She frowned. "You'll do what?"

"If I'm to be dismissed, it's best to be done with it."

She shook her head. "No one is dismissing you, child." She mustered a weak smile, but something weighed on her.

"Then why am I here?"

She turned to Mr. MacDougall. He only shrugged. In denial or acquiescence, I hardly knew.

The woman shot him a nasty look before facing me again. "Do sit, Jane. This may take some time."

Baffled but curious, I took a chair.

She squeezed herself into the one beside it, her usually serene eyes flaring with strange intensity. "Let's discuss your visions."

Her words sucked the air from the room. I'd never spoken of my visions here. Not ever. Windsor was supposed to be my chance for a fresh start. I shifted and tried to swallow. "I'm sorry, my what?"

"Your visions." Again, she looked at Mr. MacDougall.

Again, he looked away.

She sighed and leaned toward me. "My dear, we've asked you here because we need your help."

CHAPTER TWO

"MY HELP?" THE words slipped out with an unfortunate squeak.

The House Steward took his seat and leaned across his monolith of a desk. "As we improve our household efficiency and adjust our staff to align with His Royal Highness's expectations, we find ourselves... shall we say, shifting responsibilities, which, uh, traditionally..." He tugged at his starched collar and cleared his throat.

"That isn't helping, Mr. MacDougall."

I frowned at Mrs. Crossey's blunt assessment, but she wasn't wrong.

The House Steward pulled back and stared down at his steepled fingertips.

Mrs. Crossey stared at me. "Jane, I believe your visions make you uniquely qualified to help us with a particular problem. A serious problem."

She spoke with such certainty. But how could she know? It made no sense. Since words failed me, I stared at my hands. My gloves! Had they betrayed me? The soft, white leather that protected me from the images and the voices and all the emotions that had struck only sporadically throughout my life but now occurred without fail at the merest touch. There had been a few curious glances when I began wearing the gloves, but no one said anything. Most hardly seemed to notice at all. Mrs. Crossey had only pondered them a moment the first time I wore them to the kitchen.

"Those are new," she'd said as I tightened my grip on a cleaver and sliced leaves off celery stalks.

"They are," I replied, staring hard at my hands and wishing I could melt into the floor. "It's so cold in here, don't you think?"

At that she had quirked an eyebrow and offered one of her half smiles. "No, but if you're more comfortable that way." Then she'd turned back to whatever she had simmering on the stove and never said another word about my gloves. That had been two weeks ago now.

"How long have you had them?" she demanded now. Her eyes still fixed on me, taking in every twitch and fidget.

"The gloves?" I asked.

"The visions."

"I don't know what you mean." My fingers burned beneath the usually cool leather. Blood pounded against my ears. I wanted to leave this room. Get away from her and Mr. MacDougall and everyone. I wanted to be alone.

"It's all right, dear," she said. "There's no need to be afraid."

Her usually comforting manner only heightened my panic. I knew what happened when people learned my secret. It was one of my first memories at Chadwick Hollow. A lesson I'd never forgotten, and I suspect I never would.

She cocked her head to the side. "If it makes you feel any better, I have known for quite some time."

Why should that make me feel better? I tensed and shook my head. She was lying. She had to be.

Mrs. Crossey's silence taunted me.

"I... I... I don't know what you've been told," I said,

"but—"

Mr. MacDougall scoffed. "You see, Mrs. Crossey? This is all a mistake. Just as I said."

Mrs. Crossey rocked back and pinned him with a menacing look. "I will continue, Geoffrey."

The House Steward's bushy brows pulled low. "I hardly think that's wise. If certain people were here, I'm sure they would agree."

"Noted. However, certain people are not here, which leaves the matter to my discretion."

I stared, amazed and puzzled as he looked away with an almost imperceptible shake of his head.

I hoped that would be the end of it, but instead she leaned forward and addressed me with even greater intensity.

"This is all rather complicated," she said, "but you should know we are aware of your visions because you are one of us, dear."

"Of course I am." I winced at the desperation in my voice. I took a deep breath and tried again. "I've worked here six months already."

She waved me off. "I'm not referring to your service. Not exactly."

Mr. MacDougall groaned and dropped his head into his hands.

Mrs. Crossey's eyes remained on me. I shifted under the weight of that stare.

"I'm speaking," she said, "of those within the castle who understand the purpose of your gift."

"My what?" I had never considered my visions a gift. An affliction was more like it. Perhaps a curse.

"Don't play coy, dear." Her fingers flexed into fists. "As I said, I have known about your circumstances for quite some time. You see, I'm acquainted with your former headmistress. More than acquainted, actually. Miss Trindle is my sister."

That grim woman was Mrs. Crossey's sibling? I fell

back against the chair's wooden spindles. The two were so different. Miss Trindle's whisker-thin frame towered over Mrs. Crossey's shorter, stouter stature, and I could count on one hand the number of times I'd seen her smile. How could they possibly share a mother?

But then, what did I know of mothers? I didn't know how to respond, so I simply held my ground. "I don't know what you think you know or what you were told, but it isn't true."

I would not repeat that old mistake. If nothing else, Miss Trindle had at least taught me that.

"Listen to the girl, Mrs. Crossey." Mr. MacDougall's voice rattled the walls. He rose to his feet, and his gaze bored into her. "Just as I said. This is nonsense. I insist you stop this madness."

Mrs. Crossey shot up from her chair. "It is not madness. Jane, whether you like it or not, your gift marks you for a particular purpose. An important and noble purpose."

Was she trying to trick me with flattery? It wouldn't work. I knew the truth. My visions were no gift, and I had no important or noble purpose. "Whatever you think you know, you're wrong."

Her bosom rose and fell with a heavy sigh. "I wish we could give you more time, so this would be easier for you. But time is a luxury we do not have."

I listened without reacting, silently begging her to release me from this room and this interrogation. I almost wished for a permanent dismissal now. At least my secret would still be safe.

She rose and paced and pinched her bottom lip, retreating into her own thoughts. When she turned back, her eyes sparked with fresh determination. "Here is the whole of it, Jane. The Queen is in danger, perhaps *mortal* danger."

"Mrs. Crossey!" Mr. MacDougall's face bloomed red with rage. A vein bulged in the middle of his forehead. "I must protest."

She ignored him.

Yet her statement was absurd. It was beyond belief. "If that's true, why are you telling me? Go alert the guard."

"We cannot," was Mrs. Crossey's curt and ready answer. "There would be questions."

"What's wrong with questions?" She was comfortable enough asking them. Why not answer a few?

She clasped her hands. Her jaw clenched. "We couldn't explain how we came by this information."

I looked at Mr. MacDougall. He rolled his eyes, whether at me or her or the whole mess of this exchange I didn't know.

"The answers would be troublesome," she added. "Suffice it to say, we don't wish to share our secrets for reasons much like your own."

I stiffened and chose to ignore the obvious trap. "If you cannot share your source, are you sure you can trust it?"

Mr. MacDougall and Mrs. Crossey shared a look. He seemed to be screaming with his eyes, "Please stop!"

And for once, I agreed with him. This back and forth was tiresome. I would not give in and, it seemed, Mrs. Crossey would not give up. I only wanted to leave this room. This cold, airless, windowless cave of a room.

Mrs. Crossey ignored the House Steward's silent plea. She pulled a kerchief from the wrist of her sleeve and held it out to me. It was a small scrap of white linen with a border of simple lace that she always carried with her. "Take it."

Before I could move, Mr. MacDougall lunged across the width of his desk, trying to grab the square himself. "You cannot do that!" he cried.

Mrs. Crossey pulled the kerchief back before he could snatch it and stared him down. "I can, and I will."

Despair clouded his expression. Or was it fear? He pulled back.

Again, she extended the kerchief to me.

I knew I shouldn't take it. I'd been tempted many times to swipe it in the kitchen. To spirit it away for a momentary window into her past. But now that she was offering it of her own free will, I was powerless to resist.

I grabbed it, tugged off a glove, and held the kerchief's gentle fabric in my bare hand. Such a soft weave, worn smooth from years of use. I imagined I could feel every thread, every fiber, every loving touch.

I glanced up. In Mrs. Crossey's eyes, I could see she knew what she was doing.

And she knew I could no longer deny the truth.

I closed my eyes and waited for the vision.

The sun sat low on the horizon, glinting through the green canopy of an ancient oak, its gnarled branches rising like crooked fingers to the sky. In its shadow stood a gray stone house, thatched with straw that glowed gold where the sunlight brushed its edges.

A small but tidy dwelling. Five paned windows along its length. Two chimneys, one at each end, and a Dutch door beneath a bundle of dried rosemary.

I caught the scent of the herb in the whispering breeze and breathed it in.

"We're home," squealed a young girl beside me, a long blond braid swinging across her back. She kicked pebbles as a basket filled with carrots, eggs, and a fresh loaf of bread dangled from her arm.

Her blue eyes sparkled with delight, and freckles gleamed upon her nose. "C'mon, Sylvie, let's race."

I shook my head. "You'll drop the eggs. Mother will send us back to the village if you break them."

We'd already spent more than half the day walking to the market and back, and I didn't want to waste the rest repeating the errand. There were still kitchen chores to do, and I'd have to hurry to get to the woods before sundown. Mother never let me out after nightfall, and I knew he'd come this

time. I just knew…
  "Let's race, Sylvie. C'mon."
  I shook my head. "Ida Trindle, I already said no."

Ida Trindle. The name jolted me out of the vision. I opened my eyes, curled my fingers into my palms, and waited for the swirling sensation to stop. Slowly, I settled back into myself.

Mr. MacDougall leaned over his desk, his gaze as sharp as a sword.

Mrs. Crossey watched me, too, her fingers clenched in her lap.

I stared at her, trying to reconcile the stern, mature woman in front of me with the young woman I'd inhabited only a moment ago. "Sylvie?"

Mrs. Crossey's eyes widened. She nodded, a glint of triumph in her eye.

"Did you see something?" barked Mr. MacDougall.

"I saw…" I clamped my mouth shut and swallowed hard.

"Say something," Mr. MacDougall bellowed. "Tell us what you saw."

"I saw…" My voice died as the magnitude of what I'd done settled over me. I'd been foolish and now that weakness was going to ruin everything, just as it had at Chadwick Hollow. Pressure pulsed at my temples. Stupid, stupid, stupid.

Even if I kept my job, I couldn't live with the whispers or the furtive looks branding me a monster. That's what would happen if I told them. Instead, I shut my eyes and swallowed that old pain. "I saw nothing, sir."

The shine of hope died in Mrs. Crossey's eyes.

Beneath our feet, the floor trembled and the walls rattled. I recognized the sound. Horses and coaches, teams of them, descending on the castle.

The royal family was home.

I seized the excuse and shot from my seat. "There's still

so much to do. I have to get back to the kitchen. Please understand."

By the time Mrs. Crossey called out, I was already out the door, and I didn't look back.

CHAPTER THREE

AS I STORMED out of Mr. MacDougall's room, I knew I'd sealed my fate. A kitchen girl couldn't defy Mr. MacDougall without consequences.

It was still better than the alternative.

Those old pangs of shame and regret ripped through me. I could see those girls again, huddled around me. Repulsion in their eyes. Their spiteful words slicing my nine-year-old self to shreds.

I'd only wanted to impress them by telling them what I'd seen when I picked up little Dottie's rag doll in the play yard. A mother setting up a picnic on a grassy hill beside a pond. A father rowing on the water. A child basking in the loving glow of that happy moment under a clear blue sky.

A vision had never before manifested so clearly, or with so many details. I'd been so utterly charmed by it, I was sure it would charm them, too. At least I'd hoped so. Being new to the school, I'd wanted desperately to win their favor.

But any chance of that died when I told little Dottie what I'd seen. Instead of welcoming the memory, it had stirred something dark in the girl. Something that crumpled her expression and sent rivers of tears streaming down her face. Instantly, the others had rallied to protect her from me, not understanding my intent or not caring.

Dottie had told them there was no earthly way I should have known about that day and that it was pure cruelty to rekindle it when her parents had died not a fortnight later, both of them, from fever. When she called me a devil, the rest of the girls had taken up the taunt.

I'd stood there, watching their faces contort as they spewed those savage words at me until Headmistress Trindle appeared and dragged me away. She'd taken me to her office and tried to console me, but when I told her about Dottie's memory, she looked at me as horrified as the rest. "Never speak of such things again," she begged. "It's for your own good."

I'd followed her advice from that day on—until today.

I wanted to blame Mrs. Crossey for tricking me, but I knew the fault was mine. I was weak and that's why I had to leave. Before it got worse.

~ ~ ~

The royal retinue of horses and carriages had converged on the State Entrance Tower, so I set my course for the East Terrace, keeping my head down and my feet moving. A determined pace would keep questions at bay about why I was out of uniform and what a bulging carpet bag was doing under my arm.

At least I hoped it would.

I didn't want to explain myself or why I was leaving. I didn't want to think about any of it. Not now. Maybe never.

I hurried along the narrow stairwell connecting the maids' quarters to the ground floor. Through dim corridors. Past the mending room and the butler's pantry, and finally to a heavy door that opened to a small lilac patch.

Darkening clouds threatened rain, but I pressed on, my

gaze on the path ahead, threading through the manicured rose bushes and shrubs with my sights set on a gate well away from the commotion.

A familiar disturbance filled the air as I neared the fountain at the center of the terrace garden.

I lifted my finger and welcomed the soft landing of six tiny feet.

"What took you so long?" I whispered so a pair of gardeners pruning a nearby shrub wouldn't overhear.

My dragonfly danced forward and back, making her needle-like body and wings shimmer in the scant sunlight. Her movements spoke to me as clearly as any words. They told me her moods, her thoughts, her complaints. I sensed them now as I always did through our silent communication. She wasn't happy.

"Yes, I'm leaving." I looked away. "But you can come, too."

Did she think I would leave her?

She was my only friend. From the moment she landed on my knee as I sat beneath the oak tree behind Chadwick Hollow plotting my escape—I was twelve then and convinced I could fend for myself. But this remarkable dragonfly had turned her wide violet eyes up to me, and in that moment, I knew she was urging me to stay. Telling me, in her way, that if I was patient, a better path would come. And she was right, for I didn't know it then, but the headmistress was already grooming me for a life of service.

My little visitor had come to me every few months or so back then. While I walked along the stream that meandered behind the school or sat among the grove of old trees. If the visits had been more frequent, I might have given her a proper name. But *dragonfly* seemed to fit and so it has remained.

My dragonfly.

When I first learned I was to leave Chadwick Hollow for Windsor Castle, my heart broke as much at the prospect of losing her as losing the only home I'd known.

But somehow, she followed me. I found her on my first day at the castle, perched on the ledge beyond my window. It had been such a happy moment, a welcome balm for an otherwise distressing day.

Right now, she seemed to regret that decision to join me. She was in one of her moods again. Stomping as much as her tiny legs could stomp.

"I have no choice," I said. "They know about me. I mean, I think they do. Mrs. Crossey was asking questions."

My friend froze. Her pearlescent eyes locked on me.

"What do you know about Mrs. Crossey?"

The little one dipped her head.

"I didn't tell them anything. Of course I wouldn't."

Her tiny stare held mine again. No head dip, no dance. None of her usual gestures.

How did she know I wasn't telling the whole truth? How did she always know?

"Fine. I might have said something, but it was vague. They only suspect. Maybe just Mrs. Crossey, but still—"

She stamped her feet as though she were stamping out a fire.

"You do know something about Mrs. Crossey, don't you?"

Her head dipped once, then again.

"You're not making sense."

Instead of explaining herself, she flew away.

I wheeled around, my gaze following her trajectory. "That isn't nice," I called out. "You could at least answer the question."

I had no intention of letting her off so easily, but the argument would have to wait. She had found me once, so I was sure she could again, and I had reached the lower gate. The metal bar was down; an ancient-looking hinge that might have been forged when William the Conqueror first built his fortress here more than seven hundred years ago.

I knew from previous visits that the gate didn't lock from this side. Its purpose was to stop outsiders from coming in, not insiders from going out. I'd learned that lesson after my first stroll to the river's edge. I'd been forced to walk all the way back to the King George IV Gate to get back in.

Since then, I made sure to prop the door open with a sturdy rock. Out of habit, I grabbed a cobble-size limestone as I approached before realizing I wouldn't need it this time.

I dropped the stone, and it landed with a thud at my feet. As I lifted the latch, I paused for one last look back.

To think, this castle had stood on this mount for a thousand years and would likely stand a thousand more. Its time here would go on even if mine had come to an end. My jaw tightened against the unexpected emotion creeping up my throat.

"There you are. What took you so long?"

At the sound of Mrs. Crossey's cheerful voice, my head snapped forward. I found her leaning against the wall on the other side of the gate, still in her kitchen apron and with a worn issue of *Englishwoman's Domestic Magazine* opened to the recipe pages.

I opened my mouth but found no words.

"I've been waiting for you," she continued. "Come. Walk with me."

CHAPTER FOUR

I STOOD AT the gate, stunned into silence and gaping as Mrs. Crossey dog-eared the page she'd been reading and closed the magazine.

"You appear to be leaving us." She might have been remarking on the weather, not catching me mid-escape.

I didn't trust myself to speak. She looked like the same, sweet woman I'd worked alongside for so many months. The friendly mentor who had taken me under her wing and who disappeared to the Servants' Hall or the garden with a magazine while a stew simmered or the porridge boiled yet always returned well before anything burned.

But how well did I really know her? After the exchange in Mr. MacDougall's office, I realized I knew very little.

"I thought it would be easier for everyone this way," I muttered.

Mrs. Crossey rolled her magazine and shoved it into a skirt pocket. "Fair enough. But stroll with me before you go. Just for a few moments."

When I didn't move, she tried again. "There's nothing to fear. There are simply things you should know before you make this decision."

My fingers tightened around my bag's brass handle.

"What things?"

She sighed and watched a crow take flight from a nearby tree, its throaty caw echoing across the hills. "You might think what happened today came out of the blue, but I assure you it didn't. It was always going to happen. I'd hoped to wait a bit, till after your birthday at least. But this matter with the Queen changes things." She paused and rubbed her lower lip. "And then there's the matter of your visions—" Her gaze dropped to my hands. My gloves.

"I told you, I don't have—"

She stopped me with a look. "Let's stop the nonsense, shall we? If I'm not mistaken, your visions have taken a turn. Grown stronger, yes? If you don't learn to control them…" She shook her head, unable or unwilling to continue.

"Then what?" I didn't care if she interpreted my concern as a confession. I had never seen that look on her face. Not just worry, but fear.

"Without training, you could lose control. But there's no reason to be alarmed."

"I'm not alarmed. I just want to be left alone."

"All right. If that's truly your wish. But as I said, there are things you should know. About your family, for instance."

At that, she strode past me, taking the path that meandered away from the gate and down a slope, toward a grove of trees that was nearly swallowed by a fog bank rolling off the Thames.

I kicked at the dirt. "I have no family." A noose tightened around my heart.

She turned back and watched me without saying a word.

Shifting, I watched a breeze drag its lazy fingers through the oaks and yews, making their branches sway. Then from somewhere in those hazy woods, another crow cried out and broke the silence.

She tilted her head. "We all have family. That's a simple fact of life." Then she turned and continued down the path.

"I don't remember them, so it hardly matters," I called after her.

"Wrong again," she called back. "Tell me what you do remember."

I didn't have to tell her anything. I could turn the other direction, toward the village, as I'd planned.

So why was a voice inside telling me to follow her? Telling me she might have answers to questions I'd stopped asking long ago but had never forgotten? The farther she walked, the stronger that feeling tugged.

Follow her.

I looked to the east, toward the village.

Follow her.

I looked at Mrs. Crossey, making steady progress. The distance between us widened.

Follow her.

Hiking my bag up to my shoulder, I hurried down the slope.

"Tell me the first thing you remember." She didn't look at me when I fell in step beside her or act the least bit surprised that I'd joined her, as if there had never been any question I would.

"The day I arrived at Chadwick Hollow, I suppose."

Yes, I'd given in, but she hadn't won. I was only playing along. I had my bag, and once I discovered what she knew—if anything—I'd still head for the village. She hadn't changed my mind. Only delayed me a little.

"It was my ninth birthday." May tenth, 1850.

I had replayed those hours in my mind so many times over the years, searching for clues to my past. I was sitting in Headmistress Trindle's office, staring at her desk. She was speaking, but I was more interested in two boxes in front of me. One, polished mahogany with shiny brass fittings, and another, a dull wooden cube with the faded image of a girl lacquered to its lid.

When the headmistress noticed my distraction, she told me the boxes were tea caddies. She'd received the newer one as a gift from grateful parents who'd just adopted one of my classmates. The other would be given to the charitable society, where all old but still useful things went.

The memory then jumps to that night as I crawled into my cot and the headmistress caught me stuffing that old caddy into a crevice between my mattress and the wall. When she asked why I had it, I confessed I'd taken it from her desk and hidden it under my coat.

"You can't send the little girl away," I'd said. "She'll be all alone in the world. It wouldn't be fair."

The headmistress mulled that for a moment then said, "No one is ever really alone in the world. And it seems you're in luck. Since today is your birthday, you may keep it. Consider it a gift. But don't let me catch you taking things that don't belong to you again. Do you promise?"

I'd nodded, and I kept that promise. I never stopped taking trinkets that caught my fancy, but she never caught me again.

"Nine years old, and nine years ago," Mrs. Crossey muttered to herself. She nibbled the tip of her thumb and counted to herself, "Forty-one? No, it couldn't. Maybe?"

"Why is it important?" It certainly wasn't to me.

She stopped and stared at me. "It's important because your mother must have been a Fayte Guardian."

"A what?"

"A member of the Order of the Fayte. Like me. Like many of us in the castle."

Was that a joke? A test? "I've never heard of such a thing."

"Of course you wouldn't. We're very careful about that." She sniffed with pride. "The Fayte Guardians are servants in the truest sense of the word and have been for nearly two thousand years. We're protectors, you see. Present yet unnoticed and always prepared to act." She frowned. "At least we were. Before this blasted efficiency campaign."

Alarm bells clamored inside me like the bells of St. George's Chapel on Sunday morning, and in my distraction, I stepped on a pebble, its sharp edge stabbing through the thin sole of my boots. I winced and limped and made more of the pain than was necessary because I didn't know what to say to her madness.

"You are a Guardian, too," she said, watching my theatrics. "Just like your mother."

I stopped. There was that word again. Mother. "Do you know something about her?"

Her eyebrows lifted. "Only that a gift such as yours passes from mother to daughter," she said. "So, it stands to reason that your mother possessed it, which would make her one of us."

"A Guardian?"

"A Fayte Guardian. Yes." She straightened and looked pleased with herself, probably thinking I believed her.

I let it pass and instead stared at the misty hills and darkening clouds. I didn't want to argue, not if she held some clue to my past.

"Tell me," she said, "do you remember anything about her? Your mother, I mean. Anything at all?"

How many times had I tried to conjure something from my past? A face, a touch, a voice. I'd tried everything and failed. "Nothing."

Her shoulders slumped. "I suppose I shouldn't be surprised. Ida mentioned it. No matter. There are other ways."

"Other ways of what?"

"Tracing the bloodline. The Fayte track such things. Births, unions, the emergence of gifts. There are records that could be consulted, should you wish it. Once this matter with the Queen is resolved."

It had been so long since I'd indulged the desire to know my parents. But here was a chance.

I was tempted, to be sure. But only for a moment.

The woman was clearly playing me for a fool. There were no Fayte Guardians or records. These were fantasies she'd probably invented to trick me. I didn't know why she would concoct such insanity, but it hardly mattered. I couldn't stay, and it should have been as clear to her as it was to me. I'd slammed the door on that possibility when I fled the House Steward's office.

Besides, it didn't matter what she knew or didn't about my family, did it? I was doing fine on my own. I shook my head. "That won't be necessary. The past means nothing to me."

A question formed on her face, then faded. "Of course. This isn't the time to drudge up the past. Not when you have your future to consider."

"My future?"

"I can see you're in a hurry. You must have something waiting for you. Or someone? A suitor, perhaps?"

Was she mocking me now? She knew I had no money or status to recommend me, and I certainly wasn't a beauty in any sense of the word. Not fat or thin, or tall or short. Plain brown hair and plain blue eyes. Simply average in all respects and altogether bland. I snorted. "I don't need a suitor. I intend to make my own way, thank you."

"I see. Then you must have a destination in mind."

If finding a decent inn in the village constituted a destination, then yes, I had one. But I wasn't about to share that plan with her.

Instead, I watched the sky continue to darken as we neared the grove. The treetops and dense fog seemed to be swallowing what was left of the pale sunlight. I pulled my coat more tightly around myself and tried to fend off the chill as mist clung to my cheeks and dampened the hem of my skirt as it swished through the tall grasses. If I wasn't mistaken, rain would be upon us soon.

I hurried closer to the trees for protection. They were sturdy old oaks already thick with springtime leaves. I spied one just inside the thicket. A taller, wider, and lusher specimen that would surely keep us dry. But as I turned to tell Mrs. Crossey, something rustled beneath the underbrush of dead leaves and fallen twigs.

A squirrel? A mouse?

The hidden creature crept closer. I kicked the leaves in front of me to shoo it away. Then I saw it wasn't an animal at all. It was a tree root thicker than my arm snaking toward me. It stopped not more than a foot from my boots and shot up to entwine itself around my right wrist. Once, twice, three times around.

I tugged and pulled, but nothing helped.

"Stop!" I cried, but to no avail.

A black, burning fear speared through me. My chest heaved, and I gulped the cold wet air as I fought to free myself.

Still that serpent root held tight. Then a murky crimson mist rose from it and separated into tendrils that encircled my limb.

Heart racing, I yanked harder again and again.

The root's grip only tightened, and when the misty shadows closed around me, they merged into inky, solid darkness.

Somewhere in the distance, I heard someone scream.

Or was it me? I didn't know anymore. I didn't know anything.

Then, in an instant, my panic dissolved. Fear, pain, panic. Everything I saw, everything I felt, it all slipped into crimson light before vanishing altogether.

CHAPTER FIVE

SOMEONE SLAPPED MY cheek. I wanted to complain, but I couldn't move.

Another slap. Harder this time.

My eyelids fluttered. My lips twitched.

Where was I?

"Jane! Wake up!"

I recognized Mrs. Crossey's voice, but she was so far away. And frightened.

"Wake up, girl. Don't slip away."

I opened my eyes. Gray forms emerged from the blackness, only shadows then dim, hazy colors.

"There you are. Oh, thank goodness."

The woman wrapped her fleshy arms around my shoulders and rocked me. I sank into the cushion of her lap.

"What happened?" My words stuck like dry biscuit crumbs to my tongue.

"Don't worry about that now. You're here. You're well."

I let her words soak in. I was here. I was well.

But where had I been? What had happened?

The questions melted against her soft ministrations.

I closed my eyes.

"No, no, no. Don't drift off. Tell me what happened."

I shook my head, or tried to. Images seeped back. "The tree." My stomach clenched at the memory. "It grabbed me." Even as I said the words, I didn't believe them. It wasn't possible.

"What did you see?" she insisted. "Do you remember?"

"A root. Wrapping…"

Other memories returned. Streaks of red light tangled around my arm. And eyes. Fiery red eyes with thin, black pupils. Unnatural. Terrifying. I remembered falling, plunging into nothing, an endless descent.

I cringed. I didn't want to remember. I wanted the emptiness again. The nothing.

"What is it?" Mrs. Crossey shook me gently.

"I'm tired."

She shook me again until I opened my eyes. "We can't stay here. It isn't safe."

Where could I go? I couldn't move.

But Mrs. Crossey was already yanking me to my feet.

Something glinted in her hand. Her magazine? No. It flashed gold with a glimmer of violet light before she shoved it and the cord on which it was attached back beneath her collar.

"What was that?" I stared at her. An icy prickle skittered up my spine.

"Nothing." She brushed the dirt off her backside then brushed at my skirt, too. "Let's get you back inside, shall we?"

A new fear washed over me. "Where's my bag?"

"It's here. Right here."

And so it was. Behind me, where I must have dropped it.

But how could she act so calm? A tree root had attacked me. *Attacked* me. Wasn't that cause for some alarm? Or had I imagined it? "Did you see it?" I asked.

"See what, dear?"

"The tree. The root."

I bent to grab my bag and nearly lost my balance.

Mrs. Crossey threaded her arm around my waist. "There, there now."

When I was steady again, I shimmied out of her grasp. She had only touched my coat, but I had to be careful.

"Sorry," she said, pulling her arm back. Then she bent and picked up my bag with her other hand. "Let's get you back to the castle now, shall we? Away from this…"

Her voice trailed off, and I followed her gaze to the massive tree. Was it a shadow, or was its bark actually black?

Maybe it was the fog or my raw nerves, but the ridges along its contours seemed to slip and slither, like pythons gliding over its surface. I closed my eyes but they were there again, those red, grimacing eyes and crimson tendrils like talons gripping my arm. My hands shot to my face. "I don't want to go back." I stumbled back and nearly fell.

She caught me at the elbow. "I'm afraid that would be a mistake."

Her tone sent icicles through my veins.

I stared at her. Directly into her eyes. "Why?"

She didn't want to answer. I could see that.

"Then I'm leaving. Give me my bag."

"You're in no condition to go anywhere."

My legs were nearly steady. My mind clear. "I can manage."

"I'm sure you think you can, but there's too much you don't know. Not yet anyway."

Anger churned in my gut. "So tell me," I said, and probably more harshly than I should, but I'd had my fill of her nonsense.

"All right," she relented. "I know you have questions, but I can't answer them here. What I can say is I believe you're in danger if you leave this castle. If you stay, I can protect you."

"From what?"

She closed her eyes, but only for a moment. When she looked at me again, she was as somber as I had ever seen her.

"I fear whatever attacked you will do so again. And that's my fault. I should have prepared you. I've already wasted too much time."

"But how? I haven't done anything."

Another crow screamed out across the Slopes, and then a dozen or more rose from the grove's dense canopy. Mrs. Crossey watched them with obvious alarm. "We must go. You will be safer in the castle until we sort it out."

I held my ground. "But I can't go back, even if I wanted to. Not after what happened. Mr. MacDougall must be furious. He won't take me back."

She scoffed and shook her head. "Never mind about Mr. MacDougall. It's not for him to decide."

~ ~ ~

At my bedroom door, I listened before turning the knob and gave thanks for the silence within. No voices, no footfalls, nothing to indicate Marlie lurked within.

If she'd finished her errand, she was probably back in the kitchen, and for that I was relieved. Questions were the last thing I wanted to face just now. About Mr. MacDougall's summons, about my absence from the kitchen, and certainly about the carpet bag on my arm that was holding every one of my few worldly possessions.

I just wanted to be alone.

After closing the door behind me, I hung my coat from a peg and dropped my bag into the wardrobe Marlie and I shared. I fell onto my bed in an exhausted and bewildered heap, still at a loss to explain what had happened beyond the castle wall.

A fairy tale about secret protectors in the castle? Guardians disguised as servants? It was utter madness.

Then to be attacked by a tree? I wouldn't—*couldn't*—

have believed it if I hadn't awakened from that swoon with dirty streaks along my skirt and the smudges along my sleeves and gloves where the root had coiled around me like a snake.

I would have thought it a bad vision, but I'd never seen anything like those eyes in a vision before. Not a face, not a body—just piercing reptilian eyes that not only saw me but seemed to see *all* of me. My thoughts, my feelings, my fears. Everything.

I know you.

Had I imagined those words or had someone spoken them? I couldn't remember.

And what of Mrs. Crossey? Nearly as terrifying as those eyes was seeing genuine fear on her face. I might have suspected it was a ruse if I hadn't known, even in all that confusion, that she had been the one to free me from whatever that was.

What had she used? A golden charm? A talisman of some sort? My wits were so muddled it was impossible to know for sure.

Maybe I didn't know anything for sure.

Yet here I was. Back in the castle. Back in this stark, little room with two narrow beds, one plain wardrobe, and a slender window that looked out over the outside world. My safety had seemed to be Mrs. Crossey's primary concern, but it couldn't be her only one. She had intended to stop me from leaving and here I was.

I punched my pillow and threw it against the wall. Perhaps it was a mistake to return. But even now, despite the doubts and regrets, a part of me believed her.

She had said I would be protected within these walls. But from what?

More images flooded back. Red tendrils twisting around my wrist, my elbow, my shoulder. My whole arm trapped by a powerful... not heat or cold, but both at once. A feeling like a thousand angry ants marching along my limb. I'd watched, frozen and afraid, as those smoky tendrils devoured my arm. Unable to move. Unable to do anything.

Grabbing the pillow again, I pressed it to my face, closed my eyes, and screamed.

I opened my eyes and the vision faded. But it returned the instant I closed them again. Feral, snakelike eyes closing in.

My heart thundered in my chest.

Mrs. Crossey had said I could lose control of my visions. Was this what she meant?

I jumped from my bed and dashed to my carpet bag. I plunged my hand down between the folded frocks and petticoats until I felt it: my memory box.

I dropped to the floor and balanced the old tea caddy on my lap. After tugging off one glove, I trailed my fingertips over the smooth edges, the faded image of the curly haired girl. Then I raised the hinged lid, revealing the treasures inside.

Hard, determined footsteps rattled the corridor and stopped me. I shut the box and shoved it back into my bag before the room's door flew open.

"What happened? Are you leaving?"

It was Marlie, breathless and confused as she stared at me, her eyes darting around the room for some evidence. Finding none, she pushed back a few blond strands that had come loose from her kitchen bonnet. Her flour-caked fingers left a powdery streak across her cheek.

"Of course not. Why would you think so?" I shoved the bag into the wardrobe and closed the door. "Shouldn't you be in the kitchen?"

"Shouldn't you? That's what Mrs. Crossey..." Her voice trailed off, and her eyes went wide as she noticed my dirty skirt and arms. "What happened to you?"

I stared down at the stains. "I fell."

Why was she so curious? She'd never taken an interest before.

"But how did it happen?"

I stared at her, unable to concoct a plausible excuse. Instead, I changed the subject. "What did Mrs. Crossey say?"

Frustration clouded her sky-blue eyes, but she let it go. "She sent me to fetch you. Just after Mr. MacDougall pulled her into his office for a private word. He didn't look happy, and neither did she when she came back. Are you in trouble?"

"I don't know." And truly I didn't. "Did he say something?"

"Not to me. They don't tell me anything."

I gnawed my bottom lip. Would she tell me if she could? I had no reason to think so.

"I'd have a care if I were you," she added. "It isn't wise to test Mr. MacDougall's patience, not unless you... you know." She pulled her thumb across her neck and stuck out her tongue, mimicking a corpse.

"I know." I also knew if Mrs. Crossey couldn't convince him otherwise, it wouldn't make a shred of difference whether I returned to the kitchen quickly or not.

"Then, c'mon," she said. "Before he notices we're both gone."

Why was she trying to help me? Why was she taking any notice of me at all? This was all very strange. "Is that the only reason you're here? To get me back to the kitchen?"

She tensed and her smile faded. "Of course, it is. If you're let go, who knows who they'll stick in this room. My last roommate snored. I don't want to go through that again. Now, are you coming or not?"

The smart thing to do would be to go with her, but still I held back. What if she asked more questions? What if I let something slip?

"You go ahead," I said. "I need to change." I brushed at the dirt along my side, but it didn't do any good.

Her nose wrinkled. "I guess an apron can't even hide that. Don't take too long, though."

When she closed the door, I breathed more easily, though I knew it was only a temporary reprieve. I still had to face Mr. MacDougall.

CHAPTER SIX

I ENTERED THE Great Kitchen to find Mr. MacDougall standing at the center of the room, announcing the evening assignments. We were all expected to attend these daily meetings—from the head chef, to the legion of cooks, bakers, and confectioners who reported to him, to the kitchen and scullery maids, including myself.

I bent my head and kept to the perimeter, weaving past the long row of stoves and worktables until I came to the corner where I helped Mrs. Crossey prepare the servants' daily meals.

She was standing over a tall copper pot, pouring in a stream of pearl barley with one hand and stirring with the other.

"What did I miss?" I whispered when I came up beside her, catching the scent of her savory soup.

"A bit of drama, to be sure," she whispered back. "The Royals want a private dinner alone with the children. Chef is beside himself."

It was no secret the head chef, a Frenchman with an affinity for fussy meals, had been working on a welcome home feast for well over a week. Pears and plums had been soaking in barrels of imported rum for days, molded cakes and pies were being assembled in the pastry room, and a beef shank was turning on a spit in the largest of the kitchen's hearths.

The man was pacing in front of it, spewing an angry stream of foreign invectives.

"Of course, I share your disappointment." Mr. MacDougall stood to his fullest height and stared down his nose at the chef. "But do not forget, we serve at Her Majesty's pleasure, not the other way around. Perhaps some of your delicacies might be reserved for the masquerade ball?"

The man wheeled on the House Steward. "*Bal masqué? Quel bal masqué?*"

Mr. MacDougall swallowed, making his Adam's apple dance. "Surely, you've been consulted, Chef. It's to be held Friday next."

"*Mon dieu!*" The Frenchman turned on his heels, threw up his hands, and spewed a fresh stream of French insults at the roasting carcass. Then he stormed out of the room, nearly splitting the swinging door in two as he went.

It wasn't the first time those in charge of the kitchen hadn't been apprised of an important event. Though the Lord Chamberlain and his staff planned and organized most of the castle's ceremonies and special occasions, orders to the kitchen staff and servants were handled by the Master of the Household, who delegated the duty through a long line of underlings. Sometimes the pertinent information was relayed in timely fashion, sometimes it was delayed, and other times it never trickled down at all.

Cynics blamed territorial grudges and strategic undermining, but it was easy to see how information could slip through the cavernous cracks of the castle's convoluted hierarchy.

Truly, it was no wonder Prince Albert wanted to simplify the mess with his efficiency campaign. It was just unfortunate that so far the only simplifying was dismissing the maids, pages, and footmen who merely took the orders, and not the legion of managerial deputies and assistants who gave them.

But if that particular injustice had dawned on Mr. MacDougall, he didn't show it as he smoothed his wiry eyebrows before turning and scanning the room, meeting every eye, daring anyone to speak. He stopped when he saw me.

"Jane Shackle," he growled. "Where have you been?"

I looked at Mrs. Crossey. She looked away. I searched for Marlie two tables away. She was absorbed in removing a bit of grime from under her fingernail, conveniently ignoring my distress.

I was on my own.

"Me, sir?" My voice cracked and I hid my hands to hide the gloves that, despite my efforts with water and cloth, still bore the signs of my earlier struggle. "I've been right here."

I might have flushed at the lie, but I'd done so much of it today, I was growing rather used to it.

Mr. MacDougall frowned. "I will have a word with you in my office. Now."

I sent Mrs. Crossey a pleading look.

She nudged her chin forward ever so gently. *Go*, she seemed to say.

As if I had choice.

Since I was closest to the corridor that led to his room, I approached it first. And for the second time that day, I steeled myself for what awaited me. I was preparing for the worst when I opened the door to let myself in.

"You?"

My head shot up to find Lucas Wyck already within and staring back at me from the chair where I'd sat only a few hours before. He jumped to his feet and appeared to be as troubled by the sight of me as I was of him.

Mr. MacDougall came up behind me.

"Mr. Wyck," he grumbled. "Why are you here?"

The stable hand doffed his cap and dark hair tumbled

over his forehead, partially eclipsing his view. "I was hoping to have a word, sir."

"Not now." Mr. MacDougall's tone left no room for negotiation.

Mr. Wyck dropped his chin to his chest. "Of course, sir." He moved around the chair and approached the door, and in doing so came within inches of me.

The usual fear of human contact gripped me. I recoiled. To avoid looking him in the eye, I stared at his hands. Surprisingly smooth and clean for a man who worked in the dust and muck of a stable all day.

"Is something wrong, Jane?"

Mr. MacDougall's words jolted me. I realized I was still staring where Mr. Wyck had been though he was already out the door and down the hall. I wrapped my arms over my chest in defense against the prickly feeling that gripped me. "No, sir. It's just rather cold in here."

The House Steward sneered. "You've obviously spent too much time at the ovens. It's a bit warm for my taste."

Not surprising, I suppose. And it likely explained why that monstrosity of a fireplace was always dark. The man was a walking icicle.

Instead of complaining, I tried to focus on something besides the goose flesh on my arms. My attention flitted from his desk to the burgundy rug beneath me, its pile matted and frayed by the boot heels of every sullen servant ever summoned to this room.

"Sit down," he demanded as he moved behind his desk, checked his appearance in the oval mirror, and settled into his leather chair.

I moved toward the seat Mr. Wyck had vacated, then thought better of it and settled into the other. I regretted it immediately. From this vantage point, the dragon heads in the mantelpiece seemed to stare at me over Mr. MacDougall's shoulder, their snarling mouths and sharp teeth a fierce if silent warning.

He leaned back and rubbed his jaw with his skeletal

fingers. "You know, Jane, I'm not sure what to make of you."

"What do you mean, sir?" Why was he scowling at me like I was an insect he wanted to crush?

"I mean, why are you here?"

Because Mrs. Crossey stopped me from leaving. Because a tree attacked me. I couldn't say these things, of course, not without sounding like a lunatic. "I was recommended by my schoolmistress, if you'll recall."

He stared, as though deciding whether I was telling the truth. "And that's all?"

"What else could there be?" The instinct to run clawed through me again, but this time I didn't budge. I knew he wanted me to leave. I could feel it like fire beneath my skin and it made me suddenly determined to stay. To spite him, if nothing else. I crossed my ankles, clasped my fingers, and returned his stare.

He seemed on the verge of saying something then stopped and glanced away. After a long moment, he muttered, "Let's be clear: I'll be watching you. Closely. Now return to the kitchen."

I rose before he could change his mind and made my way to the door.

As I hurried to put distance between me and that man, I thought about what Mrs. Crossey had said. *If you stay, I can protect you.* I wasn't so sure. She might be able to protect me from whatever lurked beyond the castle wall, but I feared the greater danger was staring daggers at me from behind that desk.

CHAPTER SEVEN

WHEN I RETURNED to the kitchen, Mrs. Crossey was at the worktable, cutting a beef roast into chunks with her cleaver. She saw me and jutted her chin at the pile of onions, carrots, and celery beside her. So, it was to be stew in the Servants' Hall this evening. Without a word, I pulled a knife from the caddy and grabbed a fat onion.

"Careful of the paper there." She pointed to the magazine pushed to the table's corner at my end. "I'm trying something new from Mrs. Beeton."

Mrs. Beeton was Mrs. Crossey's favorite columnist in the *Englishwoman's Domestic Magazine.*

"What's it call for there in the list of ingredients? One pint of beer or two?"

I leaned over to read it. "Just one."

"Suits me." She grabbed one of three pints beside her and took a quick, satisfied swallow.

When she saw my grin, she wiped her mouth and set down the bottle. "What? A good cook always checks the quality of her ingredients. In any case, I hope you agree the change is necessary."

My stomach clenched, and I nearly lost my grip on the knife. "What change? Mr. MacDougall didn't mention anything about a change."

She gave me a puzzled sort of look. "The change in duties, of course. Collecting the firewood for the Queen's room."

"He said nothing of it. He's giving me char duties?"

"Shh!" She waved away curious glances shooting our way. She leaned in, and I caught the lingering smell of tobacco and beer on her breath. "Not permanently and not entirely. Just an hour or so a day. It's a good thing."

I snorted and probably used more force than was necessary to chop the onion in half and trim its ends.

She took up her bowl full of meat and turned to the stock simmering on the stove behind us. Carefully, she laid each chunky bit into the pot. "You won't do much good if you're stuck down here all day."

But I didn't want to leave the kitchen. At least here I didn't have to speak to anyone but Mrs. Crossey. I didn't have to be careful about what I said or did. I could keep to myself.

And char duties? It ranked even lower than scullery maid. Or was that the point? Instead of firing me, he was demoting me. It didn't matter that I did more than just clean and stock Mrs. Crossey's station as I was assigned. I cleaned and cut the vegetables, measured out the flour and salt, even helped with the biscuits when she let me.

It was extra work, sure, but I hoped it would lead to something better.

"Don't look at me like that," she reprimanded. "This will allow you to move around more freely. And to move around *upstairs*."

My knife stopped mid-chop. "What difference would that make?"

"Come now. Isn't it obvious?" At my blank look, she shook her head. "When you're up there, you can use"— she raised her hands and wiggled her fingers.

So that was her plan? She wanted me to wander the castle in search of visions? I shook my head.

Her lips tensed in an angry line. Still whispering, she said, "You would prefer to stay down here and allow the Queen to be attacked?"

She practically spat the words, as though I should be ashamed. But why? I had nothing to do with these Guardians, or whatever they were. I was a girl hounded by visions I didn't want who just wanted to be left alone. I stared at the onion in front of me, at the knife, at the constellation of notches and stains in the wood. I stared at anything so I wouldn't have to meet the stare searing into the side of my skull. I wanted to tell her that, but I already knew the argument would get me nowhere.

Instead, I took what I hoped was a more practical approach. "My gift doesn't work that way," I said with strained control. "I see the past, not the future. Even if I wanted to do what you're suggesting, I couldn't. It's impossible."

She set down her copper bowl with a clatter. "I don't believe it is impossible. Of course, we won't know for sure until we begin your training."

My head shot up. My forehead wrinkled. "What training?"

"Training that will help you learn control, for one thing. We'll begin tonight. The sooner, the better, all things considered. Meet me in front of Mr. MacDougall's office at midnight."

Midnight? She couldn't be serious. "I'll be sleeping."

She picked up a cleaver and a head of celery, and the blade landed with a thud, separating the white heart from the green stalks. "I understand it's a sacrifice, but it's necessary." She gave me a look that drained my blood. "And not just for the Queen's sake. Also for your own."

I was about to challenge the point, but I stopped at the sound of footsteps behind me. I turned to see Mr. MacDougall approaching, his usual grimace aimed directly at us.

"Is everything satisfactory, Mrs. Crossey?"

She set down her cleaver and wiped her hands on her apron. "Yes, I believe it is. Jane and I were just discussing her new duties."

He skewered her with stony eyes. "As I mentioned, I don't believe we'll need to go to that trouble."

She pulled her lips into a saccharin smile. "But it's absolutely no trouble at all. Is it, Jane?"

I didn't want to agree, but the look on her face gave me no choice. I shook my head.

His scowl deepened, and I knew he was envisioning all manner of violence against me.

"And since we've been so productive this morning, there's no reason she can't start this very afternoon."

"Today?" Mr. MacDougall and I blurted in unison.

Mrs. Crossey clasped her hands at her chest. "Absolutely. I think it would be for the best."

"I'm sure she isn't ready." The tightness in his voice caused a few nearby heads to turn.

"She's as ready as she'll ever be."

How could she speak of me this way, as though I wasn't standing right in front of her? "Don't I get some say in this?"

A strange calm came over her, and she crossed her arms in the way Headmistress Trindle would when she was struggling to control her temper. "Of course you do, dear." She stared at me, eyes widened, waiting for me to continue.

I shifted. I had her attention, but I had no idea what to do with it. "It's all happening so fast," I blurted. "Could we start tomorrow at least? So I can prepare myself?"

Mr. MacDougall's long and spindly forefinger shot up. "Yes. Good idea. No reason to rush things. Perhaps a week would be better."

I knew why I didn't want to do it, but why didn't *he* want me to do it? Why was he acting so peculiar?

"No," I said. "I think a day should suffice."

Mr. MacDougall scowled at me, but Mrs. Crossey

grinned. "Very good. Then it's settled. We'll begin tomorrow."

I waited for Mr. MacDougall to object, but he only gritted his teeth. "Tomorrow then," he snapped. He turned on his heels and stalked away.

Across the room, I could hear him bellow for Abigail, and for a moment, I almost felt sorry for her.

CHAPTER EIGHT

THE REST OF the afternoon and early part of the evening passed in a flurry of vegetable peeling and chopping, washing, and the usual clangor of a kitchen in the throes of preparing meals for the royal family, their guests, their household, and the legion of officers and servants who attended them. Though I was trying to keep my mind on my work, I wasn't succeeding.

Somehow Mrs. Crossey and I managed to assemble the servants' evening meal although she'd found fault with the dice of my carrot and the cleanliness of my station. My visits to the pantry were too long for her liking, and I'd handed her sugar when she'd requested salt—twice. Under ordinary circumstances, I would have been roundly reprimanded, but today she only sighed and shook her head.

I would have preferred the reprimand.

At a lull in the activity, I gathered the last of the bowls and utensils we had used and delivered them to the washing maids while Mrs. Crossey tended to the pots on the stove. When I returned, I took a steaming kettle, poured some of the boiling water over my cutting board, and scrubbed away the vegetable residue with a stiff-bristle brush.

"What's next?" I asked, barely able to stifle a yawn.

"Take your dinner, then get some rest. I can handle it from here."

The clock built into the kitchen's lantern roof read only a quarter past seven, which in truth meant ten past because the chef's trick of setting it ahead five minutes didn't fool anyone. It was the earliest I'd ever been released from my shift. A welcome and unexpected treat.

"We have a long night ahead of us," she added in that low, conspiratorial tone.

The training. I'd nearly forgotten. I didn't know whether to be annoyed or afraid. To be honest, I was feeling a bit of both.

"Get some sleep and I'll see you later."

"Midnight. Right." I took my leave before she changed her mind and maneuvered past a cook working on an aspic, another hovering over a sauce pot with Marlie handing him tiny bowls of seasoning herbs, and a third chopping what appeared to be the ingredients of mincemeat pie.

I hadn't realized I was hungry until I pushed through the swinging door that led to the Servants' Hall and my stomach grumbled, reminding me I hadn't eaten anything but a few slices of purloined carrot and celery since breakfast. I skirted past the handful of maids, footmen, and underbutlers already seated at the long table that nearly filled the narrow room.

I recognized most of them, including Abigail, but I kept my head down and focused on getting to the sideboard, where the beef stew was keeping warm beside a basket of buttermilk biscuits. I ladled my portion, took a seat at the far end of the table, a good distance from the others, and looked at nothing but my bowl and the wall of brass bells across from me.

A jingling above a plaque that read "White Drawing Room" sent one young maid scurrying from her spot to attend to whatever was needed upstairs. As the door closed behind her, a footman elbowed an underbutler in rolled shirtsleeves.

"Did you hear? Another girl was let go today."

The older man stabbed a chunk of meat in his bowl. "MacDougall said these terminations wouldn't affect breaks." He gestured to the empty chair where the girl had been. "So what's that then?"

The older one scoffed. "Sure. As long as it isn't *his* meal interrupted—"

He stopped when the door swung open again. All chatter ceased, and every eye shot up. At the sight of Mr. Wyck—and not Mr. MacDougall—the men focused again on their food and their gripes. But not the maids. They leaned their heads together and whispered like schoolgirls.

"There's a seat here, Mr. Wyck." Abigail patted the space on the bench beside her.

The stable hand smiled and moved toward her, but then his eyes found mine. He stopped, his smile vanished, and he waved feebly at the girls before retreating through the door without a word of explanation.

I was trying to decide whether to be relieved or insulted when Abigail leaned back from her huddle.

Her brown eyes skewered me. "What was that about, Jane?" Her smug attitude told me she already had her suspicions.

I stared at my stew. I didn't trust myself to look at her. I was sure she hadn't forgotten about her locket. I certainly hadn't forgotten about the accusations she'd lodged against me. I know I should have felt some guilt over the matter, or at least some remorse, but truly I felt... nothing. So I shoveled a spoonful of potato into my mouth and closed my eyes. If I ignored them long enough, they'd go back to ignoring me.

Experience told me the whispers and snickers would fade eventually, and when they did, I picked up my empty bowl, put it in the receptacle, and slipped out of the hall.

I hurried to my room and tried not to think about Abigail or Mr. Wyck and that look on his face. That conspicuous disdain.

Had he been so terribly put out that I had displaced him in Mr. MacDougall's office? It seemed more than that. Personal even. Perhaps his dislike for me simply matched my own for him.

But what reason would he have? I wasn't the one who strutted around like a peacock begging to be admired.

Still, even Mr. Wyck's inexplicable contempt paled beside the more troublesome events of the day: Mrs. Crossey's insistence that secret guardians occupied the castle, of which she was one and apparently so was I, and that incident beyond the wall. I cringed thinking of it and had done my best to push it from my thoughts. Was it an attack? A hallucination?

I didn't know whether to be frightened or embarrassed, but I was more convinced than ever that it hadn't been real. It couldn't be.

But what *had* happened? Had Mrs. Crossey tricked me somehow to make me stay? I tried to piece together the events, tried to remember *exactly* what had transpired, yet each time my thoughts turned more and more muddled. Except for the memory of those terrifying eyes. That remained crystal clear.

Mrs. Crossey hadn't helped. When I'd tried to ask about the incident at the worktable, she'd scowled and shoved her finger to her lips. "Not here! Not now."

I didn't know what to think of any it, or of her, honestly. Yesterday I would have trusted her implicitly, but today? I simply didn't know.

I'd played along with her plan. Pretended to accept the crazy scheme she envisioned for protecting the Queen. But part of me still wanted to run, as fast and as far away as possible.

I only wish I knew what I was running from.

That's what I couldn't get past. What if she was telling

the truth? What if any of it was true?

That was the question keeping me here. The question I knew would keep me awake and deliver me to Mr. MacDougall's door at midnight.

Maybe then I could get some answers.

But that was still hours away.

Right now, with Marlie still in the kitchen, I had a rare surplus of time to do exactly as I pleased.

My pulse quickened as I closed the bedroom door and darted to the wardrobe, found my bag, and pulled out my memory box. Even through my gloves, the wood felt warm and smooth.

I dropped cross-legged onto the floor and breathed in the box's smell. The rich, earthy fragrance—a reminder of the black tea it once held. Lifting the hinged lid, I gazed upon my treasures.

A piece of yellow yarn from Dotty's rag doll, an iron key from the school's old caretaker, a glass marble from a girl who knew the name of every bird she ever saw, and other trinkets. Each a tiny container of a memory I'd collected. I sifted through them all until I found the one I wanted.

I tugged the glove off my right hand before taking Abigail's tiny oval locket between my fingers. I rubbed the delicate filigree around the edge, and my heart raced.

Darkness gathered along the periphery. A swirling cloud that grew denser until it blotted out everything else.

Slowly, images emerged. A modest room. A cabin, perhaps. A rustic plank floor beneath me, a crackling hearth as large as the wall in front. A woman leaned over an iron pot suspended above a fire that gave a shine to her loose sable hair. Hair that resembled Abigail's.

When the woman turned to me, her smile made the corner of her cornflower eyes wrinkle and sent a riot of happy tingles through me like so many shooting stars. Trust and love for this woman engulfed me.

"Look at those big brown eyes!" the woman cooed.

"Why is my Little Abby still awake? Sleep, my darling. You need to sleep."

She touched my forehead, and the sensation raced from that point to every extremity.

And then the vision slipped away.

I closed my eyes and tried to hold onto the image. The curve of the woman's cheek, the warmth of her voice, the tenderness in her touch, and all the emotions that filled me. The memory had been so vivid this time. I had noticed details I hadn't before. Dried lavender suspended in three bunches over the hearth. The gingham pattern of the woman's dress beneath her apron. The smell of a meat broth in the pot.

The vision was so real now, as clear as any true memory.

I savored it until the details faded again, then I put the locket back in the box, closed the lid, and returned it to my carpet bag.

When everything was back in its place, I crawled into bed with my stolen memory and let it carry me away.

CHAPTER NINE

BY THE TIME Marlie returned, I'd been lying in bed for an hour, maybe more. The warm embrace of the stolen memory had faded and again I was sifting through my fragmented recollection of what had happened at the tree. I was trying to stitch the jumbled flashes into something I could understand. Something that made sense.

But none of it did.

"Jane, are you awake?"

I kept my eyes closed and didn't answer, only tightened my grip on the covers at my chin so she wouldn't see I was still wearing the same frock I'd worn in the kitchen. When she'd brushed her teeth at our porcelain basin, braided her long, tawny hair, and crawled into her own bed, I waited for the soft mewling of her snores.

Only then did I slip a stockinged foot to the floor. I paused, listening for any disturbance to her slumber.

At the next wispy inhalation, I knew I was safe. I pulled the rest of myself from bed and quietly slid my feet into my boots, laced them, and grabbed my coat from the peg by the door.

As I pulled it closed behind me, I heard the last of the hall clock's eleven chimes. Another hour before Mrs.

Crossey would be expecting me, which meant I had time.

Moving quickly, I navigated the corridors and kept to the shadows. After-hours strolls, especially outdoors, were against the rules for servants. Since it was a rule I'd broken before, I had no trouble dodging the guards and other nighttime staff.

When I finally emerged from the castle onto the North Terrace, the night air sent shivers racing to my toes. But a bit of cold wouldn't stop me from confirming what I now suspected: that I'd been tricked by Mrs. Crossey, nothing more. My fainting spell was likely caused by an insufficient breakfast or overwrought nerves, and not the nonsense she'd have me believe.

That certainty grew with every step.

I pushed through the gate and placed a rock in the opening so I couldn't be locked out, then hurried down the path, eager to see that tree and confirm it was a perfectly normal tree. That would put my mind at ease.

At the bend in the pathway, I could make out the grove in the weak moonlight despite the nightly fog drifting off the river.

A lingering fear twisted in my gut. A flash of smoky red tendrils winding about my arm. Serpent eyes glittering like tiny flames.

I pushed away those thoughts.

There was no danger.

There was nothing unnatural.

I only had to see that tree again, stand before it, prove to myself it was all in my head.

Still my heart thumped, keeping time with my footsteps.

I could see little more than the outer rim of oaks now. The fog had grown as thick as a storm cloud. My pulse raced and it was so dark I could hardly see my feet, but I couldn't stop. I had to continue. I had to get there.

And I was close. Just another few paces.

Something rustled along the ground behind me. I

whipped around, my chest pounding. I watched the blanket of dead brown leaves, searching for movement. I heard the sound again. Not rustling. It was the buzz of dragonfly wings.

I breathed easier and my tension uncoiled.

"You shouldn't be here," I said, my voice jagged with nerves.

My dragonfly landed on my shoulder and stared her question at me.

"I have my reasons," I answered.

Though I could always count on her to find me during the day, this was the first time she'd joined me for a night stroll.

She continued to stare.

"I couldn't sleep."

Even as I said it, I knew she wouldn't believe me. She always knew the truth.

She stomped her needle-like legs.

"Fine. I wanted to see this place again. Something happened today…"

Her stomping stopped. She turned back to the castle.

"How did you already know? Did you see it? Were you here?"

She sat, frozen, staring at the castle.

"Then don't tell me. But I'm going to have a look."

When I took a step into the grove, she leapt from my shoulder and flew at the tip of my nose.

"Stop that!" I swatted her away, but she came back at me again.

I tried to shake her off, but she wouldn't leave me alone. Finally, she did, and so suddenly that I wasn't sure where she'd gone. I searched the darkness, but it was impossible to see something as small as her beyond a few feet.

"Where are you?" I listened for her buzzing, but the breeze was picking up, making the branches sway and pushing the fog bank farther into the trees.

Then there was something else. Not my dragonfly's buzz, but... was it laughter? A deep, rumbling laughter.

"Who's there?" My voice cracked.

There was no answer. Then something moved among the trees. Perhaps the wind, perhaps something else.

I couldn't breathe, couldn't even move. I could only stare at what looked like something moving in the mist. A black form creeping through the darkness. A man? No, it was too large. A beast? I hardly knew, but I stared when I knew I should run.

Then, through the thickening fog two sparks of light appeared. Two wide, feral, and flickering red eyes.

CHAPTER TEN

"WAKE UP."

The words and the hand on my shoulder roused me from sleep, but just barely. "I'm fine, Marlie. Go back to bed." I groped for my blanket. "It's too early."

"It's not early, and I'm not Marlie."

The voice, clearer to me now, did not belong to Marlie. It wasn't even female.

My eyes shot open. The nighttime sky stared back. Beneath me wasn't my lumpy mattress, but cold, hard earth. Panic surged then crystallized into one horrifying question:

"Did it happen again?" My voice faltered, my tongue scratchy and dry.

The stranger peered over me, his features lost in the darkness. I blinked and squinted until the contours registered. The curve of a cheek. The hard line of a jaw. When he pushed back a shock of disheveled dark hair that had fallen over his right eye, a fresh wave of fear engulfed me. I tried to sit up, but my limbs wouldn't cooperate.

"Did what happen again?" His voice was sharp, demanding. "Do you need help?"

"No." I tried again to right myself, but a wild new

thought took hold: why was he here? Why was *I* here?

I had been on the path with my dragonfly and then... The image returned in a flash. That man or creature I'd seen in the fog. Where was he? I scanned the shadows. No sign of him. Even the fog had disappeared.

"Here." Mr. Wyck reached out to help me up.

I would have recoiled if I wasn't lying flat on my back. Instead, I stared at his hand. Those four bare fingers and a thumb hovered over me. I glanced down at my own hands. My gloves were on. At least there was that.

"I can manage." I had no idea if that was true, but I would never admit it to him.

"Don't be ridiculous. You need help."

He grabbed me by the elbow with one hand, took my wrist with the other, and pulled me to a sitting position.

I shook off his touch as soon as I had my balance, but it was too late. I'd felt the brush of his bare fingers across the skin of my wrist just above my glove. "Why did you do that?" I grabbed my knees, clenched my teeth, and braced for a vision.

But nothing happened. No images. No sensations. Nothing.

He frowned. "You don't look so good."

Of course I didn't. Something was wrong. Where was the vision?

I stared at my gloved palms, fresh dirt streaked over the old. What had happened? And how was I supposed to make sense of anything with him hovering over me? "You don't have to stay. I'm fine."

I could tell by the twist of his lip and the way he crossed his arms that he knew I was lying. My gaze skimmed the contours of his shoulders and the tug of his wool jacket's sleeves across his arms. He was stronger than he appeared at first glance. Certainly strong enough to overwhelm me, if he chose. My fear ratcheted up another notch.

"I hardly think you're fine," he said.

I didn't care what he thought. I only wanted to get away. I searched the darkness, but I didn't see anyone or anything that could help. Where were the guards? Where was my dragonfly?

I scrambled to my feet in what was possibly the clumsiest manner possible. But at least I was up, and I managed to evade the helping hand he thrust at me again.

"See, I can manage." I brushed the dust and twigs from my skirt and my gloves. My wits were returning and convincing me more than ever that there was no good reason for him to be here. Had he done something to me? Had he attacked me? I only knew I had to get away. Setting aside my fear as best I could, I said, "I appreciate your trouble, Mr. Wyck, but I assure you I'm feeling much better. I can manage from here."

"Right." He smirked.

This should have been easy. Walk out here, see the tree, walk back, and demand answers, *real* answers, from Mrs. Crossey, who was probably already waiting for me. "What time is it?"

"Bit after midnight, I suppose."

"How much after?" My gut twisted and the ground tilted again. I swayed uncontrollably.

"Hey, are you all right?" He leaned to catch me if I fell, but I managed to stand my ground.

"Of course I am." I shook off his efforts to grab my arm. "But I have to get back."

"Can you walk?" He moved closer, his expression a mixture of disbelief and concern. "I suppose I could carry you, if—"

I stumbled back, dodging his advance. "I'm quite fine on my own, thank you."

At least I hoped I was. It was taking every ounce of strength not to crumple to the ground. I took a step to prove to him—and to myself—that I could do it.

He shrugged, perhaps agreeing that I could walk or indifferent if I couldn't. "Then let's go." He set off toward the castle and had taken several paces before looking back to see if I was keeping up. "Are you coming or not?"

Oh, he was expecting me to follow. "Of course." I hobbled forward as best I could.

When we reached the castle wall gate, a tingling at my shoulders made me stop. I looked back. The trees were lost in inky darkness, but it didn't matter. I knew someone—or something—was out there, watching me.

CHAPTER ELEVEN

I TRUDGED ALONG the East Terrace garden pathways behind Mr. Wyck, who no longer looked back to see if I followed. It was a relief, to be honest. Without the obligation of keeping up a conversation, I could try to piece together what had happened.

Not that it helped.

I remembered talking to my dragonfly when something moved among the trees. Then I'd seen those terrifying eyes.

I didn't want to believe they were real, wanted desperately to believe they were the byproduct of an overactive imagination or indigestion.

But could it be coincidence that I'd fainted, and Mr. Wyck had appeared out of nowhere?

Hardly.

Something was going on. But what?

I was still silently debating the matter when we reached the kitchen door. When he opened it, I straightened, thanked him for his trouble, and sent him on his way.

Or tried to.

"I can't leave you here," he grumbled. "I should see you inside and safely to your room."

"No." The word was abrupt, perhaps even rude. "What I mean is, I'd prefer you didn't."

I couldn't tell him I had to find Mrs. Crossey. That I had answers to demand.

He tilted his head to the side and gave me a look that said my opinion didn't matter.

"Really. I feel fine." *Just leave already*, I wanted to yell at him.

"Jane, is that you?"

A round figure barreled toward us from the dark end of the corridor. I recognized her immediately.

"Yes, Mrs. Crossey. It's me."

As she approached, she looked at me and lowered her voice to a whisper. "It's hardly the hour to be traipsing about with" — she lowered her voice another octave — "a young man. What were you thinking?"

"I wasn't *with* a young man." It was impossible to hide my mortification. "I mean, it's all a misunderstanding."

"A misunderstanding?"

She was mocking me.

"Not quite a misunderstanding," Mr. Wyck piped in.

I shot him a nasty look, which he ignored.

"I found her unconscious on the Slopes, ma'am. I just wanted to be sure she got back inside. Safely."

Mrs. Crossey smiled kindly at him, then gaped in horror at me. "Unconscious? On the Slopes?" Her hands flew to her mouth. "How did it happen? Wait, you must sit down. Come with me. Let me get you some tea."

She gestured for me to follow her. To my companion, she said, "Thank you, Mr. Wyck. I'll take care of it from here."

He frowned but nodded. "I probably should get back to the mews."

"Yes, that would be wise. Good night, now." Mrs. Crossey shooed me toward the kitchen.

Behind me, I heard him say faintly, "Please do keep an eye on her."

~ ~ ~

Mrs. Crossey and I were down the hall, nearly to the Great Kitchen, when I asked her plainly, "What do you know about Mr. Wyck?"

"He's a stableboy, if I'm not mistaken."

"But what do you *know* about him?"

"Nothing, really."

I had the distinct feeling she knew something she wasn't telling me, or she'd be the one asking the question.

"Are you hungry?" she added in her distracted way. "I made scones for tomorrow's breakfast table. A new recipe I'm trying out. Mrs. Beeton recommends a tad more sugar than I'm used to. Not sure what I think of them yet." She maneuvered me to a stool beside our stove before lighting a flame beneath the kettle and lifting a towel off a platter of scones. "Go on. You look like you want a nibble."

Indeed, I did. I reached over and helped myself to a healthy portion. I was still chewing when the disapproving look I'd been expecting—and dreading—finally landed on me.

"So, what were you doing on the Slopes? Again. After I told you it was dangerous. I was very clear."

I pointed to the scones. "May I have another? They're extraordinary."

Mrs. Crossey tilted her head and gave me a look that said flattery was no answer.

I stared at the polished copper pots and pans hanging above our stove, but I could feel her glare. "I couldn't sleep. And I wanted answers."

She turned back to look at the only other person in sight: a night chef leaning precariously in a chair beside a distant cupboard, who appeared to be asleep. Satisfied that he wasn't listening, she whispered, "Did you see something?"

"No." I wasn't going to tell her anything until she told

me what she knew.

Her eyebrows rose.

I rubbed at the streaks of dirt and grass on my gloves. Considering the abuse they'd suffered, it was a wonder they were still intact. That was the last thing I needed.

"I can't imagine what you were thinking," she said. "I told you it was dangerous, and Mr. Wyck said you passed out?"

I closed my eyes, wishing I could wind back the hours. Wishing I had just stayed in bed.

"Well?" The harshness of her whisper verged on hysteria.

"Yes. I suppose. I mean I think that's what happened."

"You aren't sure?"

I shook my head.

Her cheeks lost their usual rosy hue. She bent down and stared hard into my eyes. "What do you remember?"

I laced and unlaced my fingers and shifted on the stool. I didn't want to think back. I just wanted to forget all of it. But that was impossible. She was waiting. "I remember waking up," I said at last, "and Mr. Wyck was there. Isn't that odd? That he should be on the Slopes so late? And…"

She pulled back. Her gaze narrowed. "And what?"

"When he touched me—"

"My dear!" Her hands shot to her mouth. She fell back against the stove behind her and bumped an empty pot, making it rattle and clang.

We both shot looks at the night chef. The noise hadn't seemed to rouse him.

I hurried to correct her misunderstanding. "Not like *that*." A hot flush spread from my shoulders to my cheeks. "I mean he touched my hand. My wrist, actually. My bare skin. It should have caused a vision, but it didn't. It didn't do anything."

Though she'd had her suspicions and I'd played along, my secret was now confirmed and laid bare. There was no going back.

If she noticed my discomfort at this, she didn't let on. At least not in the way I'd expected. "Nothing at all?" she asked. "Are you sure?"

I shook my head. Could it mean my visions had left me? And why wasn't that thought a relief?

"Touch me." Mrs. Crossey stuck out her arm.

I knew what she was doing. I looked again at the night cook. His chin was on his chest, and he appeared oblivious to everything. Slowly, I slipped off my right glove and did as she asked.

The instant my flesh met hers, the familiar swirling swept me away. The room twisted and colors collided into a mass of black and gray. When images emerged, I wasn't in the Great Kitchen. I was sitting in a country cottage, at a wood table beside a smoldering hearth. An open window showed night had fallen, and I was leaning over a book, a massive thing bound in worn, dark leather. I was holding a candle over its brittle pages, browned with age and tattered at the edges from use.

I leaned forward to read the script, but the vision faded. I was back in the Great Kitchen, facing Mrs. Crossey.

"A vision?" She reached over to pull the steaming kettle from the stove.

"Yes." I circled my fingertips over the spot where her hand had touched mine. So, I hadn't lost the ability. Strangely, I was glad for it. Relieved, even. But the question remained. Why had I seen nothing from Mr. Wyck?

I mulled over the possibilities while Mrs. Crossey poured the boiling water into a ceramic teapot and added heaping spoonfuls of tea leaves from her tin. "I'm concerned about the fainting. Tell me what you were doing before it happened."

"Don't you want to know what I saw in the vision?"

She shook her head. "I want to know what happened to you tonight."

I rubbed my fingers and wished I could change the subject. "I already told you what happened."

She frowned, and I knew she saw through me.

"Was anyone else there?"

I thought of my dragonfly. I thought of the shadow with the flaming red eyes. I shook my head.

She sighed. Perhaps with relief. Perhaps from doubt. I didn't ask and she didn't say as she collected two teacups and the sugar bowl. Finally, she said, "I was worried to pieces about you, you know. When I checked your room and you weren't there, I feared the worst."

She poured the tea, and I took a cup. Its heat was a comfort, and I breathed in the earthy scent.

"I didn't mean to be late for the training," I said after a sip. "Should we get started now?"

Her gaze shot up. "It's too late for that."

The Darjeeling was doing its job. I could feel the tension draining from my elbows and knees. "You're probably right. I need to sleep."

She lowered her cup to its saucer. "I'm sure you do, but you'll be lucky to get a couple hours tonight. Or should I say this morning? You'll need to pick up the Queen's firewood, don't forget."

"I haven't forgotten." I didn't see the cause for her concern, though.

She gave me a funny look, and I followed her gaze to the kitchen clock. I blinked. That couldn't be right. I blinked again but nothing changed. "It's three in the morning? It was only eleven when I went out."

Mrs. Crossey set her cup down, and I could see a tremble in her hands. She closed her eyes and shook her head. "I should have stayed with you," she mumbled. "I should never..." Her words trailed off then she lifted her chin and met my gaze squarely. "I don't know what happened to you beyond the wall, but you must promise not to venture out there again. Not alone. Not ever."

I nodded, too unnerved, too baffled by the lost time, to

speak.

She took up her teacup again with both hands and with such force I thought the porcelain might shatter. "It's too late to do anything tonight. We'll begin tomorrow. In the meantime, do your best upstairs. Pay attention to anything out of the ordinary."

I didn't want to go up there, and I told her so.

She reached over to pat my hand but stopped mid-reach and pulled back. "You're simply picking up a basket in the cellar and delivering it to the Queen's sitting room. She and her ladies may not even be present. You'll be in and out in a jiffy."

I'd been so sure her concerns were nonsense, but now I didn't know. What if there was a plot against our sovereign? What if it had something to do with that terrifying creature? And Mr. Wyck? It couldn't all be a coincidence.

Mrs. Crossey must have sensed my unease.

"It will be fine," she cajoled. "What could happen to the Queen at her breakfast table, surrounded by her ladies? Just be alert. Look for anything out of the ordinary."

Out of the ordinary? Hadn't this entire day been marked by things out of the ordinary? "Doesn't Mr. Wyck qualify in that regard?"

She pursed her lip and her gaze turned hard and unyielding. "Forget Mr. Wyck for the time being."

"But he—"

She raised a single finger. "Do you understand?"

She waited for me to nod before she continued.

"Your concern—your only concern for now—is to focus whatever faculties you possess and whatever powers of observation you can muster on the Queen and her safety. Do you understand?"

I nodded, though reluctant.

"Are you not sure?" she demanded.

Why wouldn't she entertain the possibility that Mr. Wyck was connected somehow? How could she dismiss him so easily? But the set of her jaw told me there was no convincing her, so I changed course. "What if something does happen while I'm up there? What should I do?"

"Nothing. You do absolutely nothing but bring the matter to my attention as quickly as possible. That's all."

I stared into my empty cup. The threat against the Queen may or may not be nonsense, but the dread I sensed was most certainly real.

"You can do this," she said. "You say you see the past, but the truth about your gift is that you see what you want to see. With proper training, you'll be able to sense the past, present, or future, if you want to. Not easily at first, but it will become easier."

In her eyes, I could see that she believed what she was saying. Her mind was made up, and to be honest, I had no more energy to argue. It was too late, and I was too tired. I dipped my head and muttered the only thing I knew she wanted to hear. "Yes, ma'am."

I rose and shuffled toward the corridor.

She grabbed a bundle of white folded linen from the shelf beneath the table. "You're going to need this."

I recognized the ruffles that differentiated an upstairs apron from my plain one.

"Don't worry," she said, handing me the bundle. "It will be fine."

"Of course it will." I tried to mean it.

Her lips pulled into a fierce line. "And promise you won't leave the castle grounds again."

I nodded, took the crisp linen, and hurried to my room.

~ ~ ~

I laid in bed trying to drift off to sleep but every floorboard creak, every one of Marlie's sleep mumblings, and all the tiny rattles and scrapes that filled the otherwise quiet spaces of our room conspired against any hope of restful slumber.

To be fair, the noises weren't the only things making me stare at the ceiling for those scant remaining hours before dawn. Fainting again at the wretched tree and those hours inexplicably lost would have been enough to keep me tossing and turning, but there was also Mr. Wyck. What was he doing out there? And when he touched me, why had there been no vision? I couldn't think of a single reasonable explanation.

And wasn't it convenient? Perhaps too convenient? A peek into his past could reveal whether he was the threat Mrs. Crossey feared, or if it was simply a strange—very strange—coincidence.

Not knowing was frustrating, to say the least.

The young man obviously thought himself clever, but the more I considered it as I tossed and turned in the darkest hours, the more convinced I was that our meeting on the Slopes was not a coincidence. He was up to something, and I meant to find out what.

~ ~ ~

At some point during the night, I'd given in to my exhaustion, but sleep had been anything but restful. Sometime before dawn I'd jolted awake with my heart racing and my back slicked with sweat. It took every ounce of control I had to catch my breath and remind myself it was only a dream. Yet it had been so clear. So real.

And I wasn't ready to part with it.

I pulled the blanket to my cheeks, closed my eyes, and tried to return to that imagined place, recapture that strange euphoria.

I could feel it just out of reach. It was like the grove on the Slopes at first, but then, as the path led on, it changed. The night turned colder. Darker. Only the moon and the stars lighted my way. But I wasn't scared. I was curious. Something was calling to me, coaxing me on. What was it? Who was it?

I pressed on through the shrubs and the trees until I came to a clearing and in that space stood a giant yew. The branches swayed in a breeze I couldn't feel, and the trunk's contours undulated to a rhythm I couldn't hear. A tree that was terrifying yet wondrous. A tree beyond imagining. And I knew, with a strange conviction, that tree held answers.

Then it was gone.

Like the time I'd lost on the Slopes.

Yet something had changed.

I had gone to bed feeling helpless, but I wasn't. Someone had been there who hadn't suffered the same lapse. Someone who had answers.

I only had to ask.

But I would have to be quick if I was to collect the Queen's firewood on time. When the early bells rang, calling the morning staff to their posts, I was already out of bed, washed, and dressed.

As silently as I could so I didn't disturb Marlie, I hurried out in the morning's half-light and made my way to the courtyard to search for my dragonfly.

"Are you here?" I whispered into the gray mist.

I watched the horizon and listened for her wings.

"I need you, dragonfly."

The sound of the door opening behind me stopped me cold. I braced.

"What are you up to?"

It was Mr. MacDougall. Fear gripped me and my mind raced for an excuse. I latched on to the first one to come to mind. "Getting a bit of air, sir. I didn't sleep well, and I thought I might invigorate before heading to the Queen's room."

The House Steward scrutinized me, then scowled again. "Have you been out here long?"

"I just got here, sir."

"Are you sure?"

I nodded.

He glanced around as though he suspected I might not

be alone, but when he was satisfied that I was, he seemed to relax. "Well, don't dally. The Queen appreciates a certain energy in her staff, but she won't abide tardiness. I suggest you get on with your task."

"Yes, sir." I held back. Was that my dragonfly buzzing in the distance?

Mr. MacDougall held the door. "Now, Jane."

The buzzing, if it was buzzing, faded into the morning breeze.

"Of course," I muttered and hurried inside. Any answers my friend might have were going to have to wait.

CHAPTER TWELVE

I DIDN'T WANT to go upstairs.

If my assignment had changed to parlor maid or chamber maid, at least I could hold my head high and expect a few shillings added to my wages.

But delivering firewood? I could already hear the whispers behind my back. What could I have done to deserve such a demotion, they'd wonder, and why hadn't I simply been shown the door? Why did I have a job at all when so many others far more deserving had lost theirs?

The speculation wouldn't be kind. It never was to girls like me.

And yet, I was in no position to decline.

So here I stood, at the bottom of a servants' staircase to the Long Gallery, dressed in a frilly apron but feeling worse than ever.

Just be done with it.

All I wanted was to get back to my familiar corner of the kitchen alongside Mrs. Crossey. Where I didn't have to wear a fussy apron, or pull my shoulders back, or avert my eyes from my betters.

I had no patience for any of it.

Just get it over with.

Somehow, I forced one foot in front of the other and ascended the staircase. At the door, I tightened my grip on my basket and turned the knob to peer down the wide corridor that led to the Queen's sitting room.

At least I appeared to be alone. No pages, no other maids, no wandering courtiers.

Still, I remained in the shadows to catch my breath and calm my nerves.

It was only my second time upstairs. My first was a chaperoned visit that took place on the day of my arrival, when I was still reeling from my abrupt departure from Chadwick Hollow. I wasn't as observant as I should have been. The only thing I remembered keenly was the jarring opulence. The scarlet carpet, the silks and gilt, the crystal and wood polished to a mirror-like gloss.

It had been an unsettling introduction to a world so different from the one belowstairs and the one I had known at Chadwick Hollow.

But now, just as then, I forced myself onward, cringing beneath the stares of long-dead royals and nobles peering down from the walls as I made my way toward Victoria Tower.

Do what you're told.

Those were the words I had told myself on that first day at the castle, when all the new rules and duties and chaos threatened to paralyze me.

Somehow I had gotten through that day, and somehow I would get through this.

By sheer force of will, I reached the door to the sitting room. On that first visit, it had been occupied, and I hadn't been allowed in. So this was entirely new territory. Carefully, I eased the door open.

I don't know what I expected to find inside, but it wasn't three ladies already in their day dresses—dark and modest as Her Majesty preferred—standing in a huddle at a window overlooking the castle's Quadrangle, teacups and saucers in hand.

One, taller and more serious than the others, smoothed a hand over her sleek black chignon and frowned at me. "Do say you're here with the firewood. It's colder than the winter Alps in here."

"Yes, ma'am," I muttered, feeling my cheeks burn but not daring to breathe another word. Speak when spoken to was the servants' rule, though I would prefer not to speak at all. I stared at the carpets beneath my feet and hurried to the room's fireplace. Across from it, a round table was set for four, and I could see the slender silhouette of a parlor maid arranging biscuits and toast points on a polished silver tray.

When the ladies returned to their conversation, I went to work unloading the wood from my basket, placing it in a copper receptacle beside the hearth. In furtive glances, I took stock of the room. Smaller than the formal drawing rooms by half and filled with cozy cushioned chairs. In fact, the whole room was cozier than anything I'd seen in the castle so far.

Dozens of framed photographs and painted portraits occupied the side tables and the bookshelves. Images of the royal children. The Queen and her Prince. Aunts and uncles and cousins.

One on the mantel stood larger than the rest. A silver frame containing the likeness of the Queen's mother, the Duchess of Kent and Strathearn, and not as the porcelain-skinned beauty of her painted portraits, but as a stout and stoic matron of mature years. Standing beside her in the photograph was the Queen, still fresh faced and young. Perhaps not yet crowned.

And this frame didn't gleam as the others did. Its polish was worn in places and spoke of recent handling, perhaps frequent handling, by ungloved hands. A daughter's hands, if I were to guess.

But then, I didn't have to guess, did I? If I could hold that frame in my bare hands, what secrets would it unlock?

Instantly I pushed away the thought. I shouldn't covet

royal memories.

But hadn't Mrs. Crossey said she wanted me to learn what I could? Anything to protect the Queen?

Peering into Her Majesty's past might yield helpful information.

At least that's what I told myself.

Beneath my gloves, my fingers twitched as I squatted beside the hearth, arranging logs on the iron grate and considering how best to lay my hands on that frame without being noticed.

I was so lost in my thoughts that I hardly noticed the women behind me. Not until someone mentioned the Slopes.

I set down the last log, brushed the residue from my gloves, and leaned back.

"But, Lila, are you sure she was discovered on the Slopes?" said a pale and timid woman I believed to be Lady Wallingham, the widow of the Queen's former equerry and the most recent addition to the Queen's household. "Not closer to the river? The riverbank would be more likely, wouldn't you agree?"

My breath caught in my throat. Were they speaking about me?

"It was most certainly the Slopes," replied the one named Lila, who could only be Lady Lila Bassey, a close confidant and frequent attendant of the Queen. She sipped from her cup and set it again in its saucer. "It was a farmer's daughter. She was coming over the hill to make a delivery to the kitchen. She was attacked near the trees. That's what I heard the guards telling the Master of the Household. The man was beside himself, as you can imagine."

I stared at the logs on the grate, but every inch of me was riveted to the conversation behind me.

"Odd, wouldn't you say?" The soft voice was keenly accented with a Scottish burr. It had to be Lady Merrington from the Highlands, a daughter of an earl who had returned with the royal retinue.

"Odd? How so?" Lady Wallingham leaned back, intrigued.

"Why was she found near the trees if she was coming from over the hill?" Lady Merrington said. "It's quite off the path, isn't it?"

"I hardly know the particulars," Lady Bassey said, already sounding bored with the conversation, "but no one's likely to be allowed out there now. The guards were discussing how to cordon off the area by order of the House Steward."

I recalled my earlier encounter with Mr. MacDougall. Was that why he was so curious where I'd been? Had he already been aware of the death?

"Did they say anything else?" Lady Wallingham asked, giving voice to my own question.

"Nothing I heard. They clammed up at the sight of me, but I can only imagine the distress it's creating with the Queen's masquerade only a few days away."

There was an "oh dear" and an "oh my" then silence, until:

"What a tragedy," Lady Wallingham said with a heavy sigh. "I do hope you'll write to tell me what they discover. I'll be afraid for you, both of you, knowing something is out there."

Her words flooded me with fear, an eerie foreboding of something lurking in the empty space of my lost hours.

"I'm sure there's nothing to be concerned about," Lady Bassey said, "but I will write if there are any developments. I wouldn't be surprised if you were back before they learn anything, however. When did you say your sister is due?"

"A fortnight is the doctor's guess. But the last child was early, so who's to say? My sister always enjoys a house full of people doting on her, though. I wouldn't put it past her to draw out the proceedings as long as possible."

She sighed again, then the conversation turned to the whims of difficult family members.

My mind wouldn't be diverted from the farmer's dead daughter, however. Had she been attacked near the path I was on? Had the killer been nearby as I walked about? That shadow in the trees, could it have been... but then another, even more terrifying thought occurred.

Had Mr. Wyck killed her?

Had he planned to kill me, too?

That thought—that fear—pushed everything else from my mind.

I sat there, frozen, until somewhere deep within me, a tiny voice broke the spell. *Get out of this room.*

It was reason tearing through my fears. I had to get back to Mrs. Crossey, so I could tell her what I'd learned.

I removed a match from the box beside the fireplace and took one out to strike.

"What's taking you so long?"

My heart skipped, and I whipped around to see the parlor maid hovering over me. Only it wasn't a parlor maid. It was Abigail.

Her mouth curled into a sneer. "You shouldn't still be here. The Queen is expected any moment."

"Of course." I rose to get away. Eager to get away.

"Wait a moment," she said, "I'm going to make sure you didn't take anything."

I opened my mouth to tell her to look all she liked, but the opening of the door stopped me.

Before I could step aside, *she* was in front of me. The sovereign herself.

My chin dipped to my chest, and my knees bent till they nearly buckled. "Your Majesty." *Speak only if spoken to.* I stared at the ground and hoped—*prayed!*—she hadn't noticed my breach.

It didn't work.

"My goodness. Rise, child." Queen Victoria's throaty voice belied her stature, standing as she did only a hair over five feet, but she had long since mastered the ability to command any room she entered.

I glanced up to beg forgiveness, but she was hoisting the plump Princess Beatrice in her arms while her ladies surrounded her and fawned over the royal toddler.

Without hesitation, I took advantage of the distraction, grabbed my empty basket, and rushed from the room.

CHAPTER THIRTEEN

I RAN DOWN the stairs with the empty basket as quickly as my feet would carry me. Mrs. Crossey needed my help with the servants' breakfast, but I had someone else to see first. And fast.

Dodging eye contact with every page, footman, and maid I passed, I made it to the kitchen courtyard in record time. Only then did I slow down, inching along the winding path between patches of rosemary and thyme, sage and mint.

"Where are you?" My eyes searched for movement among the morning's gray clouds. My dragonfly had to come. She *had* to.

I walked and listened for her buzz over the scraping of my boots. It couldn't be a coincidence that a girl had been attacked—killed!—so near to where I'd been. And I was more convinced than ever that Mr. Wyck's presence had not been a coincidence, either.

Had I nearly met my own untimely end out there?

A wave of nausea washed over me. I clenched my eyes against the pain, but the instant I did, I could see them again. Those strange menacing eyes.

My own eyes shot open again, and my dragonfly was in front of me, hovering not more than a foot from my nose. At last she'd come. I would have hugged her if I could.

"Did you see what happened last night?"

She circled, then paused, waiting until I offered her a finger perch.

"You were there. You must have seen something."

She skipped forward over my knuckle and back. After a moment she repeated the dance.

"I know I shouldn't be out here, but I have to know."

She was pretending not to catch my meaning or ignoring it, so we trudged on in strained silence. As we turned from the garden path to a lane that wrapped inside the upper ward Quadrangle, I wanted to yell at her, even as I sensed her irritation with me.

"No, I won't go back, not until you—"

"Who are you talking to?"

I whipped around and nearly lost my balance. Mr. Wyck stood behind me, his fists shoved in his front pockets, his jaw set in a hard, inscrutable line.

The fear of being caught talking to my dragonfly paled against the realization that once again I was alone with a person who was quite likely a killer.

"Are you following me?" My voice cracked. I cursed myself for not mustering more courage. He wouldn't dare do anything to me in broad daylight, would he? He couldn't be that bold. But still, where were the castle guards? Even my dragonfly had already fled. Realizing that, I lowered my hand to my side as casually as I could and tried not to give in to the terror taking hold.

Mr. Wyck kicked at the dirt in front of him with something like a smirk on his face. "I'm not following anybody. I like to take in the morning air over here when I can. It's better than the stable smell, if you know what I mean. But I'm sure I heard you talking to someone."

"Sometimes I talk to myself," I said. "When I think I'm alone." I gave him a spiteful look in case he didn't catch my not-so-subtle meaning.

His lips curled, but I wouldn't call it a smile. He didn't believe me, I could see that. But I didn't care. I just wanted him to go away.

As the seconds ticked by, it became clear that he didn't intend to go anywhere. He simply watched me.

I inched toward the lane, back to the kitchen and to safety. "If you'll excuse me then, I should be getting back inside." Silently I begged my dragonfly to follow so we might finish our conversation.

Behind me, I heard the scuff of his footsteps following mine.

My heart beat quickened.

"I'm glad to see you're up and around," he said, matching my pace. "I wasn't sure you would be after last night's ordeal."

A cold shudder shot through me, but I forced myself to stand straighter and return his glare. "I certainly fared better than the poor girl they found on the Slopes this morning."

He blanched. "What girl?"

Was he pretending to be surprised? Or was he just surprised I knew?

"The farmer's girl. The one who died." Saying it aloud gave me a sick feeling in the pit of my stomach again. It still hardly seemed possible.

The way his eyes rounded with horror, he thought so, too.

"Died? How?"

"How should I know?" If he was lying, he was doing a good job of it. He fell back a step and stared at the ground.

"Didn't you know?" I watched him closely, searching for a crack in his charade.

But he was good. He pulled off his cap and ran his fingers through the mess of his hair. His gaze drifted to the far side of the Quadrangle. "That must have been what they were doing," he mumbled.

"What *who* was doing?"

His gaze snapped back to me. "What?"

"You said 'That's what they were doing.' Who?"

He scowled and waved me off. "It doesn't matter."

I wanted to grab his dusty twill jacket by the lapels and shake him, but I feared it would only make him laugh. "It matters to me," I said instead. "A great deal, in fact."

His dark eyes narrowed. "Have you ever been on the Slopes before last night?"

"I have." Of course I hadn't but that was none of his business.

"Mrs. Crossey allows it?"

"She doesn't have to," I shot back. "Why should she? But what about you, Mr. Wyck? What were you doing on the Slopes?"

He stared at me without blinking for a long moment. "Are you implying I had something to do with that girl?"

Before I could answer, the sound of a conversation coming from the other side of the gate stopped me. Without warning, Mr. Wyck pressed his finger to his lips and pressed himself up against the wall so he wouldn't be seen by those coming through.

"What are you—"

He stopped me with a more forceful press of his finger against his lips. He mouthed, "Listen."

I huffed. Who was he to order me about? But I joined him at the wall and leaned forward to listen just the same.

"We've done all we can for the lass," a man said. "She's in the Lord's hands now."

"Indeed," intoned a voice that struck me like a lightning bolt. It was Mr. MacDougall.

"Sure you want me to drop you off here, sir? It's quite a walk, and you'd be understandably weary after dealing with such a nasty business. If you don't mind me saying so, the Constable should have shown more respect. We practically did his job for him, yeah? Collecting her like that instead of leaving her to the elements."

"Yes, well," Mr. MacDougall said, "the Constable did have a point. Perhaps I was too hasty in my efforts to protect the Queen. I should have more carefully considered the impediment to the investigation."

"What's to investigate? If it were an animal or such, there would have been signs of it. Had to be a fall, plain and simple. Maybe hit her head on a rock, nothing more, nothing less."

"I'm sure you're quite right, Mr. Jameson. Her appearance did suggest such an end, I must agree. And her strange pallor, it would be expected, I suppose, lying out there as she did. Wouldn't you say so?"

"I would indeed, sir."

"Good. Very good."

I heard boots landing hard on the ground and the slapping of hands against limbs that accompanied the general brushing off of dust and dirt.

"Jameson, you have put my mind at ease. I am grateful for your assistance in this matter, and if I might impose on your goodwill once more, I would be grateful for your discretion as well. I know questions will be asked and curiosity will abound, but for the girl's sake—"

"Sir, you needn't say another word. I see no reason to speak of it to anyone."

"Good," Mr. MacDougall said. "It sums up my own feelings as well. Our part is done. The rest is in the Constable's hands. Ah, Mr. Bailey! I wasn't expecting—"

"I have been waiting for you." Dismay was plain in the man's voice. But then his tone, especially these past few months, was never what you'd call pleasant. As the Master of the Household's second in command, Mr. Bailey was often charged with carrying out the more unpleasant duties of the office, and lately that meant overseeing the elimination of staff.

Were more dismissals coming?

"Ah, yes," Mr. MacDougall said, sounding flustered. "I was just taking care of that matter we discussed… I mean, the unfortunate…"

"I know what you were doing. Is it done?"

"Yes, sir. Just as you asked. Everything is as you requested."

"Good. Mr. Jameson, would you mind if I borrowed Mr. MacDougall? There's a matter concerning the Queen's masquerade, if you don't mind."

The words were polite enough, but there was no mistaking that Mr. Jameson was being dismissed.

"Of course, sir," he said. "If you won't be needing anything else then, Mr. MacDougall?"

"No, no, Jameson. And thank you again."

"Quite all right, sir. Quite all right." Then he made a clicking sound through his teeth that sent the horses lurching onward.

At that, the men said their goodbyes, and we heard the gate close and the cart trundle away. When the low voices and footsteps faded, Mr. Wyck peered around the corner. Then he stepped away from the wall.

I did the same.

But I still had questions.

"You truly did not know about the girl?" I asked as he continued to watch Jameson lead the horse cart toward the mews.

He wheeled on me. "Are you accusing me of something, Miss Shackle?"

I froze. I wasn't even sure anymore, but I hated the feeling of not knowing. Of being afraid. I did my best to stand my ground. "Should I?"

"Absolutely not." His cheeks flushed, his eyes flared, and his anger wrapped about him like a suit of armor.

It was an emphatic denial, and it was difficult to reconcile that earnest expression—that pained expression—with one who could carry out such a despicable act.

Could he look me in the eye and lie so convincingly? I simply didn't know.

"I should get back to the kitchen," I said. I had no more courage to press the matter. "Thank you for your help last night, but I won't trouble you any further."

He stepped aside to let me pass. He didn't smile or even nod. Instead, he glanced away and muttered, "Somehow I doubt that."

The insult twisted a furious knot inside me, but I swallowed my snide reply before it could slip off my tongue. Let him have the last word. I'd be lucky enough to get away.

~ ~ ~

I cursed Mr. Wyck's audacity all the way to the kitchen. And where was my dragonfly? Why wouldn't she show herself when I needed her? She knew something about Mrs. Crossey she wasn't telling me, and probably something about the girl on the Slopes, too. A dozen times I thought I caught her buzz, but each was something else. Leaves rustling. A bird chirping. A gardener whistling in the distance.

When I finally reached the kitchen gate, there was still no sign of her.

"Where are you?" I whispered through gritted teeth.

By now I was long past tardy and well into dereliction of duty, but I had to find her. I wouldn't have another chance until after nightfall. So, despite the fury I knew I would face, I went through a back corridor to the East Terrace and the Slopes, where I'd seen her last.

In the garden, I shaded my eyes and peered around the rosebushes. "Dragonfly, can you hear me?"

Nothing.

I followed the path I had taken the night before. I called out at intervals with no reply. At the castle wall gate, I grabbed the usual rock to prop it open and lifted the hinge.

As I did, I saw someone standing on the other side. A

tall, uniformed someone with his back to me, and beyond him a half dozen others wading through the tall grass with sticks.

The one in front of me turned and held out his hand to stop me from coming any closer. "This area's off limits, Miss. No one's allowed past this point."

"But why?" I faked an innocent look. "Did something happen?" I rose on my tiptoes to see over his burly shoulder. How far had they searched? Were they at the trees?

"Nothing for you to be concerned about. Just go back inside." He shooed me with a flutter of his sausage-sized fingers.

I stepped back and stumbled on a pebble. I thought he reached out to steady me, but he grabbed the edge of the door instead and yanked it shut.

CHAPTER FOURTEEN

MRS. CROSSEY WAS tending a fresh batch of porridge when I reached the kitchen. Without disturbing her, I went to a pile of day-old bread loaves on our table. A bundle of herbs, cream, butter, eggs, and sausage links sat nearby. So it would be a savory bread pudding in the Servants' Hall tonight. I picked up a knife and set to work dicing a bread slice into cubes.

"You've been in the Queen's room all this time?" Mrs. Crossey slanted a look my direction.

"Not exactly." I scraped a handful of cubes into an empty bowl before starting on the next slice. I glanced around, making sure no one was near enough to hear. "Did you hear about the girl on the Slopes?"

Clank!

I whipped around to find Mrs. Crossey fishing her ladle out of the pot.

"How did you hear about that?" she whispered back, wiping the wet handle with a dishtowel draped over her shoulder.

"The Queen's ladies mentioned it. Not to me, of course. I overheard them."

"Gossiping as usual." She sighed in a way that made her whole chest heave. "Still, you should have been finished and back an hour ago. Mr. MacDougall has already been by. He wants to speak with you."

"Just now?" I asked.

She nodded.

That must have been a quick conversation with Mr. Bailey. "What did he want?"

Her forehead wrinkled beneath a silver curl that had escaped from her bonnet. "Who knows, but he didn't look happy. Did something happen? I mean, *with the Queen.*" She gave me a pointed look.

I deposited another handful of diced bread into the bowl and dodged her gaze. "Of course not. It was only firewood." There was no point mentioning that awkward moment with Her Majesty. "I did see Abigail, however. So she's a parlor maid now?" I tried to keep the envy out of my voice, but I knew I wasn't succeeding.

"Abigail is not your concern," Mrs. Crossey snapped. "Tell me what delayed you."

"Nothing. I told you."

Mrs. Crossey set down her spoon and waved me to a more private corner. "You're lying. Don't pretend otherwise. Now tell me why."

How did she know? There was no earthy reason she should, but she did. Excuses raced through my head—some outright lies, some only partially so. I settled on a partial truth. "I needed some fresh air. It frightened me. That girl on the Slopes. What if it had been me? What if it was *supposed* to be me?"

She watched me as she mulled that over. "It is rather upsetting," she said at last.

I bit my bottom lip.

Her suspicion returned, and she didn't so much look at me as bore holes through my skull. "There's still something you aren't telling me. What is it?"

I cringed. How in the world did she know? "While I

was out, I saw Mr. Wyck."

Her eyes widened then her face reddened with fresh rage, and in that moment, I saw an unmistakable family resemblance. Headmistress Trindle had turned that same furious look on me many times over the years. "I told you," she said, "and quite clearly that you were to stay away from him."

She paused and pulled back to allow a cook to pass us on his way to the pantry. When he was out of earshot, she resumed with only slightly less anger. "I specifically said you weren't to speak to him."

"It wasn't my fault. He approached me." I could see that didn't appease her. "If it's all the same," I continued, "I hope I never speak to him again. I don't like him. He's rude, and I wouldn't be surprised if he was the one responsible for what happened to that girl."

That got her attention. "Why? Did he say something?"

"Not exactly."

"Then what?"

There were so many reasons, and they all swept through me, a churning sea of anger and frustration. But at the center of the storm, at its very core, one complaint rose above the others because it terrified me. I lowered my voice to little more than a breath. "I told you already. He touched me, and there was no vision. Absolutely nothing."

"That's your concern?"

Wasn't it enough? "Yes, and *he was there*. He was on the Slopes when the attack happened. If someone murdered that poor girl, it had to be him."

"Murdered? How do you know she was murdered?"

"What else could it be?"

"Any number of things, I suppose. You shouldn't jump to such a conclusion without good reason. Do you have any proof?"

I didn't, of course. And what was worse, now that I'd heard the accusation aloud, it sounded insane even to me. "You're right. It's ridiculous. I don't know what came over me."

Mrs. Crossey closed her eyes and shook her head. I could see her shoulders sink beneath an invisible weight. "I filled your head with fear, that's what did it. It's no wonder you're seeing danger at every turn. Maybe I was wrong to drag you into this."

"Don't say that." I didn't like seeing her this way. Broken, discouraged. "Perhaps I said more than I intended. I do want to help the Queen, especially if she's in danger."

She looked at me as though she were trying to decide if I was telling the truth. It was a surprise even to myself, but it was the truth. At least I was starting to think it was. I was always grateful for my job. I knew what ills befell many of the girls like me, orphans with no family or prospects. But the job was just a job. A simple reprieve from the streets or a workhouse.

I had no particular love for it, but being in the Queen's presence today, hearing her speak to me no less, made it all feel different somehow. Not like I was important or anything so grand, but like what I did mattered, that it had purpose. Yes, that was the word, purpose, and I hoped Mrs. Crossey sensed my sincerity.

The way she scrutinized me now, I couldn't tell.

"When you were in the Queen's room, did anything happen?" she asked.

"Like I said, Abigail was there." I considered telling her about the girl's accusation but thought better of it. "But I didn't feel anything."

"Are you sure?" There was that strange, unblinking stare again. The muscles in the woman's cheeks twitched.

"Abigail accused me of stealing, but I only wanted to touch one of the framed photographs on the mantel," I blurted then gasped. Why on earth had I said that?

"Photographs? Why did you want to do that?" Her eyes remained fixed on me in that peculiar way.

Say nothing. I pressed my lips together, but the answer

burst out anyway. "I thought I might see something about the Queen." My hands shot to my mouth. What was happening to me?

"But you didn't touch anything?"

I shook my head.

Finally, Mrs. Crossey looked away. She tapped her lips and muttered, "So Abigail is assigned to the sitting room now. How unfortunate."

When her gaze left me, so did the strange compulsion. "You did something to me, didn't you? How did you do it?"

She shook her head and led me back to our stove. "A conversation for another time."

I watched her return to the porridge and our ordinary routine, but I was now absolutely certain that this woman was anything but ordinary.

~ ~ ~

The hours passed quickly in the Great Kitchen as work progressed on the nighttime meals, the centerpiece of which was a royal reception in the Waterloo Room for a contingent of German and Austrian dignitaries.

All around Mrs. Crossey and me, cooks and sous chefs and assorted maids worked on a trio of potages, a poisson, a goose stuffed with wild mushrooms and rice, asparagus with a frothy mousseline, a mocha souffle, and an array of jellied fruits and ices for dessert.

I, however, worked on batch after batch of savory bread pudding for the Servants' Hall, baffled at the way everyone carried on without the slightest acknowledgment of the tragedy that had struck just beyond the castle wall.

There were no inquiries into the comings and goings of the staff to discover if anyone had witnessed anything that might be useful to the investigation. There was no call for vigilance. Nothing.

It was all so peculiar.

I would have thought no one even knew except by mid-afternoon the whispers and huddled conversations, meaningful glances, and conspiratorial visits to the pantry were unmistakable.

But rather than discuss it, it was as if everyone was holding a collective breath. Was it possible they all believed, as Mrs. Crossey seemed to, that it was merely an unfortunate accident?

I certainly didn't. And I couldn't stop myself from watching every door that opened and eying every person that strolled through our midst. Perhaps my suspicions would come to nothing, and if that was the case, then no one would be happier than I.

Until then, I watched and I listened and I waited.

After the final batch of bread pudding was dispatched to the oven, I gathered my dirty bowls and utensils for the washing maids. I cleaned the cutting board as Mrs. Crossey assembled the leftover ingredients. "I can return those to the pantry, if you like," I said.

She wiped a bead of sweat from her forehead. "No. I can take it from here. You've done enough for today."

I had?

She gave me one of her motherly looks. "You need to rest," she whispered. "We have a long night ahead."

I was too tired to argue. After two nights of little sleep and a long day on edge, the thought of crawling into bed made me weak in the knees. I yearned for my pillow. I nodded and scraped the last sausage nubs free from the board. "Midnight, then?"

She shooed me from my place and took the cutting board. "Midnight. Mr. MacDougall's office."

I grabbed a clean dishtowel, wiped off my gloves, and headed for the door.

"And, Jane," she said, a warning in her voice, "no side trips tonight."

CHAPTER FIFTEEN

AFTER MIDNIGHT, AFTER all the meals have been served and all the sous chefs and cooks and maids and pages have retired for the night, a certain stillness descends on the Great Kitchen. The busy worktables and stoves stand empty, the copper pots and pans hang silent, and an eerie darkness fills the lantern roof windows that usually glow with sunlight.

At least that's how it seemed when I slipped in at the witching hour on my way to meet Mrs. Crossey. The only soul in sight was the nighttime cook, who was already propped back in his chair beside a stockpot, a simmering beef broth by the smell of it, probably for the next day's use. He appeared to be asleep.

Lucky man. Every time I drifted off, I inevitably returned to images of the attack. As if they were always there, waiting for me. And now, to know a young woman had lost her life out there certainly didn't help.

As much as I didn't want to believe Mrs. Crossey's warnings, that girl's death had given them credence.

I tried to console myself with the reminder that the Constable and his men were investigating and the castle guards would be on high alert. It was the only thought that gave me comfort as I waited in the darkness, watching the moon creep across the starry sky through our room's sliver of a window.

It had seemed an eternity before that glowing crescent finally crested, when I could slip out of bed—quietly so as not to disturb Marlie's sleep—and make my way to meet Mrs. Crossey.

Passing the snoring cook on tiptoes, I had nearly reached the corridor that led to Mr. MacDougall's door when the sound of slow footfalls stopped me short.

I turned, expecting to see Mrs. Crossey, but I saw no one save the sleeping cook. I listened again but heard only the thumping of my own heart. Then the cook's long, sonorous snore.

My fears really were getting the better of me.

"Roaming again?"

The familiar tenor stopped me mid-stride. I resisted the urge to run. It would do no good anyway. With his larger size, he could catch me if he wanted.

Carefully, I turned to find Mr. Wyck leaning against the wall, his arms crossed and his lips tucked up in a sly grin.

"I'm not roaming." I hoped the irritation in my voice masked my trembling.

He pushed off the wall. "Then what else could you possibly be doing here at this hour?"

My cheeks burned. I tried to swallow and failed. "What's it to you?"

He straightened, making his already greater height even more so. He sensed my fear. I could see it in the way the light danced across his dark eyes.

I swallowed hard and backed away.

"Oh, there you are!"

The cheerful voice sent me spinning again. In the darkened hallway near Mr. MacDougall's door, Marlie appeared. My roommate strode toward me with a bright smile and a happy bounce in her step.

I stared at her, dumbstruck. Hadn't I left her sleeping in our room? I was certain I had, but here she was as wide awake as ever. She looked from me to Mr. Wyck then approached us both. In an exaggerated whisper, she said to me, "Did you find the leftover scones? I found some lemon curd." She lifted one of the canner's prized jars and waved it.

"I was just about to." I didn't know why I was playing along or why she was pretending to be my friend, but there seemed no other choice.

She glanced coyly at Mr. Wyck. "Will you be joining us for a midnight snack, then?"

Was she flirting with him? I wanted to stop her, warn her, but I could only stare in horror.

To my relief, he retreated to the shadows. "I was just on my way back to the mews."

"Are you sure?" She wagged the jar again. "There's more than enough to share."

Let him leave!

She paid no attention to my silent plea.

He backed away until he was at the door. "No, but thank you."

"Your loss," she demurred. "And you won't tell anyone where this jar disappeared to, will you?" She gave him a dopey, guilty grin.

"Won't say a word. If you'll excuse me."

He pushed out the door and disappeared into the darkness. Only when he was out of sight did I realize I was holding my breath. I let it go with an audible gush of relief.

"Well, that was unexpected," Marlie said, dropping the cheerful act but only slightly.

"You shouldn't have done that," I said. "You could have been hurt. We both could have."

"I hardly think so," she said.

I started to argue but stopped. I couldn't tell her what I suspected, not without raising questions. "Why are you here?" I said instead. "I mean, how did you know I'd be here?"

She jutted her chin in the snoring cook's direction and jerked her head toward the hallway. "We should go before Pierre wakes up."

It wasn't an answer, but I followed her anyway into the dark corridor. At Mr. MacDougall's door, she stopped, produced a key from her pocket, and slid it into the lock. I heard the tumblers turn. "After you." She held the door open wide.

I stared. "Is Mrs. Crossey with you?" I looked both ways along the hallway, searching for the woman. "I was supposed to meet her."

Marlie stepped into the office and gestured for me to follow. "I know you were." When we were inside, she set the jar on a side table and scratched a match against its box before lighting a stub of a candle that was sitting there. The small light bathed the office in a dim amber glow. "She told me to get you."

"She did?" Was Marlie part of Mrs. Crossey's scheme, too? Then a more terrible thought struck. "Why isn't she here? What happened to her?" Had she been attacked? Had someone else?

"Nothing happened to her. She's fine. She just wanted to get things started. So everything would be ready when you arrived."

I looked around the office, confused. "Then where is she?"

"Come here and I'll show you." She moved behind Mr. MacDougall's massive desk and set the candle on the mantel, then squared herself to the overhead mirror. She glanced back at me. "You're going to want to watch this." She placed both hands atop the left dragon's snout and pressed down with enough force to break it.

"Marlie!" I scrambled forward to stop her, but it was too late. The wood snapped. I stared, horrified. "You broke it."

"Don't be silly." She was practically laughing.

I looked more closely, and she was right. The snout wasn't broken, just bent as though attached to a hinge.

Then she pressed both hands against the mantel's long shelf and pushed. Incredibly, the entire structure, from floor to ceiling, slid back into the wall and pivoted to reveal a slender opening.

"What is that?" I didn't know whether to be amazed or frightened but couldn't help feeling a bit of both.

"C'mon, we need to hurry. Don't touch anything." She grabbed the candle and motioned for me to follow as she slipped into the dark crevice.

Reason told me to stay put. How could I trust that Marlie was telling me the truth and who knew what was on the other side of that wall? The smart thing to do would be to go back to my room and forget about hidden passageways and this midnight rendezvous. There was no way secret protectors were operating in this castle, and certainly no way that I could be one of them. It was all part of some elaborate prank.

That would be a more logical explanation, but where was the logic in what happened to me beyond the wall? The attack by the tree and the fainting. That dark figure with the glowing red eyes and the girl. That dead girl from the Slopes.

Maybe there was a rational explanation for all of it.

Maybe I only had to follow Marlie to find out what it was.

I peered inside and saw the candle's hazy glow and Marlie's silhouette descending a spiral stone staircase.

"C'mon," she whispered, her voice urgent.

I didn't move. Everyone knew castles had secret passages. Why should Windsor be any different? It was no reason to be alarmed.

So why couldn't I force my feet to move? As unlikely an ally as Marlie was, I never knew her to be malicious. Aloof, maybe, but not malicious. I couldn't believe she'd lead me astray.

I poked my head farther into the darkness. "Where are you going?"

If she answered, it was lost among a sudden thunder of footsteps and men's voices in the hallway.

"They came this way? Are you sure?"

"That's what he said."

I didn't recognize the voices, but I knew that distinctive clamor of swords knocking against buckled boots. It was the castle guards.

Someone pounded on a door near enough to make the office walls shake.

"Anyone in there?"

I heard a door open and more footsteps.

"What's that noise?" Marlie called up.

"The guards are in the next room." I stared at Mr. MacDougall's door. Had Marlie locked it? "What should I do?"

A distant door slammed, and the footsteps grew closer.

If they found us, how could I explain any of this? My heart thundered in my chest.

"Get in and close the mantel," Marlie demanded. "Just push it back until it's back in place. Hurry."

When the office door rattled from a guard's pounding, there was no more time to hesitate. I ducked into the dark space and pressed my weight against the wood. To my surprise, it glided easily and came to a soft stop against the wall.

I heard more pounding, but it was muted now. "Anyone in there?" came the question before the door burst open.

"No one here, either, Captain." A guard's voice was muffled but clear.

After a moment, I felt the shudder of the door when they slammed it shut.

We were safe. For now. It was my only thought as I leaned against the wall and tried to steady my breath. I didn't notice Marlie coming back up the stairs until she was beside me, her candle casting its soft light on what appeared to be a stone-block room barely large enough for us to stand side by side.

"Are you all right?" Uncertainty laced her voice.

I honestly didn't know, but I nodded anyway.

"Good," she said. "Because there's a lot to do, and we're already late."

CHAPTER SIXTEEN

FIRMLY GRIPPING MY skirt, I followed Marlie down the corkscrew staircase. My wariness grew with each descending step. Where was she taking me? A cellar? A dungeon? My mind raced with possibilities, each more unsettling than the last. When I tried to ask, she cut me off with an emphatic *shhhh!*

So, I swallowed my words, followed her lead, and counted each step as though my life depended on it. Ten, eleven, twelve…

Down we went, and nothing changed. Not the bare stone walls or the ragged slate steps. Not the blackness that swallowed where we had been or the void that hid what still lay beyond. Not the back of Marlie's head, with her neat knot of hair beneath her bonnet, or the scuff of her boots and mine. Seventeen, eighteen, nineteen…

The only thing that was changing as we made our way down to wherever we were going was the temperature. It continued to drop and raise goosebumps across my arms and along my spine. By the twenty-fourth step, I could see my breath like a hazy cloud before me.

At the thirty-second step, Marlie paused and looked

back. Not at me, but past me, to the darkness above. Her eyes flashed with concern. She whispered, "I would appreciate it if you didn't mention the guards to Mrs. Crossey. I promised her I could manage this, and, if it's all the same to you——"

"I won't say anything," I whispered back, surprised by her timidity. "You have my word."

Her brightness returned. "Thank you. You know, I'm glad she's finally told you, about *you know*. It's been dreadfully hard not being able to say anything about it. Sometimes I thought I might burst. But Mrs. Crossey said it was important not to say anything too soon. So, I didn't, but now that you know I hope we can be proper friends." She flashed a toothy grin and waited.

I forced a smile in return. "Yes. Of course." She wanted to be friends now? After all this time? But she wasn't moving. She was still staring, so I added, "I'd like that."

At that, she grinned wider and made a happy shrug with her shoulders. "I'm glad."

I had no idea what to say or to think so I just counted. Eight more steps brought us to the last stair.

Marlie lifted her flame and cast its scant light across what appeared to be a stone cellar. I couldn't judge its size because the far wall was set too far back in the shadows. Each step revealed a few more paces of the same side walls, the same floor, but no end. Only darkness. "Where are we?" I whispered, gazing into the void.

She walked past me with a mischievous grin. "We're almost there."

Before I could argue, Marlie ventured deeper into the tunnel, her candle casting its sphere of light against the crude stone walls.

I paused. The smart thing to do would be to climb back up the stairs to a world without hidden passageways, underground tunnels, or secret agendas.

Back to a world I recognized.

Marlie turned back, her candle held high. "Are you coming?"

I stared up at the dark space above me. Mr. MacDougall's mantel was up there, lost in the shadows. In front of me, Marlie's flickering light illuminated the spattering of freckles on her nose.

To think I'd thought I understood this girl, a girl no older than myself who I had worked beside and slept beside all these months. The roommate who kept to herself, as I did, and seemed no more remarkable than a loaf of bread.

But just as Mrs. Crossey and Mr. MacDougall had shown themselves to be something more than what I knew, Marlie Carlisle was proving there was more to her as well. Was she also a Fayte Guardian?

Ahead, Marlie lifted her candle again. "Well?"

I stared into the subterranean void that stretched behind her. It would be foolish to forge ahead without knowing where the tunnel led, but I had come too far to go back without answers. I steeled myself and lifted my chin. "I'm coming."

If she noticed the fear in my voice, she didn't show it. She only said, "Good," with a distinct note of relief.

And with that, she resumed the underground journey and her recitation of all the trouble there would have been if the guards had found us, which led to anecdotes about the times she'd been caught after curfew and a number of uncomfortable discussions in Mr. MacDougall's office.

At least I think that's what she was saying because I was hardly listening.

Instead I was concentrating on the tunnel and searching each new length of stone wall and flagstone path the candlelight revealed. Who could have built this place and why? And where on earth were we going?

I lifted my collar over my nose to lessen the rank smell of moist earth and mildew that was so thick at times it choked me. The extra layer didn't help much, but at least the stench dissipated as we moved deeper along the path.

"Is it far?" I asked.

"Not really."

I took her answer to mean we weren't close, either.

When we approached a door of rustic wood and heavy iron hinges, I stopped.

But Marlie didn't. She didn't even slow. Apparently, this wasn't our destination.

"How much farther?" I asked as I hurried to catch up to her.

"Not much."

She wasn't convincing.

When another door came into view, I brightened again.

But again, she didn't stop. The other doors—I counted ten in all—I passed without excitement or expectation.

Instead, I hugged myself for warmth and wished I had brought a coat. The air that had already been cool and damp at the beginning of the tunnel was downright cold now and the air was filled with the scent of forest trees and underbrush.

We walked in silence, with only the scrape of our boots against the flagstones, but by the time we reached the thirteenth door, I couldn't stand it anymore. "Where do all these doors lead?"

"All over," Marlie answered. "Some to places inside the castle, some elsewhere. But no one uses them. They haven't been needed for ages."

Needed for what? I was about to ask, but Marlie stopped and held out a hand to stop me. "Rat."

I looked down as a brown rodent scurried across our path a few paces ahead. I tensed despite myself. A single rat hardly posed a danger, but I still didn't like them. When the animal disappeared into a crevice on the other side, Marlie pulled her hand back and resumed her pace.

Now the walls began to change. The large, sharply cut stones gave way to a smaller, less uniform variety. Some were thin and narrow, others thick and wide. The variety created sloping, uneven layers that made the walls appear to undulate. It was a wonder they stood upright at all. "How long has this tunnel been here?"

"As long as the castle, I suppose. Maybe longer."

"It looks so old. The stones..." I trailed a fingertip over the worn edge of one that protruded beyond the rest. I was tempted to remove my gloves. Could there be memories locked in these stones? I was mulling the possibility when I stumbled into Marlie's back. She had stopped when I wasn't looking.

Marlie scowled over her shoulder. "Please watch where you're going."

"Sorry." I shuffled back and realized the tunnel had come to an end.

Before us stood a wide door, wider than the others and made of a finely polished cherrywood that narrowed to a point like a leaf's apex ten or so feet above our heads. Twin pillars of a whitish stone flanked it, and upon each was engraved a winding vine of chiseled symbols.

"Take this." Marlie thrust her candle at me.

I took it, and she grabbed the door's scrolled brass handle in one hand and pressed a lever above it with the other. From somewhere deep in the stones and the wood, something clanked and clicked, and the door groaned open.

She entered, and slowly, reluctantly, I followed.

It was as if we'd stepped into a cathedral. Above us, the vaulted ceiling was supported by pillars that soared far above our heads. Thirty feet, maybe forty, all terminating in an arched ceiling framed with heavy beams. The polished marble beneath our feet reflected and amplified our candlelight, though I could also see small blazes in the mouths of stone dragon heads set into the walls at intervals around the room. Between the stone dragon heads hung tapestries, mounted cross swords, daggers, and medieval crests.

"What is this place?" I murmured, my voice low and

reverent.

"Officially, it's the Great Hall of the Windsor Order of the Fayte, but we usually call it the Library. This part anyway." Marlie set the candle on a wooden pedestal beside the door.

The Library. It was an apt name. Ahead of us six curved wooden towers formed a circle that stretched almost to the ceiling. Each tower was divided into dozens of shelves. Some were stuffed with books and boxes, tattered scrolls and loose pages. Others looked as though they'd been scraped bare.

Gazing up, I wondered how anyone could reach the highest shelves until I noticed a scaffold contraption made of brass ladders and pipes, pulleys and levers, all cobbled together with caster wheels at the bottom and handles at the sides so the entire structure could be pushed from one tower to the next along a brass rail that connected the towers like a shiny necklace.

"Robes, Marlie. Don't forget the robes!"

I knew that voice booming from somewhere farther ahead, somewhere deep within this mysterious hall. It was Mrs. Crossey.

Marlie rolled her eyes and mumbled, "Of course, I wouldn't forget the robes."

She blew out her candle as the Library's light was sufficient and looked at me. "Pick any one you like."

I followed her glance back to the door and saw behind us a tidy line of indigo robes hanging from their hoods.

When I didn't move, she grabbed the closest one from its hook and thrust it at me.

"You have to put it on." She wrinkled her nose in apology. "Everyone has to wear them. It's a rule."

There was that word again. "Who is everyone?"

"The Fayte Guardians, of course." She shook the robe, urging me to take it.

The Fayte Guardians. But who were they? I didn't voice the question. I lost my nerve and stuffed it back into the pit of my stomach. I took the robe.

She grabbed another and slid it around herself, lifted the hood over her head, and tied the laces at the collar.

I followed her example, shrugging the soft linen over my shoulders and lifting the hood over my head.

She nodded her approval. "Are you ready?"

"How would I know?"

She chuckled as though I were joking. I wanted to tell her my reservations were real, but she was already striding down the aisle that divided the ring of bookshelves.

I swallowed hard and fell in step behind her.

Within the ring were four sturdy tables. The two to my left were bare, but one on the right was piled with books. One massive tome lay open, as if someone had just stepped away from it. It looked remarkably like the one I'd seen in the vision I'd pulled from Mrs. Crossey's memories. I moved closer to try to make out the brown-ink scrawl, but I couldn't decipher a word.

"You're familiar with ancient Gaelic, then?" Marlie asked.

I stiffened, chastened that I'd been caught snooping. "Not really. Is that what this is?"

She nodded. "Just some old recipes."

"What sort of recipes?"

"I was looking for something medicinal for the Queen," she added. "For her stomach."

It was no secret that since Her Majesty had returned from Balmoral Castle, she had eaten little more than a smidgen of semolina pudding and tidbits of bread. Such a development ordinarily sent Chef into fits, but even he knew that when the Queen passed on her usual feasts, she was likely suffering. Perhaps from a toothache or a digestive complaint, though she never complained outright.

But what aid could Marlie find in such an old book? "Did you find anything?"

"Thankfully, I did. The Council cleared our shelves of

the oldest volumes a few years ago to be stored at Balmoral, but I hid this one among the assignment records because it's one of my favorites. There's a recipe for every ailment you can imagine. That one there is a delightfully spiced carrot soup with the soothing qualities of chamomile. I was thinking one could easily add a touch of white willow bark to relieve aches and pains as well."

Tonight my roommate was full of surprises. "I didn't realize you knew so much about cooking."

"Not so much about cooking, but plants and herbs? Those I know a bit about. That's where I can do a bit of good."

Her pride was evident, and I wanted to know more. "Chef sets the menus. Doesn't he decide what Her Majesty eats?"

She giggled. "He thinks he does. That's all that matters."

The twinkle in her eye didn't betray her secret, but it told me enough.

When we emerged from the ring of towers, I saw the Library—grand as it was—was still just an anteroom to an even more remarkable space. A temple of sorts, but where an altar might be, there stood a fountain formed of white, nearly translucent stone.

Beside it stood a lone figure in a robe, which wasn't indigo like Marlie's and mine, but a rich and vibrant purple. The hood was up, obscuring the face, but I knew those thick wrists reaching out from the ends of the bell sleeves and the reddened fingers that gripped the fountain's edge.

It was Mrs. Crossey.

As we neared, she raised her hands from the fountain and lifted her hood to reveal a long and loose shroud of silvery hair I had only seen in wisps that sometimes escaped the muslin cap she usually wore. She held out her arms, lowered her chin, and said, "Welcome, Jane. Welcome to our sanctuary."

CHAPTER SEVENTEEN

AT THE SIGHT of Mrs. Crossey behind the fountain, my courage faltered.

"Come, child." She motioned to me. "Come closer. Don't be afraid."

But I was afraid. I had no idea where I was or what I was doing here.

Marlie nudged my elbow, urging me onward.

Hesitantly, I followed her along the path of black and white stones laid into a braid along the polished floor until we reached the fountain's pedestal base.

"What is this place?" I whispered when we reached Mrs. Crossey.

"It's many things," she replied, amusement teasing her lips. "Tonight, however, it's where we'll see what's what."

I nodded as though that made sense, but it made nothing of the sort. Instead, I searched for answers along the gently curved walls, taking in all the long and narrow tapestries. There were a dozen or so weavings, some depicting people in indigo robes engaged in household tasks and others portraying more pastoral scenes.

The grand weaving behind the fountain, however,

stood taller and wider than the others, and in the foreground, a woman in a purple tunic with her auburn hair pulled back behind her shoulders had lowered herself on bended knee beneath the glowing touch of a pale woman as tall as the oaks and as slender as a reed whose white hair flowed to her waist over a diaphanous gown that seemed to shimmer even as I stared at it. It was her ears, however, that drew my attention. They were too large for human ears, protruding as they did through her cascading hair, and their tops were not round, but pointed sharply toward the sky.

"Who is that?" My voice was hardly more than a breath.

Mrs. Crossey's lips spread into an affable smile. "Legend has many names for her, but to us, she is the Lady of the Fayte. In this moment, she is creating the first Fayte Guardian, bestowing her gifts on the Warrior Queen herself."

I had never heard of the Lady of the Fayte, but I knew about the Warrior Queen. Queen Boudica of the Iceni tribe had been a frequent topic in Chadwick Hollow's history lessons. That Queen's rebellion against the Roman invaders failed in the end and the woman lost her life, but her fierce loyalty to our homeland inspired an enduring pride in the hearts of Britons—especially Headmistress Trindle.

I pointed to two girls in the background. "Who are they?"

"Boudica's daughters," Mrs. Crossey said. "Some say they have played an even more important role than Boudica in our history. They appear in that weaving as well." She gestured to a smaller tapestry to the right that showed Boudica standing between the girls. "Do you see what she's doing?"

"Offering them wine?"

"Not exactly." Mrs. Crossey looked away and smoothed her robe. "Perhaps that story, the story of our legacy, is a subject better left for another time. If you would, please remove your gloves and dip your fingers into the basin."

I pulled back. "Why?"

"No harm will come to you here, Jane," she said, her voice calm and reassuring. "But you must do as I ask. We'll move slowly. If there's anything unpleasant, we'll stop. Let's give it a try, shall we?"

Marlie scoffed. "But you can't. It's not a New Moon and no one's here."

Mrs. Crossey held out her hands. "We're here."

"But it's impossible," Marlie railed. "The rule—"

"I understand about the rules," Mrs. Crossey said in a way that made it clear Marlie should stop. "I'm choosing to break this one. And while we might not have the benefit of a proper moon, we do have Jane. If she's as powerful as it would seem, it could prove useful."

Marlie fidgeted. Her gaze darted back toward the Library. "If that's what you think is best. I should probably leave you to it, then." She inched back from the fountain.

Mrs. Crossey hung her gaze on my roommate. "I would prefer you didn't leave."

Marlie froze.

"I need you here. Jane isn't initiated. You must be the witness."

Marlie threw up her hands. "But you're the Master Scryer. Can't you initiate her?"

Mrs. Crossey's stony expression gave way to a soft chuckle. "I'm already breaking one rule, I'm not going to push my luck."

Marlie trudged back to the fountain's edge. "Fine. What would you like me to do?"

Mrs. Crossey straightened. "Prepare your Faytling, and we'll begin."

At that, Marlie and Mrs. Crossey each pulled a black cord from beneath their collars. At the end of each hung a small cylinder, a golden filigree cage wrapped around a pinkish stone. They laid the jewels over the front of their robes before lowering their fingers into the fountain's basin.

Mrs. Crossey caught my eye. "Now, if you would, dip your fingers into the pool."

Slowly, I tugged away my gloves and slid them inside my robe, beneath the waistband of my skirt. I held my hands over the water then lowered them in.

At that moment, the clear water turned a soft lavender hue. Startled, I yanked my hands back and the color disappeared.

The rise of Mrs. Crossey's eyebrows told me the change had surprised her, too.

"What happened?" I clasped my dripping fingers to my chest.

"Did you feel something?" Mrs. Crossey asked.

I shook my head.

"Then it must be an indication of your gift. Let's try again,"

I didn't want to, but I did as she asked and lowered my fingertips into the pool. The water again turned lavender.

In that instant, my fingers seized, my arms seized, my whole body seized. I couldn't move. I couldn't even think.

But as quickly as that paralysis set in, it passed. I could move and breathe, only the racing of my heart remained. "What was that?"

Mrs. Crossey ignored the question. Her eyes were closed, and she dragged her fingertips in lazy figure eights along the water's surface. "Great Lady of the Fayte," she intoned, "please hear us as we humbly seek your counsel."

There was a long silence, then Marlie whispered, "It's happening."

I glanced up to see the pendants resting on Marlie's and Mrs. Crossey's chests pulsing with violet light, weakly at first then stronger and in perfect unison.

For a full minute we remained that way—Mrs. Crossey twitching at times, frowning at others. When she pulled her fingers from the basin, Marlie and I did the same.

Marlie leaned forward, her fingers gripping the fountain's edge. "It's never felt like that before. What does it mean?"

"I believe it's because of Jane," Mrs. Crossey said.

"What do you mean?" I asked. "What happened just now?"

Mrs. Crossey wiped the water from her hands. "I was trying to communicate with the Lady. That's the pool's purpose. The water forges the bond and opens a doorway of sorts. We call it *converging*. It's how she alerts us to potential hazards and dangers."

"Or used to anyway," Marlie grumbled.

I looked at her. "What do you mean?"

She glanced at Mrs. Crossey. "She just stopped. For years, there was nothing. Then a few months ago, out of the blue, she returned. Sort of. But it's different now. The messages are vague and confusing. Sometimes they don't make any sense at all. The Supreme Elder warned us that something was wrong. That perhaps we'd displeased her. Some are even saying his firing is proof of it."

"Now, now," Mrs. Crossey said. "It's certainly unfortunate that he was let go the way he was, but it doesn't mean his interpretation was the right one. It was only a theory, and until the Council of Elders assigns his replacement, we are free to explore other explanations."

"I suppose," Marlie said, though she hardly seemed convinced. "Then did you sense the Lady just now? Did she convey a message?"

Mrs. Crossey shook her head. "Not a message, not exactly. But the threat is present and getting stronger. It's closer than before. Perhaps even within the castle."

I didn't know anything about a Lady of the Fayte, but I was beginning to understand something about threats within the castle. Again, my mind turned to the peculiar Mr. Wyck.

"There's more, isn't there?" Marlie said, her frown lines

deepening.

"Perhaps, but I'm not sure what to make of it," Mrs. Crossey said. "The message is: A face is not a face. Or rather a false face. It's a bit confusing."

Again I thought of Mr. Wyck. Perhaps he wasn't who he said he was. An impostor?

Marlie shook her head. "As vague as ever."

"I'm sure it's not intended." Mrs. Crossey rubbed the water from her hands. "We are communicating with another realm after all. Words and symbols are not always so clear."

I looked up from drying my own hands. "What do you mean *another realm*?"

Marlie frowned. "What would you call it?"

An odd fear gripped me. "Call what, exactly?"

Marlie turned to Mrs. Crossey. "You said she was Fayte. How can she not know—"

"Enough, Marlie."

My roommate stopped, but whether it was Mrs. Crossey's reprimand or the woman's glare that did it, I couldn't say.

"The Lady's realm is a hidden world," Mrs. Crossey said by way of an explanation, "a world beyond our own."

"That's nonsense."

Marlie scoffed.

Mrs. Crossey sighed. "I can see how it would seem so, but I assure you it's not. Let's leave it at that for now."

Marlie's head shot up. Her eyes sparked. "Mrs. Crossey! I know what the message means."

"You do?" The elder woman looked skeptical.

"The false face? It's the Queen's masquerade."

Mrs. Crossey tapped her lip. "Of course! The masquerade..." She nodded, the idea sinking in.

"It has to be," Marlie said. "And if we know when the attack is to take place, we can prepare. We can put everyone on alert."

There it was again. Everyone. "How many Fayte

Guardians are there?"

"Not as many as there used to be, unfortunately," Marlie said. "Not since the efficiency campaign began."

Mrs. Crossey was pacing, still tapping her lip. "We can't tell anyone, at least not yet."

"But we must," Marlie wailed. "I know she isn't initiated yet, but the message came from the divining pool. So it shouldn't matter."

A deep crease split Mrs. Crossey's brow. "It could matter a great deal to some. They'll question the message, or worse. Many believe as the former Supreme Elder believed. Once we find the threat, once it can be confirmed, then we can share it with the others. Until then, this information must remain between us. For now, at least."

"But we can't do this alone," Marlie wailed.

"With Jane's gift, I think we can," Mrs. Crossey said. "And this should help." She lifted the cord with the golden pendant from her neck and offered it to me.

I stared at the dazzling cylinder. It was still glowing faintly. "What do I do with it?"

"Just wear it. For now."

Marlie shifted and touched her own pendant. Reverently. Protectively. "Are you sure that's wise?"

"Jane is going to need all the help she can get," Mrs. Crossey said. "At the moment, a Faytling is the best we have to offer."

Faytling. It was a beautiful name for such a treasure. I reached for it, my fingers itching to wrap around that delicate vessel.

Perhaps Mrs. Crossey sensed my eagerness because she pulled it back and said, a bit sternly, "With the gloves, I think. At least until we have a better idea of what you can do."

I wasn't going to argue. I tugged on my gloves, and she extended the jewel once again.

Taking it gingerly into my palm, I held it up for closer

inspection. Its inner light brightened then faded again. "What an odd little thing," I whispered as I stared, transfixed by the jewel.

Her eyes twinkled. "It appears to like you. That's a good sign. A very good sign, indeed."

~ ~ ~

"You didn't hear a word I said, did you?"

I glanced up from the edge of my bed, where I was admiring my new treasure. "I did. You told me to put the Faytling away and get some sleep."

She stood at the mirror over our washbasin and tied off her night braid with a ribbon. "Lucky guess."

It was a lucky guess. Nothing she'd said since we returned to our room had registered. Ordinarily I'd be happy for the conversation. It would be a welcome break from the usual silence that filled our room. But I couldn't tear my attention away from the Faytling.

I lowered my gaze back to the jewel and marveled at its smooth edges. Its delicate curves. "Can I ask you something?"

"Of course."

"When did you get your Faytling?"

"Not till I was eighteen, at my initiation."

"Did you already know about the Guardians by then?"

"I was eight or so when my mother first told me. I didn't really understand it, though. She told me we had special jobs in the castle to take care of the Queen. I thought she was talking about being a maid in the kitchen."

"That's all she told you?"

"A little later, when I started collecting herbs, she told me that might be my special job, just like it was for her. She also told me it was fine to talk about herbs and the things we did with them at home but that I shouldn't mention them to other people." She looked up at the ceiling and shook her head, remembering. "She told me I knew so much about herbs people could become jealous and that it would be a kindness to spare them that. It's embarrassing to admit that I fell for it. I was so gullible. I guess I just thought it was normal to have cabinets full of twigs and dried leaves and a mother who could whip up a special tea or poultice when you were sick. She knew so many recipes, and they were all up here." She tapped her temple. "Never wrote down a single thing."

"Couldn't you write them for her?"

Marlie slumped forward and clasped her hands together. "I wish I had. I guess I thought she'd always be around."

"I'm sorry." I wished I'd kept my question to myself.

She smiled to reassure me. "It's all right. It's been years now. She and my father were both taken the same winter. They were older, you see. My mother used to call me her Twilight Child because I came so late." She chuckled to herself. "I never cared about that, though. They loved me more than any parents ever loved a daughter, I'm quite certain of that."

"You're lucky." I meant it kindly, but there must have been something in my voice that made her shift and change subjects.

"Faytlings are wondrous things, aren't they?" She was watching me gaze at the one in my hand. "So beautiful, and yet—"

"Mysterious."

"Exactly. Such wondrous little things."

"I can't stop looking at it. I've just never seen anything like it. The metal is so delicate, as if it's woven somehow. And the stone. Does it look like it's getting brighter to you? Does yours do that?"

She flipped her braid to her back and strode toward me, her ivory chemise billowing behind. I thought she was going to pull her own talisman from her neck so we could compare, but instead she covered Mrs. Crossey's Faytling with her hand. Careful not to touch me, but still blocking my view.

"I'm serious about putting it away. It needs to get used to you before it'll work properly."

Mrs. Crossey had mentioned the same thing, but it didn't make sense. "How does metal and stone get *used* to someone?"

"Don't ask me." She flipped her hand away. "It's just how it works."

It wasn't logical, but nothing about the Fayte Guardians seemed logical. Mrs. Crossey had told me not to fuss with the Faytling. To simply wear it overnight then to wear it to the Queen's room in the morning.

I'd agreed, but what I really wanted to do was take the thing in my bare hands and see what secrets I could pry out of it. These past few weeks, as my visions became clearer and more intense, the subtle yearning to peer into a past that didn't belong to me, that desire to borrow a few fleeting moments of comfort, now clawed at me with ferocious hunger.

I tried to get my mind off it by changing the subject. "That ceremony, it's been happening like that since Boudica's time?"

Marlie dropped onto her bed. "They used to be far more interesting. The old stories say there were once threats from the other world that required the Lady's direct intervention, but not anymore. The modern world pushed the sprites and pixies and all their kin too far out of reach."

"Sprites? Pixies? Is that what the Lady is?"

"Of course not." Marlie laughed. "Sprites and pixies are dull little things, barely smarter than troll or a goblin. No, the Lady is one of the Ancients. That's what we call them. Others call them fairies or fay. She told us her people used to live on the island, long ago, before men arrived. They left before Boudica's time, or at least most of them did. It's hard to say. She never spoke much about it, and now she hardly speaks to us at all. Just enough to keep the Queen out of harm's way."

"Why do they care so much about our Queen?"

Marlie shrugged. "It's the promise she made to Queen Boudica. As long as there are Fayte Guardians pledged to serve, the Lady will offer her guidance and gifts. It's the Fayte Covenant."

"Gifts, like talents?"

"I suppose. But honestly, most Guardians can't even remember how to use their talents, if they ever had any at all. Mostly what we do is keep the Queen healthy and in good spirits. When more is required, a properly placed guard usually suffices. The time that fellow tried to shoot the Queen when she was pregnant with Princess Vicky, for instance."

My head snapped up. "I heard about that. Edward Oxford was his name, wasn't it? The newspapers said he was too simple for ill intent."

Marlie rolled onto her back and stared at the ceiling. "Sure, that was the story. The Fayte Guardians made sure he didn't succeed. Same thing with that boy Jones, and there were a few others. But this threat, the one Mrs. Crossey has seen, is so vague. It's strange."

I turned the Faytling over in my hand. It was all very strange, indeed. "So, after I wear this, what will it do?"

"Hard to say. Some people say they don't do anything anymore."

"Anymore?"

She yawned and shrugged. The late hour was catching up to her. "Supposedly the stones are cut from crystals in the Lady's own realm. They're supposed to amplify the natural gifts of those with Fayte blood, but like I said, no one really believes that anymore. Mrs. Crossey is about the only Guardian left who does. Most of them think the magic died away when the Lady stopped Converging with us. Some don't believe it ever existed."

I held up the jewel and stared. "What do you believe?"

After a long pause, she answered. "I know the legends and I've heard the stories, but I've never seen anything like what happened at the divining pool today. I don't think I would have believed it if I hadn't seen it with my own eyes. How did you do it?"

The awe on her face startled me. "I don't know. I didn't try to do anything. I just did what Mrs. Crossey asked me to do."

She nodded, as though my answer made sense to her. I wish it made sense to me. "So, your Faytling doesn't do anything?" I asked.

Gently she took hold of her talisman and cradled it in one hand. A dreamy look came over her. "I think it does. When I'm collecting roots and herbs for a remedy, sometimes it sort of glows and I can sense it, as if it's guiding me somehow." Then she snapped out of it. "I'm probably just imagining it, though."

"Maybe, but who's to say? You can't be too careful when the Queen gets indigestion."

That made her laugh, and I laughed, too. It felt surprisingly good. When had I last laughed like that? I couldn't even remember.

When the room was quiet again, Marlie asked, "If tonight was any indication of the kind of Fayte power inside you, it will be very interesting to see the effect the Faytling has on it. Whatever strengths you already possess, I imagine they're going to get stronger."

"My strengths?"

"The things you're good at. Your gifts."

I nearly laughed again at that. What was I good at? Not much, unfortunately. Maybe lying. Stealing. Keeping secrets. I smirked but said nothing, just closed my fingers more tightly around the jewel. The visions were already getting stronger, and Mrs. Crossey had already warned I might lose control. Cold fingers scraped down my spine. "Do you think it could be harmful?"

"I don't think so." She stepped away from me and

went to her bed. With one hand, she pulled back her covers, and with the other, she again touched the place on her chest where her own Faytling rested beneath the fabric. Was it for comfort or courage? "Just wear it," she said. "Then we'll see."

"You're right. We'll have to wait and see." I lowered the black leather lace around my neck, dipped the pendant beneath my collar, and slipped into bed.

But something else tugged at my thoughts. "Before the ceremony, when you tried to leave, why did Mrs. Crossey stop you? Why can't she do the ceremony by herself?"

Marlie rolled onto her side toward me. "I'm sure she can, but it's against the rules. Not just for her, but for anyone."

"Why? Is it dangerous?"

Her lips twitched. "I've never seen anything that was dangerous, but something happened a long time ago. No one talks about it, but I've heard stories about a young scryer, just a little girl still new to her talent, who was trying to communicate with the Lady but who welcomed in someone—or something—else by mistake."

"Who was it?"

Marlie shook her head. "No one knows, but it frightened the Council enough that when they found out, they prohibited any scryer from ever Converging alone after that."

"It's never happened again?"

"No, it can't. But like I said, we shouldn't be talking about it. Please don't mention it to Mrs. Crossey. I've probably said too much already."

Why did everything have to be so secretive? I knew it was an argument I wouldn't win, so I wished her a good night, closed my eyes, and tried to fall asleep.

Despite my efforts, all my questions still burned like flames within me. There was so much I didn't know, but there was knowledge in the Faytling. I sensed it.

I knew I shouldn't, but at the sound of her soft snores,

my resolve weakened. I ignored the common sense telling me to be patient and the voices of Mrs. Crossey and Marlie telling me to leave it alone.

Something else whispered, *go on… touch it.*

So I did.

With my bare fingertip, I stroked the cold metal filigree once and waited.

I ran another finger across it, then two.

Nothing.

I wrapped all four fingers and my thumb around the talisman, nestling it in my palm. I half braced and half begged for a vision.

Absolutely nothing.

I let it go and rolled onto my back to stare at the ceiling, disappointed and frustrated, until sleep finally took me.

CHAPTER EIGHTEEN

MY NEW DAILY routine deviated little over the next few days. Wake with the first morning bell, collect firewood for the Queen's sitting room, help Mrs. Crossey prepare the servants' morning meal, start the servants' evening meal, return to the Queen's room to collect the afternoon tea service, and finally help Mrs. Crossey finish the servants' evening meal before being released for the day.

Then, after snatching a couple hours of sleep, the real work began at midnight.

The first night we descended to the Library and spent our time testing the accuracy of my visions. I'd never had reason to doubt them, but Mrs. Crossey wanted to be convinced.

To begin, she produced an assortment of items from her pocket that belonged to individuals I'd never met. An ivory pipe that had belonged to her father, a silver spoon from a neighbor, and buttons that were the property of various royal attendants. She seemed relieved, if not outright pleased, when I correctly identified each owner.

The second night she pulled out the same items with new instructions: instead of sifting through the past to discern an identity, I was to look into each owner's future. That effort proved less fruitful. With each attempt, the visions only led to the past, no matter how much I tried.

"Let's try something different," she said after several failed attempts. "What does the belonging tell you about the owner? Do you sense any emotion? Happiness or sadness? Anger or frustration?"

Although thoughts, feelings, and occasionally sensations had been accompanying the visions produced from my memory box trinkets for weeks now, those produced by Mrs. Crossey's items were scattered at best, even with the Faytling gripped tightly in my fist. Her father's pipe rendered only a vague, forlorn feeling. The spoon, a surge of eager, happy thoughts centering on the sweet smell of ripe strawberries. The buttons produced nothing discernible at all.

The one emotion all the trials shared, however, was Mrs. Crossey's disappointment—in me—though she tried to hide it behind kind and encouraging words.

After two hopeless hours, she sent me back to bed with a reminder to keep the Faytling close and not to be discouraged. "Even a natural-born gift requires practice to master," she said. "You have only begun to master yours."

Perhaps if she hadn't been so agreeable, I wouldn't have lain awake wondering what I was doing wrong. And perhaps if I hadn't lost so much sleep, I wouldn't have stumbled on the edge of a rug the next day and nearly dropped the tray that held the Queen's empty teapot and cups. I watched in horror as a handful of silver teaspoons bounced over the tray's edge and tumbled across the carpet.

Luckily, the Queen was already off to the stables for her afternoon ride, so only her ladies and Abigail witnessed my mistake. The latter wasted no time rubbing it in.

"Do pay attention," she whispered harshly when she came up beside me.

"Of course," I said, embarrassed and angry at my

clumsiness. I already suspected she'd been placed in the sitting room for the sole purpose of spying on me. I imagined the delight she'd take in relaying this bit of news as I bent to collect the scattered spoons.

As I was on the floor, the door opened. I shot up, expecting to see the Queen, but it was only a page. At least I assumed it was a page, for I could see nothing more than the top of a black cap over a tower of dress boxes.

"What, pray tell, is that?" inquired Lady Bassey, who looked up from her knitting needles where she sat beside the window.

"A special delivery, madam," came a boy's voice from somewhere behind the packages. "Costumes for the ball."

"Our costumes!" Lady Wallingham jumped up from where she sat across from Lady Bassey.

Before the boy could set down the stack, she was beside him, searching for a tag.

"Which is mine? Oh, I hope the dressmaker used the golden silk. A proper Cleopatra must have golden silk."

She lifted a box and read the card. "Lady Merrington? But she's not even here. Why does she get a costume?"

"Set it aside," Lady Bassey instructed in her usual matronly way. "Now let's have a look at what we have."

The two of them pounced on the remaining boxes like kittens with a new ball of string.

Soon, both were holding up exquisite gowns—a white and pale rose ensemble suggesting a Greek toga for Lady Bassey, and for Lady Wallingham, one of golden silk studded with turquoise and carnelian jewels around an Egyptian-inspired collar.

Both costumes were such marvels of construction it was difficult not to stare, but as Abigail was preoccupied with tidying a cabinet on the far side of the room and the ladies were engrossed in their gowns, I gravitated toward the mantel and the photograph of the Queen and her mother.

If ever there was an opportunity, this was it.

My fingers drifted to my chest, where the Faytling rested beneath my white pinafore and black frock. I tugged it over my collar and held it tightly in my gloved hand. After trying all night with Mrs. Crossey's random belongings, I couldn't resist the urge to see what I might learn from something that belonged to the Queen.

I told myself it was in Her Majesty's best interest. I'd pledged to protect her, after all, and to use my visions in that effort. Having a better understanding of her past would only help in that pursuit, wouldn't it?

At least that's how I justified my trespass, even if I couldn't quite silence the part of myself that knew I wanted to do it anyway.

I checked behind me. The women were still engrossed in the costumes, so I carefully pulled the cord from beneath my collar and freed the talisman.

"What should I do with Lady Merrington's box?" Lady Wallingham asked as I worked off both gloves and wrapped my bare right hand around the golden cylinder.

I reached for the silver frame with my left, watching both ladies and Abigail over my shoulder to be sure they paid no attention to me.

"I honestly don't know." Lady Bassey pressed her gown to the front of herself and swayed back and forth. "The Queen can sort it out later."

"The Queen can sort out what?"

At the sound of that feminine yet commanding voice, I whipped around. Yet I had neglected to remove my hand from the talisman, and in my haste ripped the cord from my neck. Horrified, I watched as the golden Faytling dropped to the floor. Quickly, I stepped in front of it to hide it from view and curtsied with the others.

The Queen frowned and straightened to her full yet still diminutive height. "So, you approve of the dresses, do you?" A shadow of a smile tugged at her pale cheek.

"Oh yes, Your Majesty," Lady Wallingham gushed. "The Cleopatra gown is exquisite."

"And you, Lady Bassey? Does your costume meet with your approval?"

Lady Bassey, composed as always, lowered again into a formal curtsy even as she continued to hold the gown to her breast. "A splendid and unexpected gift, ma'am. Your generosity is most appreciated."

The compliments brought satisfaction to the Queen's lips, and since she didn't look my way, I managed to shuffle the talisman and its cord along the floor with the toe of my boot to a place behind the table until I could retrieve it.

The Queen turned to the page standing beside the door. "Is there something you require, young man?"

The boy stared straight ahead, straining not to make eye contact with his sovereign. "The Lady Merrington's gown, Your Majesty. Shall I remove it?"

The Queen glanced at the unopened box and waved her hand. "Yes, take it to her room. Thank you."

The boy bowed, collected the box, and disappeared through the door. But as the door closed behind him, someone on the other side caught it and pushed it open again. It was a man sporting a bushy rim of black hair that dipped down into an impressive pair of mutton chop sideburns. He bowed deeply.

"Your Majesty, you summoned?"

"Mr. Galding. Yes, do come in. I understand you have been making inquiries at the Crystal Palace on our behalf, yet I don't recall asking you to do so." She proceeded to a deeply cushioned chair with a pleasant view of the Quadrangle, then settled into it with a good degree of fussing and shifting of her voluminous skirts.

When she was done, she appeared entirely at ease, but the same could not be said for poor Mr. Galding. The man's cheeks had turned crimson and his forehead slick with perspiration. The way he gripped and abused the brim of his top hat, I wondered if it would ever recover.

Somehow, despite his shaky demeanor, the man

managed to approach her and bow. "Your Majesty, I have done so at the request of the Master of the Household by way of his deputy." His voice wavered. "I was asked to secure an entertainment that I was assured would please you and His Royal Highness. A sort of a surprise, you see."

While all eyes remained on the Queen and Mr. Galding, I bent down and grabbed the Faytling. I tucked it out of sight before rising quickly, thrusting my hands into my pockets, and scanning the room to see if anyone noticed. Mr. Galding still stared at the Queen. The Queen stared at Mr. Galding. The ladies-in-waiting stared at them both.

Abigail, however, stared directly at me.

She fixed me with a venomous glare. "What did you pick up just now?" she whispered.

"Nothing," I whispered back and prayed the fiery burn on my cheeks didn't give me away.

She appraised the tea tray—the cups, the teapot, the sugar bowl, the silver spoons. She frowned when she discovered nothing missing. "I saw you pick up something. Is it in your pocket, you good for nothing thief?"

I froze. I couldn't tell her about the Faytling. She'd never believe it was mine.

"Girls!"

We both whipped around at Lady Bassey's reproach.

"What's this?" The Queen's question was directed at us.

Abigail and I hung our heads and muttered apologies. Lady Bassey motioned Abigail closer and whispered something in her ear, which sent the girl off toward the door. She shot me a final sneer before departing.

Then the ladies' attention went back to the Queen, and hers returned to Mr. Galding.

"Tell me of this entertainment." She held the man in her icy gaze.

"It's an instrument, you see." He swallowed hard before continuing. "A remarkable machine that transforms steam into music. The inventor calls it a calliope, and he intends to debut it at the Crystal Palace. I was asked to, I mean, I was rather hoping to persuade the Palace's director to allow me to borrow it for the ball."

The Queen frowned at first, then her eyes grew wide. She clasped her hands to her chest. "It's a capital idea," she gushed. "Did you hear that, ladies? An instrument that creates music from steam. Won't His Royal Highness be pleased?"

Lady Bassey set aside her gown. "Yes, two things he loves so dearly: music and machinery. I'm sure he will be delighted. Don't you agree, Lady Wallingham?"

The younger woman perked up from where she was standing in front of a mirror with her golden gown pressed to herself. "Oh, yes, Your Majesty. I do agree, indeed."

"It will be a marvelous addition to our masquerade," the Queen said with smug satisfaction.

Mr. Galding raised a short, chubby finger with some hesitation. "If I may, ma'am. I did express that wish to the director, but there is a problem."

The Queen's amiability slid away. "What problem?"

The ladies looked up from their preoccupation with their gowns. Mr. Galding again worked his hat brim through his fingers.

"Be assured both the instrument's owner and the director are eager to arrange the command performance," he said. "But, you see, a pipe was damaged during the voyage from America. A replacement has been commissioned, but it will not be ready in time for the ball."

"The event is still days away. Send whatever is required to our own shops, if you must."

The man, with obvious consternation in his eyes, shook his head. "Your Majesty, I have made such an offer, and even with our own shops, and even if it could be completed sooner, the inventor is the only one capable of installing the pipe properly, I'm told, and his ship is not expected in until the day after the masquerade. But, if I may, I have what I hope will be an acceptable alternative."

The Queen harrumphed and reached down to her knitting basket beside her chair. She grabbed her knitting needles and a scarf on which she was working. "What is the alternative, then?"

He cleared his throat and seemed to be trying to rally his confidence. "An acclaimed chamber quartet from Vienna is in London, preparing for a series of performances at month's end. They come highly recommended and arrangements could be made for them to perform at the masquerade. Then, once the calliope's owner arrives and the instrument is fixed, a private performance could take place."

The Queen's lips twitched as she mulled his suggestion. After a long pause, she sighed. "That would be acceptable, I suppose. Please see to it." With her decree delivered, she turned her full attention to the mound of yarn and half-finished scarf heaped in her lap.

"Very good, ma'am." With relief, he turned to leave.

"Mr. Galding?"

He wheeled back, his smile gone.

"Do not mention anything about this contraption to His Royal Highness. In fact, don't mention anything about your visit to the Crystal Palace at all. If we cannot present this wonder at the ball, I should like to at least make it a surprise for my husband."

The man's ebullience returned. "Yes, ma'am. You can be assured of my utmost discretion."

At that the Queen raised a thin eyebrow toward her ladies. "I hope you, too, will abide by my wish."

Both ladies dipped a submissive chin and uttered their assurances.

"Good." The Queen settled back into her cushion and resumed her knitting. "Is there any tea?"

I straightened and touched the silver teapot's side. It was still warm to the touch. I looked to Lady Bassey for guidance.

She nodded, which I took to be permission to speak.

"Yes, Your Majesty. But not a fresh pot, I'm afraid." I winced, not knowing if that had been an acceptable response or not.

"Fine, fine," she said.

I lifted the pot and poured into a gold-rimmed teacup adorned with the Queen's insignia.

She watched me place a sugar cube in her cup and raised a finger. "Don't be stingy with those. I'm feeling a sweet tooth today."

I nodded and deposited another cube into the cup then stirred with one of the tiny silver spoons, making sure to use one that hadn't dropped to the floor. I extended the cup to her.

Again, the door opened, but I forced myself to remain focused on the cup I balanced over the Queen's cushioned armrest. I watched her glance at the door and heard someone enter, but no one spoke. Not until the Queen sipped from her cup and said with strained cordiality, "You may speak, Mr. MacDougall."

I nearly fell forward but quickly caught myself and wheeled around to find Mr. MacDougall's imposing figure standing at the center of the room with a smug Abigail by his side.

He cleared his throat and clasped his hands behind his back. "I am terribly sorry for the interruption, Your Majesty. I only need a word with the maid."

My stomach dropped to my heels.

He looked at me squarely. "Join me in the hall."

All eyes turned on me, including the Queen's, and I didn't need a Faytling's help to divine their thoughts: that I was exactly what Abigail had said I was, a thief. Nothing but a good for nothing thief.

CHAPTER NINETEEN

MR. MACDOUGALL STOOD in the corridor as I closed the Queen's sitting room door behind me. Abigail stood by, her gaze darting from the House Steward to me and back again.

"I saw her take something, just like she took my locket," Abigail wailed. "I *saw* her."

He regarded her outburst with a spike of his overgrown eyebrows then slid that regard back to me. "Abigail is under the impression you took something that doesn't belong to you."

Every inch of me froze in guilty fear. "I did not, sir."

His cheek twitched. It was his only response.

"I'm sure it's in her pocket," Abigail pressed. "Make her show you. You'll see for yourself."

He crossed his arms over his narrow chest. "Perhaps Abigail is right."

The minx smirked. "Of course, I am. I *saw* it."

Mr. MacDougall grimaced. "That's enough, Abigail." He turned back to me. "Do please show us the contents of your pockets."

I stared at her, at the ugly ruts anger had carved

between her eyebrows and the pinched wrinkles above her nose. Had she always been so bitter, or had I done this to her?

I had known it would be a risk when I snatched the locket. But it was the way her fingers always seemed to wrap around it at her collar in an absent-minded sort of way. And the dreamy look that came over her as she touched it. I knew it held precious memories, and I wanted them. Eventually I could think of nothing else.

That's what compelled me when I passed the open door of her room and saw the thing dangling from the hook by her washbasin. I'd paused to check that the room was empty and that no one was nearby, then I'd slipped in and grabbed it. I was just turning the corner to the stairwell when I heard a door of another maid's room open and then Abigail's voice.

She had seen my back as I rounded the corner, but she had no proof I'd taken anything.

Despite my gnawing guilt, I stood firm. "I will do it," I said defiantly, "but only to prove she's wrong." I slipped both hands into my skirt pockets and pulled them out, leaving them to flop at my sides like a bloodhound's ears.

Abigail's smug expression turned to befuddlement. She searched the crimson carpet around my feet. "It's a trick. She must have put it somewhere else. A sleeve maybe? Her gloves? Check those ridiculous gloves!"

I dangled my wrists at my sides to show I had nothing stashed there then held out my hands so Mr. MacDougall could see nothing was wedged within them.

The House Steward glowered at Abigail. "It appears you are mistaken. Again."

Her lower lip shot out in a pout. "She stole something. I know it."

He turned to me. "What do you say, Jane?"

I fought back my guilt. I would make amends to Abigail, but not here. Not now. "Sir, I didn't steal anything from the Queen's sitting room." *That* was the truth, and I clung to it.

He closed his eyes and touched his right temple with a fingertip as though a headache was brewing there. When he opened his eyes, they were bloodshot. The skin beneath his eyes appeared sunken and gray. I almost pitied him.

"Abigail, no more—"

"But, Mr. MacDougall—"

His hand rose to stop her. "No. More. You must refrain from these baseless accusations. Or else."

Her shoulders slumped.

This may be her defeat, but it was not my victory. I knew that well enough.

"Jane," Mr. MacDougall said in his low, menacing way, "if you have deceived us, I assure you, it will not go well for you."

Then, instead of dismissing us, he turned and strode away.

Abigail looked as surprised as I was. Then her expression darkened. She stepped closer and leaned her face into mine. "You aren't going to get away with this."

I shuffled back till I was flush against the door. "You've got it wrong."

But even as I spoke, I saw her gaze drift from me and a sappy smile spread across her lips.

When I looked, I nearly groaned. Someone was walking toward us from the main drawing rooms, and while he was still yards away and his head was down, I recognized the rolled-up shirtsleeves, the dusty boots, and the deviant hair curled beneath his tweed cap. He seemed to halt, as though he was about to stop and turn back but then thought better of it and proceeded toward us.

When he was close enough, Abigail said in a singsong voice, "Good afternoon, Mr. Wyck."

"Afternoon," he answered with a quick glance her direction. When he looked at me, his lips tensed. "Miss Shackle."

"Mr. Wyck," I replied.

He didn't stop. In fact, he seemed to quicken his pace.

Only when he disappeared around a corner did Abigail turn back to me, her eyes wide. "What's going on between you two?"

"Nothing."

"I doubt that."

Was it a trap? "We're acquainted," I said carefully.

"Is that so? Then perhaps you could introduce me? I mean, properly."

There it was again, that stupid, starry-eyed look all the maids got when he was around. I didn't know what to say, so I ignored her question. "I should be going. Mrs. Crossey will throw a fit if I'm not back to help with the evening biscuits."

Abigail crossed her arms. "Yes, I suppose she will. Think about it, though. You owe me that much."

"I don't owe you anything." I walked away, taking the opposite route from Mr. Wyck. With every step, I could feel her eyes on me like burning daggers, but I didn't stop until I opened the door to the servants' stairs, carefully closed it behind me, and made sure I was alone. Only then did I bend down and fish the Faytling from the ankle of my boot.

~ ~ ~

I found no sign of Mrs. Crossey back in the kitchen.

"You missed a dandy of a tantrum," Marlie whispered. She'd left a bowl of fresh strawberries at her worktable to join me at mine, which was uncharacteristically bare.

"Mrs. Crossey threw a tantrum?" Alarmed, I scanned the kitchen, looking for the woman.

"Not her. Chef. The orangery delivered a crate that sent him into screaming fits. Mr. MacDougall calmed him by sending Mrs. Crossey into town to find something more suitable."

"She's gone?" I was already envisioning an afternoon

of leisure. An unexpected boon.

"She is, but you can lose that grin. Mr. MacDougall wants you to report to the wash room."

"Please, no. Not the wash room."

She shrugged and I could see it gave her no pleasure to relay the unwelcome news. It was a dismal assignment, and she knew it.

Frankly, I wasn't surprised. Mr. MacDougall had found no proof of my guilt but had found a way to punish me nonetheless.

For the next few hours, my naked waterlogged hands and I worked alongside the small army of washing maids that scrubbed piles of grimy pots and pans, as well as the hundreds of dirty plates and bowls, cups and utensils carted into the dank, windowless room on carts.

At least it gave me time to think.

While the washing maids gabbed about their many complaints and gossiped endlessly, I mentally replayed the confrontation with Mr. MacDougall and Abigail, and her ridiculous desire for an introduction to Mr. Wyck.

As if I could manage one even if I'd wanted to.

Which I didn't. I may regret taking her locket, but I drew the line at matchmaking. Certainly with him. What did she find so appealing about him anyway? What did anyone?

He wasn't exactly awful to look at, if you didn't mind that messy hair or that brooding, faraway stare. It was more the way he strutted around as if he owned the place. Honestly, why had he even been near the Queen's rooms?

The question pricked me.

What *was* he doing there?

And why had he given us—given *me*—such a funny look when he passed by? That strange look of consternation.

Two words snapped to mind. Getting. Caught.

They stayed with me the rest of the day and by the time I joined Mrs. Crossey in the Library, I could think of nothing else.

"It's him," I said as we collected our robes from the hooks, after explaining the events that had led me to be standing in the corridor with Abigail. "I don't know why or what he has against the Queen, but it has to be him."

She pulled her robe around herself and tied it closed. "I'm quite sure I told you to disregard Mr. Wyck."

"But you also said to watch out for the Queen. He's up to something. Why else would he be there?" I fastened my own robe.

"And what of the foretelling? How could 'a face is not a face' apply to him?"

Why was she protecting him? "He could be here under false pretenses. Or hiding his true intentions."

She shook her head. "Let's not deviate from the plan."

Her plan. "The masquerade ball?"

"Precisely."

But that was still days away. "Why should we wait when the threat is already obvious?"

She reeled back. "Because it's not obvious. Not to me, and it shouldn't be to you. You shouldn't be reckless with your assumptions."

It was absurd that she wouldn't see reason. "Then what do you suggest?"

"I suggest we take the time we have to strengthen your ability. To continue to see how we might use the Faytling to advantage. Now come with me."

I trudged along behind her to a table, where she proceeded to lay out a variety of new items she pulled from a leather pouch—a handkerchief, a cuff link, a hairpin, and a slender wooden comb.

"Where's the Faytling?" she demanded.

I pulled it from beneath my collar and let it hang freely over my chest.

"Hold it and touch an item then tell me what you can about the item's owner."

More games. Fine. I did as she asked and discerned that

each item belonged to a different servant who worked within the castle. The identities came quickly, much more quickly than they had before, but I still couldn't divine any anger or malice.

And why should I? Not a single item belonged to Mr. Wyck.

"Don't pout," she said sharply. "It's unbecoming."

I looked away. Good sense told me I should drop the matter, yet I couldn't help myself.

"Why can you not at least include something that belongs to him?"

"It isn't necessary."

I clenched my teeth. She had accused me of not taking the threat to the Queen seriously. But I had to wonder, did she?

"Even you must see there's something off about him. Doesn't it bother you that he was out there the night that poor girl was killed?"

"You were there as well. Did you have something to do with it?"

That frosty stare stopped me cold. "Of course not. You know I didn't. What could I possibly have against an innocent farmer's daughter?"

"What would *he* have against such a girl?"

"I don't know. But when I touched him, I felt nothing. It's like he's hiding something."

She grimaced. "Be that as it may, until we know more, we owe him the benefit of the doubt."

"Then what do you suggest we do?"

"I suggest we do what we've been doing." She glanced down at the scattering of belongings on the table. "The faster you learn to use your ability to sense danger—real danger—and who's behind it, the better off we'll be. Until then, I say whatever prompted that young man to be on the Slopes, you should feel lucky for it. There's no telling what might have happened to you if he hadn't come along when he did. And for now, we'll assume our culprit intends to use the ball as an opportunity to get close to the Queen. Do you agree?"

She wouldn't continue until I nodded.

"Good. Now get yourself to bed. You need to be well rested and ready for work tomorrow."

She gathered up the items she had brought and stuffed them back into her pouch. She turned to me again.

"Close the fireplace behind yourself, if you would." She gazed up to the tops of the towering shelves and grabbed the rolling ladder. "I've a bit more work to do here."

~ ~ ~

The morning of the ball, I found Mrs. Crossey in our usual corner of the Great Kitchen, staring into her porridge pot.

"The cellar master says there's no need for firewood in the Queen's sitting room this morning as she'll be breaking her fast in her own room." I had intended to keep the irritation out of my voice, but there it was, ringing out like the clang of a copper pan slamming to the floor. It was childish to sulk, but I couldn't help it.

I had risen before the early bell to see the Queen and her ladies preparing themselves, to be part of the festivities—even in that ridiculously small way.

Mrs. Crossey ignored me.

"You might have mentioned it last night and saved me the trouble," I added, looking for some response.

Still nothing.

"Mrs. Crossey?"

Finally, she turned. "Oh, good. You're here. I wanted you to do something for me, now what was it…" She tapped her lips and glanced around.

I stared at the mountain of apples on our table. "Peel the apples?"

She looked at me, and I pointed to the bowl.

Her eyes widened as though she were seeing the ruby

red fruit for the first time. "Yes. Apples. Exactly. If you could just give them a good coring, that would be grand."

She went back to staring at her pot without another word. Not about the firewood or the needless trip to the cellar. Nothing. I sighed. Best to let it go. I searched through the collection of knives. Not finding the one I wanted, I turned back to her. "What happened to the paring knife? It was here last night when I cleaned."

"The paring knife?" She frowned. "It must be there. I set it beside the bowl."

I looked again. "I don't see it."

She wheeled on me, a deep crease between her eyebrows. "Open your eyes, girl. I put it right... Oh." Her gaze drifted to the edge of the stove, where the paring knife lay. Her anger disappeared. "I don't remember putting it there." She handed it to me.

"Are you all right?" I took the handle and studied her face. Fat red blood vessels shot through the whites of her eyes and her eyelids drooped.

She shook her head. "It's nothing. Not enough sleep, I suppose."

How long had she stayed in Fayte Hall?

"Oh, you won't need to collect the firewood this morning. The Queen and her ladies will be breakfasting in their own rooms."

"I know I..." I stopped mid-sentence. It didn't matter. I stepped closer to her and lowered my voice. "But shouldn't I check on things up there? See that everything's all right? With the Queen, I mean."

And to be sure Mr. Wyck wasn't wandering the halls again, though I knew better than to mention it.

She turned back to her porridge, took hold of a giant wooden spoon, and stirred. "Let's just keep to our plan."

Our plan. Of course.

Discouraged, I picked up an apple and used the slender paring knife to shave off the shiny red skin in long thin strips.

For hours we worked in silence, until Mr. MacDougall came around the corner, scowling as usual and holding a freshly starched parlor maid apron in his grip.

"Jane, please report to St. George's Hall. You'll be helping with receiving duties this evening."

There was a definite frown on his face, as though my assignment was not of his choosing nor his preference.

"Thank you, Mr. MacDougall." Mrs. Crossey gave him a keen look that made him look away.

He sneered as he set an apron on a clean space on the table and moved down the aisle to set another in front of Marlie. Addressing her, he said, "You will be assigned to reception duties as well." He didn't even look her in the eye before moving on to talk to a young cook overseeing the roasting of a pheasant turning on a spit.

"You heard him. Off with you now," Mrs. Crossey said.

I glanced at the clock overhead. It read a quarter till four. "It's still early. The ball is hours away."

"The time will pass quickly, I assure you. Use it wisely." She gave me a knowing look and I could almost hear her thoughts: *Use the time to find the menace.*

It hardly seemed likely that someone plotting against the Queen would be hanging about the cloak room, but I knew an argument would get me nowhere. I gathered up the crisp, ruffled apron.

Mrs. Crossey moved closer.

"There's a footman stationed in the Grand Vestibule," she whispered. "An older gentleman. Chester is his name. Marlie knows him. You can trust him."

She turned back to the stove to stir her savory beef stew, steeped in the fragrance of rosemary and thyme. "Remember, you're only collecting information. If you sense something—anything—you find me or Mr. MacDougall. No one else. *Do* nothing else. And for goodness' sake, don't forget the..." She patted her chest to indicate the Faytling.

I swallowed hard and tried to calm the butterflies that had taken hold of my stomach. "I know. I can do it."

At least I hoped I could.

CHAPTER TWENTY

GARLANDS OF WHITE hydrangeas, peach roses, fuchsia tiger lilies, and sprigs of deep green foliage adorned the wood-paneled walls of St. George's Hall. At the center, a bouquet on a round table towered over the tallest men, and ivory silk hung in wide ribbons from the ceiling to the walls, intersecting the colorful coats of arms belonging to the Knights of the Garter. The sight of it all stopped me cold.

"Don't let Mr. Bailey see you gawking like that, or we're done for," Marlie whispered, referring to the Chief Deputy of the Household. "We're already late."

And so we seemed to be. A veritable army of footmen and maids had formed a line that stretched a good length of the immense hall, and pacing in front like a sergeant was the portly and monocled Mr. Bailey, scratching at his fussy beard and mustache as he bellowed orders like a military general.

Marlie waited until his attention was directed toward the far end of the room before she joined the line and assumed the same chin-up, chest-out position as the others. I followed her lead, though the line was so long I found myself straddling the vestibule doorway.

"I am aware of the discontent over our decreased numbers," I heard him say as he turned and paced back our direction, "and that some have expressed concern over our ability to uphold our usual excellence in service. To that opinion, I say, hogwash. I am confident this staff is more than capable. Furthermore, allow me to remind you it is not only our duty to perform our tasks as they have been assigned, but rather our privilege to do so, for the sake of our Queen and country."

I turned away, unable to stomach this insipid speech from a man with lily-white hands who had obviously never touched a broom or scrub brush in his life.

As rousing as he was trying to be, I could not help but think his time would have been better spent foregoing this lecture and letting us simply get on with our work. At least when he paced back the other direction, it left me free to take in the flowers and the silks. But then a group of workmen ascending the Grand Staircase caught my attention. They were muscling up wooden crates from the lower floor before disappearing into a side room.

I leaned toward Marlie and motioned their direction. "What are they doing?"

She only grimaced, her stern look imploring me to be quiet.

But it was too late. Mr. Bailey was already striding toward us.

"My apologies. Did you have something to add to the discussion?" Each syllable dripped with sarcasm.

"No, sir," I muttered, but I couldn't tear my eyes from the parade of crates being carted through the hall because one of the delivery men was indisputably Mr. Wyck.

Mr. Bailey wheeled around to see what I was staring at when Mr. MacDougall appeared at the stairs, carefully watching and directing the men and crates.

Mr. Bailey's brow furrowed. "MacDougall!" he called out. "Deliveries are to be routed through the kitchen. I was quite clear!"

Mr. Wyck and the other workmen stopped and stared at Mr. MacDougall, who looked at Mr. Bailey with such puzzlement I had to snicker.

I had never seen Mr. MacDougall called out, and from the scattering of gasps and giggles, I wasn't alone.

The House Steward adjusted his tie and swallowed hard. "Of course, sir. I was under the impression we were to—"

"Never mind," Mr. Bailey barked, waving off Mr. MacDougall's attempted reply. "I'll go over it again."

As this transpired, I watched Mr. Wyck. My fingers found the Faytling resting at my collar, and I squeezed it gently through my gloves. *If you are capable of doing anything, do it now!*

The ground shifted and a swirling sensation licked at the space around me. A vision? I waited, eager for something.

But nothing manifested. The feeling only teased. A wink at something beyond my grasp.

"Are you from the kitchen?"

The question jolted me from my near swoon. I tried to focus on the dour man in a footman's uniform standing before me.

"That's us." Marlie shot me a nasty look before turning her sweetest smile back to him.

I nodded and saw that Mr. Bailey had crossed the vestibule to huddle with Mr. MacDougall. He seemed to have forgotten us altogether.

"I'm Chester." The footman touched the scarcity of silver strands the years had left him and cleared his throat. "Have you ever received guests before?"

Marlie and I looked at each other and back at him. We both shook our heads.

He frowned with mild exasperation. "Well, come on then."

He led us through the Grand Vestibule—past the place

where Mr. MacDougall and Mr. Bailey had been, though where they'd gone I didn't know—to a side gallery filled with chairs and side tables at the front and, behind two sets of folding screens, an area where guests could deposit coats and shawls and whatever sundry items they wished to store for the evening.

Chester directed us to a secretary desk set at an opening between the screens.

"This is your station. You shall accept the items from the guests and hang or shelve them as necessary. Take a ticket from that desk"—he motioned to a stack of gold-embossed stationery and a quill—"write the number of the rack hook or shelf... You can write, can't you?"

I had been strolling through the makeshift aisles, acquainting myself with the racks but wheeled around. "Of course I can write."

He cleared his throat. "Just making sure. Now, that door there"—he motioned to a large one along the back wall—"is the resting room for ladies."

"And the gentlemen?" I asked. "Do they have a room as well?"

He nodded with a degree of impatience. "The anteroom behind the vestibule has been set up for their purposes."

I looked at Marlie. She shrugged.

He rolled his eyes. "Shall I acquaint you with it as well?"

His opinion that we were not the most helpful of attendants was clear, and to be fair I was inclined to agree.

Marlie and I nodded in unison.

"Follow me, then," he said.

He covered the distance to the door in long, hurried strides before disappearing into the vestibule once again. If he was trying to lose us, he couldn't have done a better job of it. When he glanced back to check that we followed, I could swear there was disappointment in his eyes to find us still in pursuit.

Finally, he turned a corner and opened a door, releasing the scent of cigar smoke and pipe tobacco, newspapers, and hair pomade. I peeked inside and found a formal room arranged with high-back chairs and side tables topped with crystal ashtrays, decanters, and tumblers.

"The gentlemen's room—"

A commotion around the corner stopped him. I turned to see Mr. MacDougall storming down a flight of stairs.

"No, no, no!" the man cried over his shoulder. "It must be now. It cannot wait."

Another man still hidden in the staircase called out from behind him, "Sir, we cannot leave our posts."

I recognized the voice even before I saw the man emerge into view, a dark sweep of hair escaping beneath a tweed cap, as usual. It was Mr. Wyck.

"This cannot wait. The shipment must be unloaded immediately."

The two of them disappeared down the turn of stairs descending to the lower floor, and I craned my neck to watch until I could no longer see them.

"What are you doing?"

I hadn't heard Marlie come up behind me. She was looking down the stairwell, trying to see what I was looking at.

"Who's down there?" she added.

"No one. I thought I saw something, but I must have been mistaken." It was better not to tell her what I suspected of Mr. Wyck. One question would lead to another, and I had no sufficient answers. Not yet anyway.

"We should get back," she said. "We can't miss the early arrivals."

"Of course." I was growing more certain, however, that the threat we sought was already here.

When I fell back, she stopped and whipped around with a scowl. "What's taking so long?"

What, indeed.

"I forgot something in the kitchen. Go on, I'll be right

behind you."

Before she could object, I darted back to the stairs. Only when I'd reached the bottom did I pause to look back, so I was sure she wasn't following me. No sign of her.

Good. But where had Mr. Wyck gone? The narrow stairwell had corridors leading in all four directions. I scanned each, and one looked as promising as the next.

"Careful, boys, careful."

Voices! It was Mr. MacDougall somewhere along the corridor to the right.

I looked around the corner and saw him, standing beside a door opened to the castle's North Terrace. He was ushering through the workmen, each carrying a crate emblazoned with the word "fragile" in bright red letters. Some crates were large, some small, and they all were being taken to the same place.

But where was Mr. Wyck?

I edged closer. One man, then another, and another. I had seen these men in the Servants' Hall, but not one of them was the one I sought.

Suddenly, he was there, stepping over the threshold, his arms embracing a crate.

I leaned farther to get a better view, but nothing appeared out of the ordinary.

Then Mr. Wyck spied me. I shot back behind the wall, but it was too late. My heart thundered in my chest as I searched the corridor for somewhere to hide. Could I get up the stairs and out of view before he reached the corner? Hardly. Then I heard Mr. MacDougall call out.

"Not that way, son," the man said. "We must stay clear of tonight's preparations. Backstairs only to the Rubens Room, if you please."

"Yes, sir," Mr. Wyck grumbled.

I exhaled the breath I didn't know I'd been holding and waited. After a long moment, when I no longer heard footsteps, I peeked around the corner again to see the door still open, but no one coming or going. I ventured closer and heard the voices outside.

Keeping to the shadows, I saw Mr. MacDougall and four of the men, Mr. Wyck among them, standing around the cart, where one enormous crate still waited. It was as big as a stove and even taller.

"We'll have to take it up in pieces," one of the men said with a rough rub to his beard.

"Absolutely not," Mr. MacDougall said. "It cannot be dismantled."

"How about a pulley?" another suggested, pleased with himself. "We could hoist it up to the room."

His neighbor wheeled around with a grimace. "And how do you suppose we'd manage that without plucking out the window?"

The one who had made the suggestion scratched his head. "Yeah, guess that wouldn't work."

"Guess not," his neighbor scoffed.

Mr. Wyck, who had been standing apart from the others with his head down, jumped into the cart, tipped the large crate, and watched it balance on its edge.

"What do you think you're doing?" Mr. MacDougall said with obvious concern.

Mr. Wyck didn't respond until he had set the crate back down. "What I'm thinking is, there's a dolly in the stable that we use to move feed sacks. We could use it to move this box."

The way Mr. MacDougall's eyes widened I thought he might embrace Mr. Wyck, right then and there.

"Capital idea. You there, go get it." He gestured to the bearded man, who nodded and jogged off.

When he was gone, Mr. Wyck leaned against the cart. He looked at his two colleagues then at Mr. MacDougall. "It shouldn't take more than a couple strong backs to get this up to the Rubens Room. I know Mr. Jameson would prefer someone get the horses out for their exercise before the crowds arrive."

Mr. MacDougall appeared to have been lost in thought but perked at the mention of a crowd. "What? Oh, yes. Of course. Go on along then. One of you stay behind, though. Yes, how about you?" He indicated the bigger, burlier one with the beard.

Mr. Wyck stepped up. "I'll stay."

The other two stable hands looked at him like he was crazy for volunteering. Mr. MacDougall looked suspicious.

"I've lugged feed around the stables enough to have a pretty good handle on that contraption. I can manage it, with Charlie's help, of course."

The scrawnier one grinned and shuffled back from the cart, tugging the other one with him. "As long as you're sure, mate. We should be getting back, now that you mention it."

Before Mr. MacDougall could argue, they hurried down the lane.

"What in the world are you gawking at?"

I wheeled around to find Marlie behind me.

She was eying the cart. "What do you suppose that is?"

"I believe it might be something called a calliope."

"A what? Oh, now I see what you're up to." She turned to me with a wide, knowing smile. "Mr. Wyck?"

"Hardly." I didn't enjoy lying to her, but I couldn't tell her the truth. I couldn't risk her confronting him on the spot. He would only deny it, and then where would we be? "I just wanted to see the instrument in the cart. I heard it's rather remarkable. A piano that makes music out of steam. Can you imagine?"

"Does it now?" She looked back at the large wooden box. A slow, creeping grin spreading across her face. "And I'm sure Mr. Wyck is of no interest whatsoever. C'mon. There's time for this later. We've got work to do."

Reluctantly, I allowed her to pull me away.

When we reached the receiving room, the footman was there, looking apoplectic. "Where have you been? You cannot leave the chamber unattended. If you have a question or need—"

"Sorry, it couldn't be helped," I said. "We won't leave again." I looked at Marlie. "At least not at the same time."

The footman grabbed his lapels and appeared to have more to say before thinking better of it. "Fine," he relented. "Do you have any questions?"

I brushed past him and entered the chamber. "We take the coats and cloaks and whatever else and hang them up or put them on a shelf. Fill out a ticket and give it to the guest. Is that right?"

"Yes," he said with a huff. "Now if anything should go wrong, you can find me near the entrance."

If something went wrong, I doubted he would be any help at all. "Where will Mr. MacDougall be?"

He scratched his head. "It's difficult to say. He moves about. Why do you ask?"

"It's just…" I looked at Marlie. She shook her head. I knew what she meant. The less we spoke of our true mission, the better.

Marlie stepped forward. "It's just that we want to be sure he sees us doing a good job. The kitchen is fine and all but…"

A liveried man swept through the door. "There you are, Chester. A carriage is on its way."

Chester rolled his eyes and glanced our way. "And so it begins. Get to your places, girls. It will be a long night, I assure you." He straightened his cap and hustled off with the other footman.

I leaned closer to Marlie. "Thank you for your help there."

She smiled and winked. "That's what friends are for."

The words stopped me cold. Friends? Is that what we were?

CHAPTER TWENTY-ONE

THE CLATTER OF the approaching carriage jolted me from Marlie's surprise declaration. Guests to the Queen's masquerade ball would be funneling in soon and there was no time to waste. I hurried to the chamber door to see the first arrivals. I hoped that's what I appeared to be doing anyway because I was really searching for Mr. Wyck and Mr. MacDougall.

There was no sign of either man.

Instead, I saw footmen, a dozen of them or more, arranging themselves into tidy rows on both sides of the red-carpeted staircase as a carriage stopped at the main doors. Along the lower steps, more footmen assembled—until a frantic Mr. Galding appeared and waved them away.

"Not here, men," he cried. "You're needed in the ballroom. There aren't enough footmen in the ballroom."

An underbutler approached. "Sir, these men are required here. The Chief Deputy to the Lord Chamberlain made the order himself. Assign pages to the ballroom, if you must."

"Absolutely not," Mr. Galding wailed. "Pages are useless in the ballroom. I was assured there would be adequate staffing, but there is not. You have commandeered *my* footmen."

From behind the two men, Mr. MacDougall appeared, his arms held wide, false cordiality oozing from his expression. "Gentlemen, we all agree there are too few men to do the job adequately, but we must do the best we can under the circumstances. Shall we remove ourselves to the Guard Room to discuss it?"

As he herded the other two into a side room, a gray-bearded man in regimental attire ascended the stairs from the arriving carriage, a golden mask dangling from his gloved fingers. Behind him, two paces or three, came a stout matron in a pale-pink gown with a matching mask festooned with white ostrich plumes that obscured half of her face.

"That's the Earl of... Oh, what was it? Berg-something. No. Mon—no, that's not it, either. It'll come to me. A stickler, for sure, I remember that about him. Complains about everything and always has to request something peculiar when he attends a dinner. Last time it was a fruit chutney to spread on his roast pheasant. Curry wasn't even on the menu! He does it to aggravate, if you ask me."

Marlie prattled on, but I stopped listening.

I was too busy watching the entry and the vestibule, searching for Mr. Wyck, who would be restricted to the common areas now, dressed as he was. I was so focused on examining the shadows that I didn't even notice Chester approach with a pair of gentleman's gloves, a scarf, and a pale-pink stole.

"She'll take them," Marlie said, motioning to me and proceeding to gawk at the couple, not even trying to be subtle in the way she craned over the man's shoulder.

"What? Oh, yes, of course." That was Mrs. Crossey's plan, wasn't it? I was to touch the belongings, wait for a vision, and tease out any threat to the Queen. That the most credible threat was, at this moment, still carting about pieces of a steam instrument gave me some comfort.

Yet how could I keep Mr. Wyck away from the Queen once I did spot him? That was the question that plagued me as I folded the scarf, the gloves, and the stole and placed them on a shelf. I was so caught up in those thoughts, I considered skipping the vision altogether, but curiosity got the better of me.

I had never read an earl before, or the wife of one, and my fingers twitched with curiosity.

Carefully, I slipped off my right glove and picked up one belonging to the earl. Its leather was of a reddish brown, and I was admiring its softness when a white flash nearly overwhelmed me.

From the flash, an onslaught of images emerged. I focused on the present, and soon I could see the woman in pink harping in the carriage, then a cold and stingy lump of grisly beef on a plate alongside a bare potato, then a ledger with a meager and dwindling balance.

I dropped the glove. Woe, regret, and resignation filled that man, but malice? No, at least none I could sense.

I breathed deeply, releasing all that I could of that vision. With more reluctance, I took up the woman's stole and blanked my mind again. Just as quickly, another swirl settled over me.

Sadness. Disappointment. I saw the man slumped at the carriage window, dark rooms that were cold and bare, rough hands stitching rips in a gown long past its prime.

Sorrow, so much sorrow, but nothing suggesting danger to the Queen.

"Where's the ticket?"

Marlie's question broke the spell.

"The ticket? Yes, of course." I swallowed the residual emotions and set down the stole, grabbed a gold-embossed card from the stack, and scribbled the shelf number.

"Here." I handed it to her.

"Well? Did you see anything?" She leaned close, her

eyes wide with expectation.

I shook my head.

"Maybe this one then," she said. "He looks unsavory." She handed me a caped Ulster folded over her arm and a gauzy shawl. "You must be quick, though. There's a line now. We can't keep them waiting."

"Quick. Right." I found a hook for the coat and shawl and ran bare fingers over the sleeve.

Polished leather shoes, an embrace with a comely maid in a hallway shadow, an older woman—a wife?—waiting in the drawing room.

Nothing to do with the Queen. I set the coat aside and took up the shawl.

A sick child in bed, a tear-stained letter, a vial of laudanum hidden among a shelf of perfume bottles. Despair and desperation, but again nothing directed toward Her Majesty.

I grabbed a ticket, scribbled the number, and hurried back.

The eye roll the footman gave me when I put the card in his hand told me I was still taking too long, but at least he didn't complain. Not to me anyway.

And that's how the time passed. A footman delivered a bundle, and sometimes I detected something close to danger, but each time, when the vision clarified, the bitterness focused on a spouse or an in-law or a neighbor. One old curmudgeon was particularly irritated that his wife forced him to attend the ball at all, as he staunchly believed masquerades were silly, juvenile affairs.

Not a single guest, however, presented violent thoughts or ill will toward the Queen, and I wasn't surprised.

The chime of the first hour came far too quickly. Between visits from the footmen bearing items to check, I scanned the crowd beyond the door for Mr. Wyck. It was next to impossible, though. Curious guests wanted to linger in front of the crisscrossed swords, the mounted pistols and daggers that climbed the vestibule's walls, the suits of armor astride stationary steeds that flanked the staircase like the ghosts of medieval knights, or any of the myriad treasures tucked here and there.

"What's wrong with you?" Marlie asked the next time she handed me a coat. "Do you need a water closet break?"

I cringed at the bluntness of her question. Yet it was the perfect excuse. "Yes, as a matter of fact, I do. Cover for me. I'll be right back."

I hurried out the door before she could stop me or complain then disappeared into the mingling crowd.

I kept to the perimeter, worried that I would stick out in this throng of well-heeled guests. But no one looked my direction. Or, if they did, they didn't look for long. I was only a servant after all.

I could go anywhere.

That thought carried me through the crowd to the corridor that would lead me to the stairs and, I hoped, the Rubens Room above.

There was no time to spare. I had to find Mr. Wyck before he reached the Queen.

Up the stairs and down the hall, I passed no one, which was odd. Where were the usual pages, porters, and footmen that were ubiquitous in this part of the castle?

Finally, I found the room I sought and paused at the door, listening for voices. Nothing. I pushed the door open a crack and peered in. Sunlight poured through the open window, glinting off the gilt furniture and dozens of gold-framed portraits.

But there was no one. Not a soul.

I opened the door wider and spied the crates in a far corner beside a window. After checking that there was no one behind me, I slipped inside and closed the door. I padded to the crate and examined them. Nothing unusual. Only a dozen or so closed wooden boxes, the Crystal Palace's seal intact.

Disappointment set in. I would have liked to have seen

this marvelous new invention, this steam instrument they
called a calliope.

Behind me, a door closed. I whipped around, searching
the shadows. Was someone here? My heart quickened.

Footsteps in the hallway. I rushed to the door, threw it
open, and saw a man dressed in a lavishly trimmed pirate
coat with black trousers and shiny boots. I would have
assumed him to be a guest who had lost his way if it wasn't
for the distinctive flop of tousled chestnut hair I spied
beneath his feathered tricorn as he rounded the corner.

I gasped and pulled back into the shadows.

The figure stopped at the sound and turned. His face
was obscured by a silvery mask, but it was unmistakably
Mr. Wyck.

He stared my direction for what seemed an eternity,
then turned and continued on his way.

The shadows had saved me.

I breathed with relief, even as the implications sank in.
He was dressed for the ball. That's how he intended to get
close to the Queen. That was his plan.

My heart raced. The Queen was not only in danger. She
was in danger *now*.

I rushed back to Marlie as quickly as I could without
drawing undue attention.

"You're red as a cherry tart," Marlie said when I found
her. "What happened?"

"I have to get to the Queen before he gets to her." My
voice came in a breathless torrent.

Color drained from her face. She grabbed my hands
and pulled me to a secluded spot beside the window.
"Before who gets her?"

"Mr. Wyck. He's dressed himself up as a guest. He's
headed for the ball. We have to go. Before it's too late." I
knew I wasn't making sense, but there was no time to
explain. We had to move.

Behind her gentle brown eyes, I could see Marlie
sorting and scrutinizing my words, weighing them for

merit.

I grabbed her elbow, breaking my own rules of touch. "We must go!"

She stared at my hand on her arm then looked at me. I could see she understood now. "The Queen isn't there. Not yet. It's too early. She won't appear for another hour, if I had to guess."

"We cannot guess!"

"You're right," she said. "Wait here."

She hurried to the door and hailed a footman. When he approached, she whispered to him. Then he whispered to her. He pulled back, his eyes narrowed to pinpricks. She nodded. He sighed and leaned in again. A moment later, he pulled away and returned to his post.

Marlie returned to me. "The Queen isn't expected in the ballroom for a half hour, at least."

"What else did he say?"

"Nothing of importance." Her glance skittered away.

I didn't need a vision to know she was lying. The way she refused to meet my gaze was proof enough. I would have demanded to know what was said if I thought she would tell me, but I knew she wouldn't. I had my suspicions, though.

That footman—was he Fayte? Were there others around us? Mrs. Crossey refused to tell me their number, and I suppose it had been my own fault for not pressing the question. Perhaps Marlie had told him what I'd said. Perhaps they could help.

That thought filled me with hope. "He can assist, can't he? The Fayte Guardians will help?"

Her fingers flew to her lips. Her face contorted in horror. "Don't speak that name. Not here. Not *ever*."

"I'm sorry." But I wasn't. Not really. What did she expect? The Queen's life was at stake.

She nudged me back to the shadows beside the coat racks.

"He said he'd do what he could." She scanned the

room to be sure she wouldn't be overheard. "But there simply aren't enough of us to do much of anything without being noticed."

Her concern was evident, but it still made little sense. Someone intended to harm the Queen, and these people were worried about being *noticed*?

"Who cares if they're found out if it means saving the Queen?" I tried to match her whisper, but my frustration was getting the better of me.

"It's not that simple," she said. "There are rules. He will do what he can."

How could she accept that? But there wasn't time to argue. If they weren't going to do something, I would.

And I already had a plan.

CHAPTER TWENTY-TWO

I HAD REACHED the Grand Staircase when a hand landed on my shoulder. I whipped around.

"Sorry," Marlie said. She pulled back and flashed her palms. "I forgot."

"Don't try to stop me." I knew it was risky, but my mind was made up.

"That's not what I'm doing. I'm going with you."

I didn't expect that. "What about the cloak room?"

She flicked her hand over her shoulder. "I told Chester you needed help."

I frowned, puzzled.

"With a female issue," she elaborated.

"A *female* issue?"

She stifled a laugh. "He didn't dare ask anything after that. But it's fine. Everyone's in the ball or milling about in St. George's Hall. There's nothing to do now but wait, and I wasn't going to let you do this alone. But what exactly *are* you doing?"

A page in full red-and-gold livery strode toward us with a silver platter and cloche. Once he passed, I whispered, "I'm going to the private apartments."

"The Queen won't be there. She must be in the Throne Room by now."

"I need to get something, and if I don't hurry, it'll be too late."

We had to get through the kitchen and up the east stairs to stay out of sight. The detour would add several minutes to the trip, but I couldn't risk being seen—or stopped—by Mr. MacDougall.

She gnawed on her lower lip and touched her Faytling, but she didn't move.

I was losing what little patience I had left. "We have to *go*."

Something desperate flashed in her eyes and she gripped her Faytling more tightly. "I think there might be another way. If it works, we can cross the Quadrangle in half the time."

Tempting as that sounded, lanterns had been set up along the interior lanes for the carriages. Anyone gazing out an inner window would be able to see us. Mr. MacDougall, Mr. Bailey, even Chester. "It's too risky."

"But no one would see us."

"Are you insane? Everyone could see us."

She straightened herself and shook off her hesitation. "You're wearing Mrs. Crossey's Faytling, aren't you?"

My fingers brushed the crystal talisman hidden beneath my collar. I nodded.

She ducked into a dark alcove near the stairs and motioned for me to follow. "There's an old trick Mother taught me. She told me they used to do it to move through crowds quickly, but that's when the Guardians still relied on their magic. No one does now, not in ages. I used to do it until Mr. MacDougall caught me and threatened to revoke my Faytling if he caught me doing it again. It should work, though."

"What should work?" So far, she wasn't helping. She was only confusing me, and time was slipping away.

She pulled her Faytling over her head and slipped the

vessel, cord and all, into the palm of her right hand.

I did the same.

"Now, think to yourself, 'I'm invisible,' 'I'm unseen,' or something like that. The words don't matter as much as the intention."

"You can't be serious." If she thought this was funny, I certainly didn't.

"I'm absolutely serious. Just watch." She lifted her right hand to show me the talisman, then she disappeared. She completely vanished.

I searched around. "Where are you? Marlie, where'd you go?"

After a moment, she reappeared behind me, grinning with triumph. "I'm right here. See? It works."

"But how?" I searched the space behind her and around her, hoping for a reasonable explanation, yet suspecting it was just as she'd said. Magic.

"It's the Faytling. It works best when there are distractions around and in short spurts, but I think it can get us there."

Think? That wasn't reassuring.

Still, the minutes were ticking by. I did as she said, gripped the Faytling inside my glove, and mentally repeated the word "invisible." It might have been the effects of the talisman or just my nerves, but the view in front of me turned murky and unsteady, like the onset of a vision.

Was it supposed to feel like this? It didn't matter. As long as it worked, we had to keep going.

I followed her past the line of footmen, and to my astonishment, they didn't look at either of us. It was as if we weren't there at all.

We passed through the open doors and made our way through a break in the line of carriages before crossing the wide lawn of the Quadrangle.

If Marlie was having the same sideways feelings I was, she didn't show it. I, on the other hand, was struggling to keep up. Was this part of the Faytling getting used to me? Every step proved more difficult than the last, as if my boots had been weighted with stones. And I couldn't shake the feeling that we were being watched. I searched the windows, looking for faces staring at us, seeing through our trickery.

I saw no one, however. It was only my imagination. My nerves. And I forced myself to keep moving. To keep pace with Marlie despite my reluctant limbs. I swung my arm forward for momentum and though it felt like my arm, what I saw moving beside me was a hazy, silvery outline of what might have been my arm. Only it couldn't be because my arm was still locked at my side. Panicked, I returned the silvery shadow back to my side. I clenched and stretched my fingers in amazement, but the spell was broken by a voice—*that* voice—whispering in my ear, "There you are."

A blackness rimmed my vision that constricted, making the tunnel of my sight smaller. Ever smaller. No. I wouldn't give in. Not this time. One foot in front of the other. I pressed on. Again and again and again. I stared at the ground without blinking. Afraid to blink. I watched my feet, but every nerve sensed him. He was near. I could feel it. That voice.

Finally, Marlie stopped when we'd crossed the Quadrangle lawn. "Where to now?" When she glanced back, her face crumpled with concern. "Oh goodness, what's happened?"

In an instant she was at my side, supporting me by the arm, and I didn't try to push her away. I didn't have the strength.

"You're burning up," she said, and it was true. I felt none of the usual evening chill. Instead it was as hot as the hottest summer's day. He was here. He was everywhere. But who was he? What was he?

I tried to speak but my mouth was dry. It was difficult to even breathe.

"Hurry, let's get you inside. Just a few more steps. There we are. C'mon."

She opened a door beside the King George IV Gate and pushed me over the threshold. I stumbled into a wall and stood there, feeling cool plaster against my cheek.

"Here now. Give me that." I could feel her finger fishing inside my glove until she hooked the Faytling and pulled it out. The instant the talisman left my grasp, a weight lifted from me. His presence left me. I could breathe. The heat subsided. I looked around to see it wasn't a dark room after all. It was a lighted corridor, a long one with plain white doors on either side. A servants' area by the look of it.

"There now, your color's coming back." I could hear the relief in her voice.

"What happened?" I muttered, wiping perspiration from my forehead.

She lifted Mrs. Crossey's Faytling. "The spell, I'm sure. It doesn't typically have such an effect. It should pass quickly, though. There's a linen room near the end of the hall where we can rest."

"There's no time. And I'm fine." I wasn't, not exactly, but whatever had happened, whatever I saw or thought I saw, was over now and once I had what I needed, I'd feel better. "What's the quickest way to Lady Merrington's room?"

Marlie's forehead crinkled over her nose. "Lady Merrington? Didn't she return home?"

"She went to see a sister, but it isn't her I need. It's what's in her room."

"You need something from her room?" Her words shook with alarm.

Her glance darted away, but before it did, I could see the question there. It would be foolish to think she hadn't heard the gossip about me. The accusations, especially from Abigail. In all our months as roommates, she had never asked if they were true or mentioned them at all. I had hoped it meant she didn't believe them.

Now I wasn't sure.

"You must trust me," I said.

Slowly her glance returned to me. "Fine. Where is her room?"

I bit my lip. I wasn't sure exactly, and I was still so weak. But my energy was returning, slowly. "Near the Queen's room."

"Next to it?"

"No. Two doors away. Maybe three. I'll know it when I see it." I gnawed my lip. I didn't like lying to her, but it was the only way.

Marlie grumbled under her breath, gave me back the Faytling, and led the way up a bare staircase that opened to the western end of the Long Gallery. "After you," she said.

I poked my head out and saw no one along the crimson-carpeted corridor. A blessing.

I tugged off my gloves and approached the first door, placing my bare right hand upon the porcelain knob. My shoulders pulled back and my chin lifted as if of their own accord. A sour sensation twisted my middle as the identity came to me. Lady Bassey.

I yanked my hand away and moved to the next door and the next.

Marlie gave me wary looks as we pressed on. I scrutinized each door, waiting for the dawn of recognition.

Then a door down the hall opened. My stomach clenched.

It was only a page.

I straightened and squared my shoulders. *Act like we belong. Act normal.*

When the boy closed the door, I begged silently, *Go the other way!*

He walked toward us.

My panic surged and nearly buckled my knees, but he only nodded as he passed.

We stopped at another door, between a Chinese vase

and a Roman bust. "This is it." I leaned close and listened for sounds within. Nothing. I turned the knob and peeked through the crack.

No one.

Eagerly I slipped in, with Marlie close behind. She closed the door and latched the lock behind us, but I wasn't paying attention anymore. I was staring at what had to be the most glorious bedchamber I'd ever seen. A four-poster bed draped in quilted burgundy silks stood steps from a window covered in sheer curtains and a richly carved secretary with a matching chair. Along the eastern wall was a cheval glass and a wardrobe that rose nearly to the ceiling.

I spied the box on a settee beside the fireplace.

"What's that?" Marlie peered over my shoulder as I lifted the lid.

I peeled back the tissue paper, layer by layer, until I came to a midnight blue bodice sparkling with glass beads sewn into the shape of peacock feathers around the neckline. Gingerly, I lifted the garment by its short, capped sleeves.

Marlie gasped. "What are you doing?"

When the dress was freed from the box, I pressed it against myself, the way Lady Bassey and Lady Wallingham had. A strange sensation washed over me. Excitement? Fear? Both? It felt right and wrong and everything in between.

"I'm going to wear it," I said. "To the ball."

Marlie's usually ruddy cheeks blanched. She was afraid. For me, and for herself. Maybe she was right to be. I was stealing, after all. Even if my only intent was to protect the Queen.

But there was no time to second-guess this plan or formulate another. "I have to," I added, to reassure her and myself. "It's the only way."

She closed her eyes, and I imagined she was wishing she were anywhere else. With anyone else. When she opened them again, she was different. Not fearful, only determined. "Then you're lucky I'm here," she said, "because you'll never get into that by yourself."

"Of course I can." I could manage. I'd been managing on my own my whole life.

She waved away my words. "Don't argue. Just let somebody help you for once."

I closed my mouth and handed her the bodice.

~ ~ ~

"Tight enough?" Marlie gave a final tug on the bodice laces.

I struggled to breathe but nodded.

"You said you were the same size as Lady Merrington," Marlie grumbled.

"Close enough." The garment was tight, but I managed to twist at the waist, making the midnight blue silk swish around me. I wiggled my toes in the low-heeled slippers, which looked exquisite but had certainly been intended for narrower feet. The Faytling, black cord and all, was tucked within my plain cotton corset, leaving my neck and most of my shoulders bare.

I caught Marlie eying me. "Do I look all right?"

"See for yourself." She motioned to the cheval glass.

I nearly gasped when I saw myself. The gown was snug, but draped nicely, and Marlie had taken my hair out of its usual braid and secured it atop my head with the help of a comb made of mother of pearl and peacock feathers that we'd discovered in the dress box, along with long silky blue gloves and a matching fan and mask.

What was most appealing, however, was the way the candlelight glinted off the beads, making the gown sparkle like the crystals that hung from the castle's chandeliers. I couldn't help but smile at the far more elegant version of myself staring back at me in the reflection.

Is this how Lady Merrington would feel wearing this

gown? Was this how they all felt, all the noble ladies who paraded around the castle in their sumptuous attire?

"It is a beauty." Marlie was still watching me.

I looked away from the glass and wished away the red-hot flush creeping over my collar and cheeks. "It certainly is, but that isn't the point. It's necessary, that's all."

I was addressing her, but I was trying to convince myself. I had a job to do and gazing into a mirror wouldn't get it done. I went to the door and grabbed the knob.

"Wait," Marlie cried. "You can't leave."

I whirled around, ready to defend my plan. Ready for anything. "Why not?"

"You need these," she said. From her fingers dangled the fan and blue silk mask.

CHAPTER TWENTY-THREE

I MOVED QUICKLY along the Long Gallery, past the formal drawing rooms to a staircase that would lead to the eastern end of St. George's Hall, where I could slip into the crowd.

I paused at the end of the stairwell, Marlie at my side.

"This is it," she whispered, the words nearly lost beneath the strains of a minuet drifting from the ballroom.

This *was* it. She could accompany me no farther without calling attention to herself. I was on my own.

Which was fine. It was. I didn't need her or anyone. It wasn't difficult, what I intended to do. I would simply stroll in and act like any other guest. Just one of the legion of ladies sashaying across the floor without raising an eyebrow or drawing a second glance. I was only a lookout. That was all.

My courage increased by degrees. I squared my shoulders and did what I imagined Lady Merrington would do, what any lady of the court would do: I raised my fan strategically to my nose to cover what the mask did not, focused on the path ahead, and strode into the hall as if I belonged there.

I kept close—but not too close—to a cluster of masked guests lingering at the hall's massive hearth. I gazed where they gazed. I wandered where they wandered, and slowly we made our way to the ballroom.

Then, not a dozen paces ahead, I spotted a black tricorn with a white ostrich plume and that usually disheveled hair tied back with a burgundy ribbon in the Georgian style.

Mr. Wyck!

I broke from my unsuspecting colleagues and followed him like a beacon through the throng. As if he sensed my pursuit, he paused and turned back. I lifted my fan to obscure more of my face and saw that silver mask that dipped below his nose. He adjusted it and smoothed the velvet lapels of his coat and the white ruffles cascading from his collar.

I ducked behind a large matron in a marigold gown with bright silk flowers pinned to her sleeves. She scowled at me. I curtsied. "Pardon, madame." But I didn't move until Mr. Wyck resumed his progress toward the ball. Then I hurried as well.

At the double doors, he halted and turned again. I hid behind a man wearing a top hat, then a man's hand thrust in front of me, stopping me in my tracks.

Mr. MacDougall skewered me with his gaze.

Even so, for the first time in my life, I was happy to see him.

I leaned in close and positioned my fan to obscure my words. "It's Mr. Wyck. He's dressed as a guest. A pirate. You must stop him."

His eyes widened in surprise then narrowed to a scowl. "Jane, is that you? Where on earth did you get that dress?"

Wasn't he listening? Who cared about a dress? "It's him, sir. The one who means to harm the Queen. I know it."

Why wasn't he doing something? Why was he still standing here?

"Did you steal that dress, Miss Shackle?"

Why did he care so much about a dress when the Queen's life may be in danger? I leaned closer, so close I breathed the musty smell of him. "Sir, *he* is the threat to the Queen."

Even as I uttered the words, I knew they didn't matter. The scorn on his face told me he didn't believe me.

He stepped back and directed me, rather harshly, toward a quieter alcove.

Several guests and footmen watched, their eyes wide but they didn't dare to intervene. I was too stunned to resist—but only for a moment.

I wouldn't let Mr. Wyck get to the Queen. It was an instinct. New but powerful. I wouldn't—couldn't—fail our sovereign, and I wouldn't fail Mrs. Crossey or Marlie. I pushed past Mr. MacDougall and hurried through George's Hall.

The tricorn was no longer visible, but Mr. Wyck couldn't be far, and I already knew his destination. I could still stop him.

I hurried through the crowd as swiftly as the lovely, yet dreadfully unsteady, shoes allowed. Mr. MacDougall followed, but his larger size and dignified station made it more difficult for him to get through the throng.

By the time I reached the ballroom's doors, I could no longer see Mr. Wyck. I slid in behind two other couples and made my way along the perimeter of the dance floor to the Throne Room, where the Queen and Prince Albert would make their appearance. The doors were still closed. The royal couple hadn't yet arrived. I wasn't too late.

Encouraged, I pulled back to a bare space along the wall and was searching the room for that black tricorn when someone tapped my shoulder. I snapped up my fan and prepared to excuse myself for being in the way.

But when I turned to offer an apology, the sight of the masked pirate stunned me into silence. Even hidden behind my blue silk mask, I trembled beneath Mr. Wyck's startling gaze.

He held out a gloved hand. Such a large hand. "May I have this dance, mademoiselle?" His words flowed easily yet they stole my breath.

I stared at his hand, trying to compose my thoughts.

Finally, I mustered the breath—and the nerve—to speak.

"What game are you playing, Mr. Wyck?" I hardened my glare to match the steel in his own.

His eyes flashed. "So, you've found me out."

Was that condescension in his voice? I didn't know, but I had to admire his cool demeanor. Was he truly so comfortable among these peers of the realm? I had to wonder why that was.

"I have," I said, "as you have guessed me."

Beneath his rigid mask, amusement teased his lips. "Indeed, I have, Miss Shackle. Shall we dance?"

He watched me for some time. Was he toying with me? Or did he intend to distract me, so he might carry out his devious plan?

Again, a desire—no, a *need*—to protect the Queen surged through me. I would keep him from his plan, whatever it took. Placing my own gloved hand in his, I said, "Yes, I would very much like a dance."

His arrogance faltered for a moment, but he recovered quickly and led me to the center of the floor. Without another word, he placed his right hand on my waist and held my hand with his left. When I looked up, he was staring at me with startling intensity. Then, he dipped his chin and picked up the waltz.

To be fair, he was a passable dancer. Good, actually. I had prepared myself for a degree of fumbling, but there was none of that. In fact, I wondered if my own skill held up, honed as it was in Chadwick Hollow's main room on holidays and occasions when the headmistress felt festive and played the pianoforte for our enjoyment.

When I missed a cue and stepped on his foot, I knew

instantly the error was my own. "Terribly sorry," I muttered, mortified.

"For what? I didn't feel a thing."

He was lying, but I smiled despite myself. If he was simply biding his time, he was at least being amiable as he did so. A twinge of guilt twisted within me. I knew I shouldn't be enjoying this. I was only distracting him to keep him from the Queen. That's what I told myself as we twirled on the polished stone floor like a scene from a fairy tale, so much opulence swirling around us, the candlelight making every gilded surface glow.

He took in the crowd. So many people, but no one took note of us. Each was lost in his or her own world as we were lost in ours.

"Blue suits you," he said.

I looked up. "Pardon?"

"The color. The dress brings out the color of your eyes. I suppose it would be indelicate of me to ask how you came by such a costume or how you came to be here."

And then I remembered myself. We weren't dance partners, and we certainly weren't friends. We were adversaries.

"Yes, I suppose it would," I said, cautiously. "As it would be indelicate if I were to ask the same of you. I'm sure your mother taught you better manners than that."

A shadow darkened his expression. "She didn't have the chance. She passed when I was young."

The confession struck me like a slap across the face. Despite my dislike of him, he didn't deserve my cruelty. His pain reminded me of my own. My own loss.

Don't be fooled. It's what he wants you to think.

But could he be so devious? If he knew my past, he could easily use it against me.

Then I saw Mr. MacDougall prowling the edge of the room, watching Mr. Wyck and me. My anxiety eased. He may not be the ally I would have chosen, but he was Fayte, which meant he would help me if it meant helping the

Queen.

Mr. Wyck must have seen the House Steward as well because he tightened his hold on my waist, a sensation that wasn't entirely unpleasant but made me glad to know Mr. MacDougall was near.

Finally, when our waltz ended, I stepped back and curtsied, thanking him for the dance.

He didn't release my hand. He tightened his grip instead. "You wouldn't leave me after just one dance, would you?"

I glanced up into his dark eyes, disarmed but curious.

"It's just that if you don't have anyone else on your dance card," he continued, "I should like to keep your company. Unless you object to mine."

Again, he was playing with me.

Again, my mind reeled and I wished my thoughts didn't fixate on the spot where his fingers touched my glove. I wasn't flirting. I was protecting the Queen. As long as we danced, he could do her no harm.

The fact that part of me enjoyed the dancing was of no consequence at all.

"As it happens," I said, "I don't object."

The musicians struck up a lively polonaise. Before I could say another word, he guided me across the floor. In the middle of the dance, the music dwindled to a slow and muddled stop.

Across the floor, the Throne Room doors glided open. Two heralds appeared, one lifting a polished brass trumpet to his lips to sound the announcement of Her Majesty's arrival.

At its conclusion, the musicians launched into the opening measures of *Homage to Queen Victoria.*

From my vantage point, I could see a uniformed Prince Albert but not the Queen, though I knew she must be there as well, only too diminutive to be seen.

Beside me, Mr. Wyck watched, too. I had to wonder at the diabolical plans that must be grinding behind that determined expression. If ever there was a time I wished I could read his mind, now was it. *You scoundrel! You may be able to block your thoughts, but I already know your intentions.*

I had him and there wasn't a thing he could do about it. Emboldened, I leaned into his shoulder. "You will finish our dance, won't you?"

I was prepared for him to manufacture a reason to dash off, but instead he squared his shoulders to me and bowed deeply. "I wouldn't dream of leaving your side."

I fanned myself, admiring his ruse. Such confidence in his villainy. *You have met your match, however, Mr. Wyck. I assure you.*

We stood as the crowd parted, allowing the Queen and Prince Albert to take their seats of honor beside the musicians.

"You do seem quite interested in Her Majesty," he said in my ear. "Any particular reason?"

I shot him a look. This was brash even for him. "I suppose I am interested. Yet no more than anyone else."

He smirked. "Is that so?"

What he meant by that I could hardly guess, but it didn't matter. My only concern was stopping him from getting anywhere near the Queen.

Once the Royals were seated, the musicians struck up a new polonaise, and the dancers resumed their progress around the dance floor—Mr. Wyck and I among them.

I quickly settled back into our familiar rhythm. To his credit, he seemed more focused on me than the Queen, which I found flattering despite myself. Through the boisterous turns of the next dance, I was so engrossed in our movements that I didn't even realize he had maneuvered us almost directly in front of the Royals.

We took a turn to the left, and when I looked back at the Queen, I saw the chair beside Prince Albert empty.

Where had she gone? I scanned the room.

Then a woman's scream stopped everything. The music, the chatter, the movement.

Wild glances darted to a commotion at the St. George's Hall doorway.

I rushed closer and found a woman in emerald satin clutching a footman's lapel. Her mask of glittering green leaves hung loose at her neck, but her cries were lost beneath the growing volume of murmurs. She turned from the visibly shaken footman to scream at the crowd, "On the staircase! I saw her! She's dead!"

Gasps replaced the murmurs.

And where was Mr. Wyck? I turned to find him behind me, looking as stunned and frantic as I. In the distance, I could see the Queen's chair still empty. Beside it, Prince Albert stood flanked by a pair of footmen and two guards.

A black feeling gripped me.

Again, I searched the crowd, standing on tiptoe to see over the sea of heads. Still no sign.

With heart racing and head swimming, I grabbed the sides of my skirt and ran to the door.

Pushing through, my gloved fingers clawed at shoulders and elbows to allow me to pass. I ignored the angry looks. Who cared if I was making a spectacle of myself? I had to get to the staircase.

Finally, in St. George's Hall, I spied two footmen in heated discourse. As I neared, they pivoted on their black heels and stood at attention.

"Where is she?" I demanded, ignoring the usual formalities. "Where is the Queen?"

They frowned and exchanged confused glances.

"For goodness sake, don't just stand there." But then I remembered: They didn't see me—a servant like themselves—they saw a lady, a guest.

I tried again in short, commanding syllables, "There's been trouble. Where?"

The young men remained silent, but their glances darted to the vestibule. I took up my skirt again and pressed on. Once I'd reached the entry room, I could see a cluster of attendants congregated on the staircase.

Please, no. Please!

I ran toward them, ignoring the pains shooting from my toes.

The men were staring at the ground, at something I couldn't yet see, but then there was a pair of lady's boots.

Not the dainty slippers of a Queen.

Worn leather boots. A servant's boots.

Something deep within warned me to stay back. A blackness clawed through me.

When I reached the stairs, two footmen pulled away from the huddle, and I saw the face of the figure draped across four steps. I froze.

It wasn't the Queen, as I had feared.

The lifeless body upon the stairs was Mrs. Crossey.

CHAPTER TWENTY-FOUR

HOW I REACHED Mrs. Crossey's side I'll never know, for it was impossible to think beyond the single question pounding at my skull: Was she dead?

I squeezed past two footmen.

"She's still breathing," one said.

I nearly fainted with relief.

"The physician is on his way," said another.

"Excuse me, miss."

Someone tapped my shoulder, but I didn't look back. I wedged next to Mrs. Crossey. Her eyelids fluttered. Could she see me?

But even if she did, what would she see? A stranger. How could she know me dressed and masked as I was?

If I spoke to her, these men would know I was an impostor.

But I had to risk it. I leaned in under the pretext of smoothing back a lock of her hair that had fallen across her cheek. Then I dropped to my knees and covered my face with my hands, pretending to be overcome with emotion.

"It's me, Mrs. Crossey," I whispered next to her ear,

hoping beyond hope she would hear. I peeked through my fingers at her face. No movement. Not even a twitch.

I feared the worst.

Her breath remained shallow and weak, though I could see no evidence of harm.

A footman whispered, "Could it be the—"

Another shut him down with a harsh *shhh!*

"But the girl. On the Slopes," another said.

They were thinking the same thing I was.

More voices encroached. Dr. Holland, the Queen's physician, had arrived. My time was up.

I would do no good if I were discovered. Not to Mrs. Crossey, not to myself, and certainly not to the Queen.

An idea struck. It was a risk, but it was my only option.

Slowly, I bent over Mrs. Crossey and whimpered, hoping to appear so distraught that the footmen didn't notice my hand slip over Mrs. Crossey's and my finger slip into her sleeve. I searched the space. Yes! The handkerchief was there.

I clutched it in my palm and rose, still pretending tears. They weren't difficult, for the emotion was real.

I held that linen with all my might, wailed into my fists, and bolted up the rest of the stairs in what I hoped would appear to be an outpouring of despair.

A footman called after me, but I didn't stop. Didn't even slow until I had cleared their view. The last thing I heard was the physician demanding space around Mrs. Crossey so he could examine her.

When I was out of view, I stopped. The anteroom serving as the gentlemen's drawing room was ahead. Hope shot through me. Might Mrs. Crossey's assailant have ducked in there, eager to blend into a crowd? I poked my head in, interrupting two men chatting near the doorway.

"May we help you?" The question came from a stout fellow with a handlebar mustache, the pinch between his salt-and-pepper eyebrows a clear indication I had disrupted their leisure.

"A woman has been attacked. On the staircase. Did anyone come this way?"

The man eyed me with suspicion. "Attacked, you say? Are you sure?"

I wanted to shout at him, *Of course I'm sure, you imbecile!* Instead, I swallowed that rage and answered as calmly as I could, "Yes, sir, I'm quite sure."

His companion, another portly and sour-looking individual, removed the cigar from his lips. "There was a drunk fellow a moment ago who stumbled by."

There had been someone!

"Who was it? When?"

The mustached one frowned. "A few moments ago. He couldn't have gotten far, clumsy as he was."

"What did he look like?"

The other man inhaled from his cigar and glanced up at the ceiling, trying to remember. "Hard to say. A bit round in the middle, and he was wearing a mask, you know. Gold or silver. Goodness, I don't recall."

That was no help at all. I backed away. "Thank you for your help." Though it wasn't much. "If you'll excuse me."

The other man held out his hand to stop me. "Miss, if there's danger at hand, you should stay here. Let us call a guard. Come now, we'll get to the bottom—"

I continued my retreat. "I'm sure it's just a misunderstanding."

"Miss, please—"

"Thank you for your concern, gentlemen." I wheeled around and hurried along the corridor even as they continued to call after me.

I took the first turn I came to and then the next, eager to dodge them in case they followed. When I realized where I was, I found myself in a dark and unfamiliar alcove. Nothing looked familiar. I tried a door and found a storage closet. I tried another, and it opened to an opulent—and thankfully vacant—chamber.

But which one? I had no memory of it. I looked behind

me. I couldn't go back that way. The men may have summoned the guards, and guards would undoubtedly have questions.

Where else could I go?

What I needed was to collect my thoughts. A moment to focus on Mrs. Crossey's handkerchief and—I hoped—discover the identity of her attacker.

Because one thing was now painfully clear: it wasn't Mr. Wyck.

I stepped into the chamber, closed the door, and slumped against the nearest wall. The full weight of my failure pressing me down.

I had been wrong all along.

And what if Mrs. Crossey succumbed? I didn't want to lose her because I'd been too stubborn to see the truth. I pulled off my mask and threw it to the ground, along with the fan. What good was a disguise if I was too stupid to see what was right in front of my face?

The handkerchief was my only hope. I tugged the small square of white linen from the elbow of my left glove. If Mrs. Crossey had seen her attacker, perhaps I could see it in a vision.

I tugged away both silky gloves and gripped the linen. *Please, Mrs. Crossey. Please show me.*

Vertigo set in almost instantly. My thoughts swirled into a disorienting blur, and I searched for images to resolve.

The blur continued. After a moment, the swirling increased to a dizzying pace.

I tightened my grip and increased my concentration, focusing every thought on the fabric.

Only spinning. Incessant spinning.

I dropped the fabric and keeled over, grabbing a knee with one hand and my stomach with the other. Nausea threatened to overwhelm me.

Finally, when the ground stopped shifting beneath me, I straightened and tried to compose myself. Nothing like that had ever happened. Despite the surge, I saw nothing.

I'd failed again.

~ ~ ~

With my mask firmly in place, I made good time getting back to St. George's Hall, despite spending a good deal of it searching for a way back that avoided the Grand Staircase.

Once there, I faced a relentless stream of exiting guests. I wove and ducked between people and nearly collided with a footman.

"Where is everyone going?" I asked him.

"Leaving, miss. They're all leaving." He bowed, swerved around me, and hurried on.

Leaving? All of them? I suppose I shouldn't have been surprised considering the commotion. But what of the Queen?

I hurried into the ballroom against the tide, and it seemed an eternity before I reached the window that overlooked the northern slopes. The musicians were still milling about, packing their instruments, dumbstruck by this abrupt end to the festivities. The royal seats, however, sat empty.

Were they gone? Were they safe?

I approached a sentry beside the closed Throne Room door. I didn't recognize the man, but I lifted my fan over my lips to be sure he wouldn't recognize me.

"I do hope the Queen departed before the trouble." I mimicked the condescending tone the Queen's ladies took when they spoke to servants.

"Yes, miss. All is well with the Queen."

Somewhat relieved but still wary, I turned back to the entrance and headed to the only place where I thought I might still do some good.

~ ~ ~

I found the reception room overrun with guests clamoring for their belongings. Chester was taking tickets, and Marlie was pulling the garments. Two other maids who had been assigned to the ladies' sitting room had been recruited to help as well.

When Marlie spotted me, she pulled me into the empty sitting room.

"What are you doing? You can't walk around like that." She shook her hands at my gown.

Her complaint caught me off guard. "What else can I do? I have no choice."

"Yes, you do."

I threw up my hands in confusion, but she was already marching to a side cabinet, where she grabbed a canvas sack and thrust it at me.

"Change. I'll watch the door."

I opened the sack to find my uniform and boots within. "How did you get these?"

"I went back. I had a feeling you'd need them. Now turn around."

I followed her command and felt her tug the laces of the bodice free so I could extricate myself. The skirt I managed on my own as she stood watch at the door. After folding the silk garments as best I could, I bundled them into the bag. "How much trouble am I in?"

"None that I know of."

I tucked the bag under my arm. "But I *left*."

She shrugged. "Female issues, remember? Chester hasn't said a thing."

"Nothing?" I was relieved, I couldn't deny it. "Isn't that odd?"

"To be honest, we've been dealing with this flood of people." She craned her neck out the door. "The line is backing up again. We should get back or Chester really will have a fit."

I held the bag close and followed her back. Chester

gave me a funny look when he saw me, but Marlie stepped in.

"Look who's back. And perfect timing, too." She winked at me before approaching an impatient man who was thumping his walking stick beside his feet. "Yes, sir, how may I assist you?"

The burly man thrust his number at her. "My coat, if you please. And my wife's stole."

"Yes, sir. Coming right up." Marlie took the white slip and disappeared to the racks, conveniently avoiding Chester's suspicious glare.

When he turned it on me, I tucked the sack out of the way and addressed the next frantic guest. "How may I help you, sir?"

Over the next half hour, we worked our way through the requests, and when the last one had left the room, it was apparent we still weren't done.

The shelves and rack held dozens of remaining items—coats, shawls, hats, gloves.

"What should we do with all of it?" I asked Marlie.

"You'll need these."

I turned to see Chester carrying an armload of empty canvas sacks.

"Bag them and pin the number to identify them. Can you manage that, or will you be needing to run off again, Miss Shackle?" A single eyebrow hiked up his forehead.

"I believe I can manage," I muttered.

"And I'll help," Marlie piped in.

"Fine." He looked at another two maids who had been recruited to help. "You two, back to the kitchen. There's nothing left for you to do here."

I could hear their exaggerated sighs as they brushed past on the way to the door, with Chester close behind.

Marlie gathered the sacks and spread them out on the table. "You collect, I'll stuff and tag."

I stared at her in disbelief.

"Would you prefer the bags?" she asked. "I'll collect, I

don't mind."

"How can you do it?" I said. "How can you act like nothing happened?"

Sudden anger rushed through me. Anger at her. At myself. At whoever had attacked Mrs. Crossey and left her for dead.

Marlie's cheerfulness fell away. What remained was raw and unsettled. "Because I have to," she said. "It's the only way to help her."

I knew she meant Mrs. Crossey.

"It's going to be all right," she added.

But that was just it. It *wasn't* all right. Perhaps the Queen was safe—at least for now—but Mrs. Crossey was fighting for her life because of my mistake. If I hadn't been focused on Mr. Wyck, I might have seen the culprit. The real culprit.

And now our chance—maybe our only chance—to catch the killer was gone.

I shook my head. "It's not all right. And it won't be until I make it right."

To her credit, Marlie tried to help. She uttered sweet, encouraging words as we sorted and bagged the items left in the reception room. And then, she left me to the silence.

I was grateful. It gave me time to think.

Chester returned with a rolling cart and helped us load the bags onto it. I added the one with the costume and promised myself I'd find it later and get it back where it belonged.

"The Queen," I asked. "Is she safe?"

He nodded. "I understand she's quite well. She was taken to her rooms by the guards, where she remains in their safekeeping."

Some of the weight I'd been feeling lifted. But not all of it.

"And Mrs. Crossey? Is there news of her?"

A shadow clouded his expression. "Dr. Holland is tending to her."

"Is she awake?" I pressed.

He glanced up and seemed to struggle with his next words.

Every second of his hesitation dug the burning dagger in my heart deeper.

"Will she live?" I blurted and gritted my teeth, willing myself to maintain my temper.

"What she means is," Marlie offered in a gentler tone, "we're terribly worried. Is there any news?"

Marlie's sweetness worked. The footman softened. "She isn't conscious, but her breath is good. Strong, the physician said. At least that's how it was relayed to me. There is reason to be hopeful, but the extent of the injuries cannot be known unless… until she awakes."

It was not the news I had hoped to hear, but it was better than it might have been. I took what solace I could in that.

"Where is she?" I asked.

He glanced away. "She isn't to be disturbed."

"We understand that," Marlie said, interceding again. "But when she wakes, which I'm sure will be soon."

He turned so he was facing Marlie and eclipsed me completely. "She's in a private room near the Queen. It was deemed best to keep the physician near to both."

"Of course," Marlie said. "If you have an opportunity, please let us know if there is any change in her condition. For good or…" She didn't finish her sentence.

"Yes, you can be sure of it."

We loaded the last bag onto the cart, and he wheeled it away. To where, I didn't know or care.

A clock in the adjoining room chimed ten times.

"I suppose we're done here," she said.

The chamber was almost back to its usual state. The shelves, racks, and chairs that had been brought in would likely stay until the morning staff removed them.

"I suppose we are." I was still lost in my own thoughts about Mrs. Crossey and the Queen and the mysterious figure who threatened them both.

"Shall we get back to the kitchen?" Her tone was hopeful, if not quite cheerful. "I'm sure there's still work to be done there."

I couldn't bear the thought of returning to that little corner without Mrs. Crossey. I'd probably be assigned to another cook or the washing room, but all of it would only reinforce my failings.

"You go." I mustered something close to a smile. "I'll be right behind you."

Marlie frowned but didn't argue, only nodded and slipped out the door.

We both knew I wasn't going to the kitchen.

CHAPTER TWENTY-FIVE

THE NIGHT STAFF had extinguished most of the candles on the main floor, but a few still flickered in the vestibule and St. George's Hall, casting dancing orange light against the legion of lonely blooms and garlands. I roamed among them, weaving in and out of the shadows, by turns clutching and releasing the Faytling that rested, exposed, atop my pinafore.

I craved its help to find Mrs. Crossey's attacker, if it had any to give. I begged for it, but I also feared the consequences. I'd never felt anything like that strange malaise that had afflicted me in the Quadrangle. It was far more disorienting than any vision, and Marlie had no explanation for it. How could I guard myself against another bout when I knew nothing of its cause?

But then there was so much I didn't understand. About the Faytling. About the Fayte Guardians. About any of this.

Mrs. Crossey had been struck down. That I knew. And the same could happen to the Queen. I believed that.

After nearly an hour, my prospects were dim, I knew, but I still couldn't give up. Marlie would be in our room eager to discuss and dissect all that had gone wrong, and I couldn't face her.

So, I pressed on into the dark hallways, hastening my pace whenever I passed a footman or a guard. I didn't slow for pleasantries. I didn't make eye contact. I moved with haste and purpose, so I would be left alone.

When I found myself at a door to the East Terrace, I opened it.

The night air bit my cheeks and my nose. I hugged my arms around myself but ventured on despite the cold.

The nearly full moon was high and illuminated the crisscrossing pathways to the fountain. I walked without a destination, without a purpose, simply trying to think of nothing at all.

Then I heard that familiar soft buzz. The one I had been hoping for. I stopped at the fountain's edge and waited for her to settle.

"I'm happy for the company," I whispered. I couldn't see her yet, but I knew she was close. I could feel the familiar prickle of her attention.

But there was something else, too.

I searched the shadows and saw only the usual forms. The shrubs and statuary. The benches and paths. Were there still guards stationed beyond the wall?

"It's probably just something drifting in the air," I said to her.

There was a pause, then a silent question.

"I know it's late. But I don't expect I'll sleep tonight."

She dipped her head.

"I've made such a mess of things—" My voice caught. Again the image of Mrs. Crossey lying unconscious on the stairs vexed me.

I expected a condolence or some reassuring sentiment.

What my dragonfly conveyed was more like a slap.

"What do you mean you already knew?" I blurted. "How?"

What followed was a frantic dance.

"Slow down. You aren't making sense. What about Mr. Wyck?"

"Why don't you ask me yourself?"

I froze at the sound of the throaty voice behind me. I looked over my shoulder to find him standing not ten feet away, his head cocked to one side, his hands shoved deep into the pockets of his wool coat. A regular coat, I noted. Not the velvet costume I'd last seen him in. The hat was gone, and his hair was tucked beneath a cap, not a tricorn. "I didn't know you were there," I mumbled.

"So I gathered."

He chuckled or scoffed; I didn't know which.

"What I mean is that…" I stopped. What did I mean? Before I could decide, my dragonfly alighted from her spot and flew away.

No, she was doing something else. I stared with increasing horror as she flew directly at Mr. Wyck and circled his head.

He ducked and bobbed and tried to avoid what he was interpreting as an attack. And he laughed. A full belly laugh to which I couldn't help but smile.

"Is it always like this?" He dodged another pass.

"No, actually. She's *never* like this. Dragonfly, stop this instant."

To my surprise, she obeyed and came to rest on my shoulder. I stared at her and waited for an explanation. But she only sat primly, stared at me, and sent one simple message: "Listen to him."

"What is that? Your pet?"

Mr. Wyck's questions weren't unreasonable, but I sneered anyway. "She's hardly a pet. She's a dragonfly."

As if that explained anything.

"I can see that," he grumbled. "Yet she seems rather fond of you. I've never seen a dragonfly act like that before."

Was she fond of me? I suppose she was, just as I was of her. Did that make me *her* pet? The prospect might have amused me if my heart weren't so heavy.

"You know they call you the dragonfly maid behind your back."

"Who calls me—" No, I wasn't going to let him goad me into an argument. I had no wish for one, not tonight. "Why are you here, Mr. Wyck?"

He looked away, to the darkness beyond the castle wall. "Not sure exactly. I thought I might find you here, though."

"You did?" I bristled.

"Why are you out so late?"

He was trying to sound sharp and disapproving, but I could hear hesitation in his voice.

"I needed some fresh air. It helps me think." I hugged myself, though it was admittedly a futile attempt to stave off the cold.

He noticed. "You must be freezing. Here." He shook off his coat and covered the distance between us in long, brisk strides before draping the coat around my shoulders.

My breath stopped at the nearness of him. The warmth and the smell of dirt and hay that clung to him. Stable smells I hadn't noticed in the ballroom. When he moved back, I stared at the ground. "You didn't have to do that."

"I know."

He was watching me, and for the first time, he didn't look to be on the verge of grumbling something sarcastic. For the first time, he looked… kind.

My dragonfly buzzed at my ear, urging me, in her way.

"I suppose I owe you an apology." I fumbled with the edges of the coat. Holding it close like this reminded me how it had been with him on the dance floor. The two of us moving in unison, so effortless, so… I winced. I couldn't—shouldn't—think that way. I did not enjoy this closeness. I couldn't let myself.

"Oh?" His curiosity was piqued.

My dragonfly buzzed again. *Just say it. Say it and be done with it.*

190

Fine. Stop hounding me.

I met his gaze. "I believed you wanted to hurt the Queen." The words rushed out of me. "I thought you wanted to hurt her, and that you were the one who killed that girl, and that maybe you wanted to kill me, too. I know it sounds crazy, but Mrs. Crossey told me... It doesn't matter what she told me. But I was wrong, and I'm sorry."

My dragonfly flew a full circle around my head then paused, giving me a good long look. *You did the right thing.* Then she flew away.

She might be pleased, but I was quite sure Mr. Wyck felt differently. I expected him to be angry, or at least annoyed. Instead he let his head drop back, and he stared at the stars above.

"Did you hear what I said?"

He looked at me. "I heard you."

Was he angry? But he looked more perplexed than angry.

"I was just thinking it was strange because I owe you the same apology."

"You do?"

He stared off to that faraway place again. "I thought *you* intended to hurt the Queen. That's why I was sent here, to watch you. To catch you in the act, if I could. I thought that's why you sneaked into the ball tonight. I didn't want to believe it, but the signs seemed so obvious."

His words were crazy. "How on earth could you think such a thing?"

He threw up his hands. "Why else would you disguise yourself except for some devilish purpose? And then to get so close to the Queen?"

The way he said it, it did seem plausible, even probable, that I was up to something. Except... "But why would I want to harm the Queen?"

"Why not you? Someone clearly means to— information that isn't common knowledge, by the way, yet you seem fully aware. And that girl who was killed just over the wall, so very near the spot where I found you. If that's not suspicious, I don't know what is."

"But you were there, too! You could have done it."

He all but laughed. "Do you really think so?"

"I did, until someone attacked Mrs. Crossey." I turned to the fountain and stared into the cascading waters. After a quiet moment, I turned back. "How do *you* know someone is after the Queen?"

He shifted and seemed to consider his words carefully. "Haven't you guessed?"

I had guessed many things, and they had all been wrong. I no longer trusted myself.

After another long pause, he said, simply, "I'm a Fayte Guardian."

I scoffed. He was lying. Mrs. Crossey would have told me.

Wouldn't she?

Perhaps not. The truth was, there were many things that woman hadn't told me. Too many. The castle was apparently filled with Fayte Guardians, yet I knew of only four: Mrs. Crossey, Mr. MacDougall, Marlie, and Chester, and he was still only a guess.

But Mr. Wyck?

"If it makes a difference," he continued, "I don't think Mrs. Crossey knows. My family left for Balmoral years ago. I was barely out of short pants back then." He kicked at the dirt. "And I've altered my name."

"You aren't Lucas Wyck?"

"Not exactly." Still he stared at the ground. "Officially it's James Lucas Starwyck, Jr. I go by Lucas, but Mr. McDougall thought I should alter my last name for anonymity."

It sounded like something Mr. MacDougall would do.

"Should I call you Mr. Starwyck, then?"

His dark eyes shot up and locked on mine. "Best to stick with Wyck, I think. But I wanted you to know the truth."

Was it the truth? I still wasn't sure. Why would Mr. McDougall go to such trouble?

Mr. Wyck—or Starwyck, or whoever he was—must have sensed my thoughts.

"He believes Mrs. Crossey is acting recklessly. Against the Order's interests, you might say," he continued. "With no Supreme Elder to turn to, he sent word to the Elder Council. My father sent me to see if Mr. MacDougall's suspicions were correct."

"What were his suspicions?"

He rubbed his chin and again seemed to cherry pick his words. "That you were a threat to the Queen."

"Me?" I choked back a laugh. "Why on earth would he think that?"

Mr. Wyck—for I decided Mr. Wyck he would remain—pushed back a lock of hair that fell over his eyes. "You must admit, your actions have been suspicious."

Was he serious? The way he scrutinized me told me he was. "How in the world am I suspicious?"

"You have no people here. You keep to yourself. You wander off alone and mutter to yourself."

Was that how I was perceived? A misfit with peculiar habits? "I don't mutter to myself."

"That's what people say, but I suppose it's still better than the truth. Which, I gather from tonight, is that you converse with a dragonfly who may or may not be your pet."

His mouth twitched. He was finding humor in this after all.

"I didn't realize people paid any attention to what I do." How many of my secrets were known? "But that still hardly explains why anyone would think I intended to harm the Queen."

"Why would anyone intend such a thing? You could have your reasons. Do you? Have reasons, I mean?"

"No, of course I don't. Mrs. Crossey wanted my help

to protect her. That's all I was trying to do. It's what I'm still trying to do."

The recrimination faded from his eyes. "I believe you."

Relief. It was the only feeling that registered.

"Are you all right?" He moved closer and put his hand on my shoulder. My instinct was to shrug it off, but then I remembered. He was a void. A blessed reprieve from the onslaught of images and emotions. Instead of brushing off his hand, I stripped off my gloves, let them fall to the ground, and grabbed his hand with both of my own.

My skin tingled with the chill of the night air, except where we touched. His inner heat seeped into me through his fingers, the soft pad of his palm. I couldn't remember the last time I had touched someone without some modicum of fear.

When I looked up, his eyes were wide with questions.

Of course he didn't understand. How could he?

"When I touch someone," I said, "I can see things from their past, or sometimes things that they're thinking or feeling. It can be overwhelming. But I don't feel anything with you. Why?"

"I-I don't know." He tried to step back, but I tightened my grip.

"I thought it must be a sign of your guilt. That you were causing it somehow. I thought it was a sign of magic."

He nodded, as though it made sense. As though any of this made sense.

"What do you think it means now?" he asked.

I looked up and nearly lost myself in those haunting eyes. "I wish I knew."

We stood there for so long, he and I. An eternity. Then he brushed my cheek with his fingertips. I was sure he was bending closer, dipping his head perhaps...

But the buzz of my dragonfly interrupted whatever he was about to do.

He pulled back and watched her dart in a crazy pattern

in front of us.

He lifted his hand to swat her away, but I pulled it back.

"She's trying to get my attention." Still I hoped she noted my silent reproach.

She came to a soft landing on my shoulder, and immediately I could see this wasn't one of her usual antics. She was frantic. "Calm down," I said. "I'm listening."

Mr. Wyck tensed beside me, but I couldn't think about that. Something was wrong.

"I can't go to Fayte Hall now," I muttered. "How would I get into Mr. MacDougall's office? I'll go tomorrow, when Marlie can help."

My dragonfly flew up directly into my right eyebrow.

I stumbled back. "Stop! I told you, I can't get in even if I wanted to."

She buzzed in a zigzag between Mr. Wyck and me.

I looked at him. What she was telling me was impossible, but I asked him anyway. "Do you know a way into Mr. MacDougall's office?"

"Now?"

I nodded.

"Why?"

I stared up at the stars. None of this was making sense. "I don't know. She's saying I need to get to Fayte Hall. To the divining pool."

I winced. Had I told him too much?

"I can't get you into Mr. MacDougall's office."

I turned to my dragonfly with an I-told-you-so grimace.

"But," he added, "I can get you to the Hall."

"You can?"

He nodded. "At least I think I can. There's a way through the woods beyond the wall. My father took me through it once, years ago. I think I can still find it."

I didn't know what to say but my dragonfly did. She instantly buzzed around his head in happy circles.

When she elongated the lap, I could see she was trying

to communicate again. "She wants us to hurry. But how will we get past the guards? Surely they're still there."

He took my hand. "I know another way."

CHAPTER TWENTY-SIX

WE TRAVELED, MR. Wyck and I, along the terrace paths to the south side of the castle wall. My dragonfly kept pace beside me.

Mr. Wyck eyed her at intervals. "Is she following us?"

"I think so. She hasn't told me."

"Of course, she hasn't," I heard him mutter under his breath.

I dismissed the sarcasm. His approval didn't matter.

We hurried through the shadows and endeavored to stay out of sight of the castle guards who walked the perimeter.

We made good time. When we neared the King George gate, Mr. Wyck pulled me into a shadow before the guards saw us.

"I'll go first and distract them," he whispered.

Then I watched him affect a leisurely stride, his thumbs hooked in his front pockets. "Bit late for an evening stroll, mate," one uniformed guard called out.

Mr. Wyck made a sucking sound through his teeth and tipped back his cap. "Is it? I wasn't keeping track of the time, if you know what I mean."

"You're from the mews, aren't you?" the guard asked. "You should probably be getting back that way."

"My thoughts exactly. I was just on my way down. Say—" He rubbed at a patch of stubble on his chin and worked his way to a spot in front of the guard, giving me a chance to slip through the shadowed side of the gate's opening without being seen. "They don't know anything more about that girl who was done in beyond the wall, do they? I have a friend inside"—he nudged his chin toward the castle—"she's worried. I'd like to put her mind at ease, if I can."

Something in my gut pinched at his words. Was that true? Did he have a female friend inside? The question hounded me as I tried to focus on keeping out of sight.

The guard clucked his tongue. "I don't know anything about that. The Constable's men are keeping an eye on the spot, but they're a tight-lipped bunch. You should tell your friend to stay inside, though. To be on the safe side."

"I'll do that," Mr. Wyck said. "Thanks for your trouble."

"No trouble, mate. Have a good night."

Mr. Wyck tipped his cap again and shuffled down the lane. I held to the shadows until we were a good distance away and the darkness obscured us.

We walked in silence, each in our own thoughts. I wanted to ask him about the friend. But what did it matter? It shouldn't bother me. It shouldn't make any difference at all.

"What's wrong with you?" he asked.

I shot him a hard glance. "I was just thinking of that girl on the Slopes. What do you think happened to her?"

He looked at me then my dragonfly, who still buzzed above my head. "Difficult to say. Strange things happen in these woods. Things I can't explain. But it might have been just like they said, a terrible accident."

The way he stared into the distance, I knew he didn't believe that. Just as I didn't.

"Do you—"

But I didn't have a chance to finish my question. He held out his arm to stop me. "This is it," he said. "The path is here, somewhere."

I saw nothing but the Long Walk, the arrow-straight path that led from the castle gate to the Copper Horse statue on Snow Hill two and a half miles away, with rows of elms and oaks bordering each side. "I can't see anything but the trees."

"Precisely," he said with a confident air. "Come on."

He trampled through the low grass and I followed behind, my ankles and hem growing damp along the way. Despite myself, I watched for stray roots and tensed at every snap of a twig, every crunch of a brittle leaf under foot. I scanned the shadows for anything that moved.

To my dragonfly, who was flying to my left, I whispered, "You'll warn me if there's trouble, won't you?"

"What did you say?" he called back.

"Nothing."

"Talking to that dragonfly again? What did it have to say?"

"She's a *she*, not an *it*."

"Fine. It's not much farther. I'm looking for a tree."

Just one? There were hundreds.

We passed a dozen, then he slowed as we neared an oak that stood apart from the rest. Larger and older, its gnarled branches and deep crevices reminded me of the tree I'd seen on the Slopes.

"This is the one, isn't it?"

He didn't answer at first. He was pulling a leather cord from beneath his collar. If I'd had any doubt he was Fayte, it was dispelled by the Faytling dangling at the end of that black leather cord. "It was dipped in the Balmoral divining pool, so it may not work exactly right here."

"There's more than one divining pool?"

"Of course. There's one wherever there are Fayte. You should know that."

One more thing I didn't know. But that was a topic for another time. I pulled out the Faytling from beneath my own collar. "Would it be better to use this one?"

His eyes widened. "How did you get that?"

"It's Mrs. Crossey's," I said. "She lent it to me."

His expression changed. "Did you have it when she was attacked?"

I nodded, making that connection for the first time. "Do you think that made a difference?"

"We have them for protection, among other things." His lips twitched. I could sense there was more he wanted to say, yet he didn't.

I held the amulet in my palm. If she had had it instead of me when she was attacked, she might not be fighting for her life.

"But to answer your question, yes, it would be preferable to use yours. May I?"

He extended his hand. I pulled the Faytling over my head and handed it to him.

He took it and stepped up to a deep, jagged crevice in the tree's gnarled trunk.

"Stand behind me," he said.

When I did, he touched the Faytling to the tree and muttered words I didn't understand.

A purple glow grew within the Faytling's stone and the crevice slipped apart, creating an opening nearly as wide as a door.

I gaped. My mind groped for a reasonable explanation of what I'd seen, but there was none. Had the world always contained such magic?

Mr. Wyck looked at me. "Are you ready?"

Cautiously, I peered into the hollowed-out tree then back at my dragonfly. She was still hovering behind, urging me forward. I might not trust him, but I trusted her. I faced him. "I am."

Without another word, he took my hand and led me into that dark place.

Stepping inside, I blinked hard, trying to make out something of the space around me, but I could discern nothing. Only the musty odor of moist earth, a biting cold on my cheeks, and the warmth of Mr. Wyck's hand clutching my own. He pulled me onward.

But how could that be? If it were a tunnel, it would have had to slope down.

I dropped his hand and backed out, back into the starlit night where I could make out the clear silhouette of the tree.

Mr. Wyck emerged as well and watched me lean around the trunk, searching for the missing space. "Wondering about the dimensions?" he asked.

"It's all wrong." I searched the right side again. "We stepped in, both of us, yet there should hardly be room for even one. Where is the rest of it?"

"That's magic for you. You see what you want to see. When it comes to the Other Realm, the world plays by different rules. It's best not to think too much about it."

"But how—"

I stumbled back to avoid my dragonfly, who was buzzing at my nose, or as close to it as was possible without an actual collision.

"I think she wants you to move along."

I was going to thank Mr. Wyck for that profound insight but caught the sparkle in his eye.

Fine. I pushed past him, annoyed. Perhaps he found this all very amusing, but I knew she wasn't trying to be funny. She was frantic.

"Where do you think you're going?"

I hardly knew, but that wasn't going to stop me. I trusted my dragonfly, and she was telling me to go.

Again, I stepped into the tree's black crevice, and the moonlight vanished. Again, I was in complete and utter darkness.

I gripped my Faytling with one hand and brushed the tunnel's rough bark walls with the other. "I wish there was some light in here," I muttered to no one in particular.

As soon as the words were out, a weak light pulsed through my fingers from the Faytling. I opened my hand to see the stone was glowing. Only faintly, but enough to see a narrow path of packed earth and tangled tree roots in front of me.

"How did you do that?" The question sounded more like an accusation.

"I have no idea." I was still staring at the thing in my hand.

"How many spells did Mrs. Crossey teach you?"

"I don't know any. I just…" I just wanted light, but that wasn't a spell. Was it?

Behind me, he muttered something I couldn't hear but I surmised the meaning. He didn't believe me.

I ignored him and hurried on. Even with light, it was difficult ground to cover. The tunnel was tall but narrow, not even wide enough for us to walk side by side down what was now a noticeable downward slope.

As we moved, the temperature dropped. Tree roots wove in and out of what were now rough dirt walls. I watched for unnatural movement.

After a hundred feet or so, the passage hooked to the left and we met a tall and wide door made of roughly hewn wood and crude black hinges. I'd seen that door before— or one like it—and at last I knew where we were.

"Do we just go through?" I whispered.

"I believe so, unless I'm gravely mistaken."

I shuddered at the mention of a grave. How far underground were we anyway? I let the thought go and grabbed the metal handle. I pressed the lever that dislodged a latch and the door slid open. I peeked around the edge to see what awaited us on the other side.

More darkness.

I held out the Faytling, and the white light illuminated the space, revealing walls of uneven stones.

Familiar stones.

"What's there?" Mr. Wyck whispered.

"The tunnel from Mr. MacDougall's office."

Mr. Wyck passed me and searched in both directions. "You're right, and I believe we head that way." He pointed to the left.

The tunnel bent in a long, smooth curve, just as I'd remembered, and soon we were at the massive polished door.

When I reached for the scrolled handle, Mr. Wyck struck out his arm and held it closed. "Do you hear that?" He leaned against the wood. "I hear something. Someone's inside."

I heard it, too. Some kind of chant or incantation. I couldn't make out the words, but it was a man's voice. "Mr. MacDougall?"

Mr. Wyck straightened, his shoulders squared to the door. "Maybe."

I pulled the handle by inches and peeked inside. My gaze shot to the inner sanctum beyond the towers of books, where a cloaked figure knelt between us and the divining pool. His arms outstretched in a worshipful pose.

But it wasn't the man who sent a shot of fear through me as much as the pool itself. The whole thing, from the bottom of its footed pedestal to the wide alabaster rim glowed red. Not lavender or violet as it had during Mrs. Crossey's Converging, but a deep pulsating red with a crimson cloud rising above it.

The chanting stopped.

Before the figure could turn our way, I hid behind the nearest tower. Mr. Wyck did the same.

He moved his finger to his lips, but I didn't need the warning. His wide eyes told me he was as panicked as I.

After a moment, the muttering resumed. I breathed more easily, but I knew without a doubt this was what my dragonfly had wanted me to see.

I leaned around the tower's corner and tried to listen to what was being said. Tried to determine what was happening. Tried to identify who it was beneath that robe.

It didn't help that I couldn't understand a word being said, if they were even words at all. I stared at Mr. Wyck until I caught his eye.

"Who is it?" I mouthed.

He hiked his shoulders, a silent *I don't know*.

It was all I could do not to step out and put a stop to whatever this was for I knew with every ounce of sense within me that it couldn't be good. Or was it just me rushing to judgment again? Could I risk another reckless act? I'd already caused so much trouble.

I leaned against the tower, closed my eyes, and tried to think: what would Mrs. Crossey have me do?

Don't be rash.

I opened my eyes and stared at the row of robes hanging on the wall, with one lonely black coat hanging among them. A gentleman's coat, not a servant's.

I caught Mr. Wyck's eye again and pointed to it.

His lips twisted. He didn't understand.

But he didn't need to. I knew how to get the answers we needed.

I peeked around the tower again. The robed figure was still facing the pool, away from us. The figure stood transfixed, and I could see it was certainly a man, though too short and too stout to be Mr. MacDougall.

At that instant, wispy tendrils emerged from the cloud and stretched toward the man's outstretched hands. I watched as the streaks wrapped around his fingers, working their way over his wrists and his arms.

My heart lurched. I remembered those streaks. I remembered them winding around my own limbs, holding me captive in the woods.

I thought of the shadow creature again. That furious red gaze that had snaked into my soul.

But I had to move.

I shook off that painful reminder, pulled off my gloves, and tucked them into a skirt pocket, then dashed across the aisle to the black coat hanging among the robes.

Mr. Wyck lunged at me, trying to stop me, but I was faster. I yanked the coat from its hook and sank back into the safety behind the tower.

Instantly my panic slipped away, replaced by a powerful surge of something that started in my fingertips. Even before I could pull the Faytling free from my neck, images emerged. Not just a face, but a life. A whole world of thoughts and feelings and intentions.

I swooned with the amount of information that flowed into me.

I opened my eyes and Mr. Wyck stood over me. His mouth moved, but I couldn't hear a word. Then with a *whoosh!* the sound returned.

He tugged my arm. "We have to go. Now!"

"Who's there?" the man called out from the divining pool. "Show yourself."

I scrambled to my feet, but it was too late. Fast and heavy footsteps echoed through the hall.

I dropped the man's coat, grabbed an indigo robe, and threw it around myself. I was pulling the hood low when Mr. Bailey rounded the corner of the tower.

"What is the meaning of this?" he demanded. "No one should—"

Whatever he meant to say next died on his lips as he fell to his knees and slumped to the floor.

Standing behind him, tall and proud, was Mr. Wyck holding one end of a scroll like a cricket bat.

He stared at me. I stared back. Then he threw the scroll to the ground with a crash, and we ran into the tunnel.

CHAPTER TWENTY-SEVEN

WITH ONLY MY Faytling's light, Mr. Wyck and I didn't stop running through the tunnel until we reached the row of doorways. My heart pummeled my chest as he approached the first one. I knew he was thinking the same thing I was. "Which one do we take?" I asked anyway.

He shook his head, his expression lost. "They all look the same. I don't know. I don't remember."

"Do we take one or keep going till we reach Mr. MacDougall's office?"

He stared at the door.

A rattle and slam rang through the tunnel.

"He's coming," I said.

"If he sees us, he'll recognize us."

I couldn't let that happen. I'd seen what he planned to do. I *knew* his desperation.

Mr. Wyck pressed on. "I know it wasn't the first door, or the second. We passed four, maybe five on our way to Fayte Hall."

"At least five," I added, the memory trickling back.

He paced in front of me, stopping at the sixth door and eyed it.

I passed him, grabbed the handle, and pushed it open. To my surprise, it gave easily. I stepped through. It wasn't the same tunnel we had come in. These walls were made of brick not earth.

Mr. Wyck grabbed my elbow before I could enter. "It's not the right one!"

"I know."

The clamoring grew nearer. Mr. Bailey was almost upon us.

"There's no time," I added. "We have to go."

I pressed on and the door latched behind me. I turned to see that Mr. Wyck had followed. On the other side, furious footsteps grew nearer. I held my breath until they passed into the distance again.

Relief washed through me. I would have continued alone, but I was happy I wouldn't have to. I held my Faytling aloft to spread the light. "Does any of this look familiar to you?"

He considered the stone wall, the flagstone floor for a moment then shook his head. "Not at all."

I should have been disappointed. The tunnel could be leading us anywhere. But we were safe from Mr. Bailey, at least for now.

We trudged on through the tunnel. Curving at times, but mostly straight on, and the brick walls never changed. The flagstone floor didn't, either. Then the floor sloped upward.

Only slightly at first, but then more steeply. I sought crevices in the stone to keep my footing.

"We must be getting close to something."

I hoped Mr. Wyck was right.

Then we came to the end. A dead end.

No door, just a flat earthen wall.

I stared at it, cursing it silently for now we'd have to backtrack and try a different route.

Mr. Wyck, however, was holding his Faytling to the wall.

"What are you doing?"

"Trying to get us out of here." He touched his talisman to the dirt in front of us and mumbled something softly under his breath.

The wall trembled and cracked. It wasn't pulling apart as the tree trunk had, but dirt crumbled away in a gentle avalanche. He pressed the wall and what was left there tumbled to the ground, leaving a door-sized hole.

I gaped at the moonlight beyond. "How did you do that?"

He put his Faytling back around his neck. "You're not the only one who can work a Faytling."

"I can see that." I stuck my head through the hole. There were shrubs and leaves and something that looked like part of the castle wall. "Any idea where we are?"

He crossed the threshold beside me. "Yes, actually. I know exactly where we are. Come look."

I followed him through a shaggy curtain of ivy that drooped over the hole and emerged into the moonlight. I tucked my Faytling beneath my collar.

Above us the moon hung just above the top of the Round Tower.

I breathed in the rosemary, sage, and thyme. "Moat Garden."

We had emerged from what looked like a mound of ivy against the tower's base. Even standing just a few feet away, the ivy now completely disguised the opening. When I reached back through, my hand hit solid earth. The opening was gone.

"Strange, huh?"

He watched me, limned in silvery moonlight. Moisture glistened above his brow and he seemed on the verge of leaning in, perhaps to…

I turned, afraid of where my thoughts were taking me.

"Do you think we're safe?" I was sure we were, but I was desperate to change the subject.

"Who knows?" His words weren't sarcastic, but soft.

Worried, even. "But you should get back inside."

He was right. Even now my back prickled like someone was watching us. I glanced around, but I could see only shadows.

Was my dragonfly buzzing in the distance?

"Jane, is that you?"

I turned to see a dark figure turn the corner.

"It's me," I said, not sure if I should be relieved or worried that Marlie was out at this hour and in this strange place.

"Thank goodness." She was winded. Frantic.

"What are you doing out here? Why aren't you in bed?"

She grabbed her side, trying to catch her breath. "I could ask you the same thing. What are you—" She stopped and looked at Mr. Wyck as though seeing him for the first time. "Oh, am I interrupting?"

"No," I said, perhaps too quickly. "He was helping me get to Fayte Hall."

"He helped you what?" Concern pinched her forehead.

He stepped forward. "I'm Fayte, Balmoral Fayte, actually."

"Oh?" I could see she wasn't sure if she should believe him, and the way she stepped backward didn't bode well.

"It's true, and he's not who you should be worried about. We saw Mr. Bailey at the divining pool. He was Converging, but not with the Lady. The pool, the crystals, they were all red."

Her features froze. "You're sure?"

I nodded.

"They were most certainly red," Mr. Wyck added. "You may not be aware of the significance—"

She sneered. "I fully understand the significance. Thank you."

I stepped between them and faced Marlie. "That's not all. I know what he's doing, or what he means to do. I touched his coat, and it was all there. Perfectly clear in the vision."

Her eyes glinted with fear. "Is it bad?"

I nodded. "And he saw us. Not our faces because of the robes." I looked down and realized I still had mine on. Somewhere along the way Mr. Wyck had shed his. I shimmied out of mine, wadded it into a ball, and tucked it under my arm. "He came after us, but we took one of the doors in the tunnel. It led us here."

"Here?" She looked around. "Did he follow you?"

"Mr. Wyck whacked him over the head with a scroll, so we got a good lead on him. But we heard him enter the tunnel. I'm sure he's trying to find us even if he isn't sure who we are or where to look."

Marlie grabbed her head with her hands. "Then why are you standing here? Get to our room!"

"You two go ahead. I'm going to keep an eye out."

"Are you sure?" I asked. "He's a desperate man."

Marlie leaned toward me. "It wouldn't hurt to have someone watching your back."

She was right, but I didn't move. I didn't want to leave him behind.

Marlie stepped toward the castle and motioned for me to follow. "We need to go *now*."

"She's right." He looked at me as though he could see everything—my face, my thoughts, my heart.

"I know." I wanted to say more, but I didn't know what and there wasn't time. I straightened and pretended to be brave. "Be safe, Mr. Wyck." Then I chased after Marlie.

~ ~ ~

Marlie checked the darkened hallway before closing the door to our room. "Are you going to tell me what happened back there?"

I struck a match and touched it to the nub that was left of our room's candle. "What do you mean?" I already knew, of course. I just didn't want to have this conversation.

The walk back from the garden, where we'd left Mr. Wyck, had been a silent one. We'd moved quickly through the grounds and the castle, avoiding the guards and other nighttime staff, and all that time I knew she had questions burning within her.

"We can start with your companion," she said, "but I suppose that's only the beginning of your adventures tonight." She was teasing me, but there was something else to her tone as well. Irritation.

I knew what she wanted to know.

"I know what he's going to do," I said, still hardly believing what I'd seen in that vision. Still not quite trusting myself. "I know how Mr. Bailey plans to attack the Queen."

The candle sputtered, making our shadows twist and bend along the wall.

"But the masquerade is over. Didn't he miss his chance?"

"The ball was never his plan. He's going to attack tomorrow—" I stopped, quickly calculating the hour. "Tonight, actually. When the calliope plays."

"The thing they brought in crates?"

"It's an instrument that runs on steam. That's why it'll work."

Marlie still looked dubious. "Unless he plans to hurl those crates at her, I hardly see—"

"He's going to fill it with water from the divining pool and it'll make steam. That's how it'll work. He's going to use the instrument to unleash that monster from the Other Realm." The image I'd seen was too terrible to bear. I dropped onto my bed and covered my face with my palms.

She sat beside me, to comfort me. "Listen"—she was trying to be cheerful—"we can still stop it. Before any harm comes."

"How?" I prayed she had an answer. I had already played through every scenario I could imagine and not one ended well. "The instrument is already in the castle. The performance is arranged. And who would believe a maid with a mad story like mine?"

She thought for a moment and kicked her feet like a child. "It'll be all right," she said at last. "We have the Fayte Guardians on our side. They'll help. Mr. MacDougall will know what to do."

I bit my lip.

She rose and paced the narrow space between our beds. "First thing in the morning, we'll find him, and you can tell him what you saw."

"We can't," I blurted. "We can't tell him any of it."

"Don't be silly. We must."

"We can't"—I gulped hard—"because he was in the vision, too. Mr. Bailey and Mr. MacDougall are doing this together. And if Mr. MacDougall's involved, others might be as well. We can't trust anyone."

I knew there were only two people I could trust, and one of them was staring back at me like I'd lost my mind. The other lay unconscious in a bed somewhere in the castle. "I need to see Mrs. Crossey. Before we do anything, I need to find her."

"I don't see how much help she'll be if she isn't awake."

"Maybe. But I have to try."

CHAPTER TWENTY-EIGHT

AT DAWN, I forced myself to dress, collect firewood from the cellar, and get myself to the Queen's sitting room without screaming at the top of my lungs that traitors were inside the castle.

At least when I entered, Abigail was nowhere to be seen. Only Lady Bassey and Lady Wallingham were in attendance, sitting together near the window with knitting already in their laps. They glanced my direction when I opened the door and quickly glanced away again.

For a moment, I considered telling them what I knew. I could ask them, I reasoned, to beg the Queen to skip the evening performance, to tell her that her safety was at stake.

But they'd never believe me.

I had to get to Mrs. Crossey, and the faster the better. I dropped a log onto the grate, dumped the rest into the brass basket, and slipped out to the corridor again.

To my relief, it remained empty and silent. This was my chance.

Mrs. Crossey had to be in one of these rooms, but which? I went to the closest door and leaned my ear to it.

Nothing. I tried the knob. It turned easily, and I pushed in to find the shades pulled wide and morning sunshine streaming in. The bed stood empty, untouched.

I moved to the next door and found the same.

At the fourth, I peered in to find an occupied bed. The drawn shades made it impossible to see who it was, but I took the chance. Quietly, I closed the door behind myself and tiptoed to the edge of the bed.

What a relief to discover those familiar fleshy cheeks resting against the pillows, that ruddy nose, and coils of silvery hair escaping from beneath her sleeping cap. Mrs. Crossey looked so peaceful, yet still so weak. I sank beside her, comforted by the nearness of her and realizing in a rush of emotion how much I'd come to depend on her and how close I'd come to losing her.

I forced back tears as I found her hand beneath the linens and removed my gloves. Then, lifting her Faytling from my neck, I cradled one of her hands with both of my own and the talisman nestled between us.

"Show me something that will help the Queen," I said to her or the Faytling, or both. "Something, anything to stop the attack."

Then I was falling. Spinning. Everything around me blurred until an image took shape. A hulking shadow that slowly resolved into a man. Tall and strong, with wide, hulking shoulders. Black hair, straight as a blade and long. The ends nearly reached his narrow waist, which was a stone-like gray, like his bare back and arms. From a wide leather belt hung a scabbard, his sinewy fingers wrapped around the hilt. Coal black trousers tucked into boots that skimmed his knees.

He was waiting, I knew, but for what? I sensed his impatience like heat from a flame.

He pivoted, slowly, revealing a smooth and muscular chest, the hard line of his jaw. Sharp chin. Sloped nose. Then, the fiery explosion of raging red eyes. Murderous eyes.

214

"Come closer, Jane." The voice was a low rumble that shook me to my core. "Come to me."

The spell broke.

I don't know how.

Had he done it?

Had I?

I dropped Mrs. Crossey's hand and pulled my fists to my chest, the Faytling still in my grasp.

Tears flowed down both cheeks faster than I could wipe them away, so I gave up, hung my head, and let them come.

"What's all this now?"

The voice was soft and cracked from disuse.

Mrs. Crossey looked at me, her eyelids heavy, her lips twitching almost to a smile.

"You're awake. Thank goodness you're awake." The words erupted in gasps. I wanted to grab her around the shoulders and bury myself against her. I wanted her to protect me from that vision, that man or creature or whatever he was.

"Who could sleep with so much racket?" This time she did smile, just a bit but enough that I knew she was teasing.

"Everything's gone wrong, Mrs. Crossey. The Queen is in danger, and I was wrong—about Mr. Wyck, about the ball, about all of it. It's all so much worse than I imagined."

The woman's eyes narrowed on me. "Slow down, dear. What's the trouble now?"

Her calm stilled the tempest within me. I tried again. "The man, the one who attacked you, did you see him? Was it Mr. Bailey?"

She closed her eyes. "I didn't see him." When her lids fluttered open again, she stared past me. "By the time I knew someone was behind me, it was too late. I awoke in this bed last night with Dr. Holland hovering over me. He wouldn't tell me what happened. Only that I'd fallen. Of course, I knew it was more than that, but he would say nothing else."

"Were you hit? Were you pushed?" I was imagining all manner of violence.

"Pushed, I believe. There's quite a bump where my head may have struck the edge of a step. Could have been worse, Dr. Holland said. I'm inclined to believe him, though the headaches are quite something. He told me to stay in bed for a couple of days to be sure nothing else develops."

"Develops?"

"A fever, I suppose? Perhaps a rash? Honestly, I have no earthly idea what he meant. I can tell you I've had my fill of this room, though. I'd like to get back to my own, but he says that's out of the question." She looked from the bedpost to the vanity with the cabriolet legs and the matching wardrobe with inlaid mother-of-pearl roses adorning the doors. Furnishings befitting royalty, but I could see she wasn't impressed by any of it. She shifted against the mattress. "One prefers one's own things. I'm not even allowed my magazines," she added almost as an afterthought.

"I can bring you anything you need."

"I know." She tapped the top of the bedlinen. "But what I need isn't what's important now. Tell me what *you* need."

A simple question. Such a difficult answer.

I looked up at the coffered ceiling so she wouldn't see the tears welling in my eyes. Emotion locked my throat. I shook my head. What had happened to me? How had I been reduced to a blubbering fool?

"Can you tell me what you saw when you held my hand?" Her voice was hesitant, as if she feared the answer.

I wanted to tell her about the shadowy man, but something told me I shouldn't. I tightened my grip on the Faytling and did it anyway. "I saw someone, I think it was a man, but he had horrible red eyes." The words came out in a gust, and once they were out, I could breathe. I felt free, but from what?

Her expression darkened. She stared at me, her expression blank. No, not blank, but intentionally void of the emotion I sensed churning within her. "Who was he?" she asked.

"I don't know. But I've seen him before. His eyes at least. At the tree on the Slopes. And I've seen them in dreams."

Her fingers fluttered to her lips.

I sensed her fear, but I couldn't stop. I had to tell her everything. "I think Mr. Bailey was Converging with him in Fayte Hall."

She swallowed hard and maneuvered herself up until she was sitting upright, facing me. "Do you think? Or do you know?"

The blackness returned, the emptiness that wanted to swallow my words. And then I realized. I hadn't seen him in Mrs. Crossey's mind. He was inside my own. I could feel him there still.

But he couldn't stop me. I wouldn't let him.

My determination had the opposite effect on Mrs. Crossey, however. She shrank where she sat. Her shoulders sagged, and she sighed the saddest of sighs.

"Do you know who he is?" I whispered.

She didn't look up, but she nodded. "He's the one who came before. From the Lady's world. But he's not like the Lady. He's… I had hoped never to hear of him again. I'd hoped he couldn't hurt us. But it's my fault he's here. I allowed him into this world once long ago. And now he's back."

She opened the door? What Marlie had told me came back: the little girl scrying on her own. The monster she released. "You were the child…"

She looked past me, into the distance, over miles of time and heartache. I could imagine she was seeing the moment she had cracked open the world and let a monster in. A malevolent figure with flaming eyes. She had been the child who had changed everything.

"It was me. I started all of this. I betrayed the Lady of the Fayte. That must be why she turned her back on us."

"But you were a child. You couldn't know."

"I was foolish. My scrying ability was still new, and I was so confident. So sure of its power. The Lady came to me easily in those first days. She filled me with her knowledge and her purpose. My parents warned me to be careful, especially my mother. She was the Windsor Scryer before me, but my ability quickly surpassed hers. It frightened her. She told me not to use my power, to wait until an Elder could properly train me. I didn't listen. I thought she was jealous of my power."

She winced as if that memory pained her most. "She was trying to protect me," she said at last, "but I was too ignorant to know it. So, I scried in secret. In the woods. That's where he tricked me. If only my mother hadn't followed me that day—" She broke off, squeezed her eyes closed, and pressed a knuckle to her lips.

I waited as patiently as I could until she continued.

"If she'd let him take me, perhaps that would have saved her. But she broke his binding—powerful though it was—before he claimed me. She was strong enough to do that, but it took everything she had to force him back to his world. He must have found another way. I should have known it that day on the Slopes. I felt him, I just didn't want to admit it."

My memory shot back to that moment with her on the path. That's what had happened. Those red eyes, those smoky tendrils. I had felt him invading me. Wrenching me apart from the inside, claiming me.

"Is that what he was trying to do to me? Possess me as the Lady possesses you? Is that what he wants to do to the Queen?"

"Whatever he wants, he will take it and keep taking it. He could take this entire empire, if he chose."

I thought of the dead girl on the Slopes. "The village girl?"

"I believe so."

I sat still, too stunned to speak. Too stunned to move.

She straightened again, as if filled with new purpose. "But why did you go to Fayte Hall? Did you know he would be there?"

I looked away. I had never told her of my dragonfly, and I wasn't sure I should now, but there had already been too many secrets. "A dragonfly told me to go."

The look that came over Mrs. Crossey was something more than surprise. She tilted her head to the side as though considering my words carefully. "A dragonfly *told* you to go?"

I nodded. "I know it sounds silly, but——"

She raised her palm to stop me. "A dragonfly speaks to you?"

"In a way. She comes to me when I'm outdoors."

Mrs. Crossey's eyes widened. "This wasn't the first time?"

"She visits often. She always has."

"Always?"

I nodded, suddenly sheepish.

"Since Chadwick Hollow?" she asked.

I nodded again.

"When was the first time?"

"I can't remember exactly. I've never told anyone about her before." I thought of Lucas. He had guessed it, but that wasn't the same. Was it? "She was my secret. One of them…"

"I see," she said in the way Headmistress Trindle used to when I would explain that I preferred to read in the library instead of playing with the other girls. Or when I would rise before dawn to walk among the trees in the early morning light.

"What does she say to you?" she asked.

"She doesn't speak exactly, but I understand her." At

least I thought I did.

"Has she told you to do other things?"

I pinched the bed covers beneath my fingers. "No. That's what was odd about it. She's never told me to do anything before. She's only... She's just... She just visits me, I guess."

She mulled my words then said, "I cannot pretend to understand this dragonfly of yours, but it seems she helped you discover Edward Bailey's scheme. For the moment, I think we must focus on that. When did you say the Queen would be attending the calliope's performance?"

"This evening. After dinner, I believe."

She touched her lips. Then nodded. "That isn't much time, but it should be enough. The first thing you must do is speak to Mr. MacDougall."

I shook my head.

Mrs. Crossey sighed. "I know you and Mr. MacDougall have not always—"

"It's not that. He was in my vision. He's involved. I saw him with Mr. Bailey. I'm sure they were conspiring."

"That can't be. The man is trying at times, but he is the Vice Councilor. He wouldn't be involved in such a thing."

"I can only say what I saw, and I most certainly saw him with Mr. Bailey."

"I see," she said. "I have worked with Mr. MacDougall a good many years, however, and I have never had reason to doubt his loyalty to the Fayte. The problem with visions is that what one thinks one is seeing is not always the truth of what one is seeing. I shall speak to Mr. MacDougall myself and sort it out. Please tell him I must speak with him."

"When he asks why, what shall I tell him?" Because surely I couldn't tell him the truth.

"Tell him my injuries have caused me to reconsider my position here in the castle and that I would like to discuss my resignation."

The magnitude of that statement hit me like a boulder.

"But you can't leave."

She patted the top of my glove. "It's the only subject I am sure he will find too tempting to ignore. Now go. Before it's too late."

She was right. To put a stop to the performance, I couldn't delay. I rose just as someone rapped on the door and slowly opened it.

A bespectacled gentleman with a small hook nose peered in. "I've come for your morning check, Mrs. Crossey. Is now a good time?"

"Yes, Dr. Holland," she said. "Of course." She angled her head toward me. "Go now, lass."

I knew I had to leave, but I didn't want to leave her side. As long as I was beside her, all would be well.

The physician came up behind me and cleared his throat. I stepped to the side, reluctantly giving him my place beside her.

Her gaze hung on me. "Don't fret. This will all be right as rain before you know it."

I knew she was referring to herself, but also to our problem with Mr. MacDougall and Mr. Bailey. And I wished I believed her.

CHAPTER TWENTY-NINE

BEFORE I LEFT her, Mrs. Crossey made me promise to do as she instructed. I did—reluctantly. It didn't matter that I knew Mr. MacDougall to be complicit in Mr. Bailey's scheme. It didn't matter that I thought it was a mistake. I trusted her judgment, and right now that was more than I could say about my own.

I was pulling the door to Mrs. Crossey's room closed behind me when the Queen's sitting room door opened, and a peal of bubbly laughter followed. I turned back as though I meant to re-enter the room and kept my head down, kept myself out of the way and out of sight as much as I could.

"Come now, it's a marvelous surprise." It was Lady Wallingham emerging from the room. "I'm rather pleased to be included. You should be, too."

I fidgeted with my gloves, pretending to be preoccupied as she entered the corridor.

"Don't get me wrong, I'm pleased as well," Lady Bassey countered. "I just would have preferred a bit of warning. I had arranged to ride."

"It can be rescheduled, I'm sure."

"Of course it can. But I dressed for it, and this frock is entirely unsuitable for a performance."

Performance? What performance?

"And I sent my maid into town to collect a bonnet I ordered from the milliner. I hope she hasn't already left. I rang the bell ages ago, and there's been no answer. Oh, there's someone. Yoo-hoo. Hello? Can I get your help, please?"

Was she speaking to me? I ventured a sideways glance. She was already approaching.

I turned to face her, keeping my head low. "Yes, ma'am?"

"Find Reed and send her to my room. As quickly as you can, if you please."

"Of course. Shall I say why?" I braced. It was never a servant's place to ask such things, but my curiosity—my fear—outweighed such propriety.

Lady Bassey didn't seem to notice. "The Queen has invited me"—she glanced back at Lady Wallingham—"invited *us* to a musical performance this afternoon. I require her assistance to change into something appropriate."

My pulse pounded in my ears like so many fists. "Not this evening? Are you sure?"

Mrs. Bassey's eyebrows pinched over the otherwise smooth plane of her forehead. I lowered my head submissively.

"Yes. I'm quite sure." The curtness of her words made it clear there should be no more questions, which was just as well because the full meaning of her words was now painfully clear. Mr. Bailey had expedited his plans. There was no time to waste.

I nodded once at Lady Bassey, assuring her I understood, and made a hasty shot toward the servants' stairs.

I managed to slip through the door and out of the ladies' view before stopping to catch my breath. It was a miracle my wobbly knees could keep me upright. I leaned against the wall and tried to calm my nerves. If the performance would be this afternoon, I had to find Marlie—and fast.

I dragged in a deep breath and clutched the Faytling at my chest beneath my blouse.

No time for fear. No time for hesitation.

I pushed every thought from my mind save one. Marlie. She would be in the kitchen, so that's where I had to go as quickly as my feet could carry me and without drawing undue attention. With Mrs. Crossey still out of commission, Marlie was my only hope.

~ ~ ~

I rushed along the Long Gallery's crimson corridor, past the drawing rooms and the chapel, until I reached a servants' staircase that would take me to the kitchen. I found Marlie scraping potato peelings from her table.

"There you are," she said. "Mr. MacDougall's been searching for you."

A cook stood on the other side of her, so I leaned close. "They've changed the performance time. We have to hurry!"

Her forehead crinkled. "But you said—"

"I know, but he must know we're onto him."

Disbelief, confusion, fear, they all cascaded across her face. "What do you suggest?"

I glanced over her shoulder. Cooks hovered at their stoves and oven fires, scullery maids ferried bowls and baskets of ingredients from the cellar and the pantry. Everyone was busy with something, and no one was paying any attention to us.

I leaned in again. "Make an excuse to get away. Meet me in the Rubens Room as soon as you can."

She seemed to panic then mastered herself. "I'll be right behind you."

I didn't ask how, and I didn't stick around to find out. I hurried to the corridor that ran beneath the State Apartments until I found a narrow staircase far enough away that it could get me near the Rubens Room.

I did my best to navigate the unfamiliar corridors. After several turns, I was standing outside the anteroom that had served the gentlemen during the ball. I recalled the Rubens Room was just beyond it, but the sound of voices stopped me.

"Move it here by the window."

I tensed. The voice belonged to Mr. Bailey. I expected he would be present, but it unsettled me nonetheless. Should I try to stop him now? Burst in? Cause a commotion? But he would only deny the accusation.

I needed a better plan.

But what?

"We'll draw the curtains," he continued. "The view over Eton is pleasant this time of day."

"But the sun, sir. Won't it blind the Queen's view of the calliope?" It was Mr. Wyck.

Why was Mr. Wyck helping Mr. Bailey? My old suspicions returned.

"Hardly," Mr. Bailey snapped back. "The Queen prefers a bright afternoon. Where is MacDougall? He was supposed to oversee this."

"Yes," Mr. Wyck muttered. "Where is he, indeed?"

"Are you questioning me?" Mr. Bailey growled.

"Not in the least, sir. It's just typical, don't you think? That he should find himself scarce when there's real work to do? Men like him always leave the difficult work to others. Don't you agree?" He scoffed again.

Mr. Bailey cleared his throat. "Yes, well, he and I will be having a discussion about that when this is finished."

I smiled to myself. Mr. Wyck was clever, I'll give him that much.

"Now that I'm looking at the instrument," Mr. Bailey continued, "I'm sure we're going to need another man or two."

I pulled the door open a sliver and saw Mr. Bailey standing beside a rather large rectangular box painted a shiny red with golden curlicue trim. There were piano keys on one side and brass pipes of varying heights protruding from the top. Mr. Wyck was leaning down, his hands on his knees, eying the strange contraption.

"I'm sure I can handle it, sir," he said, his gaze still on the instrument. "This part here, is it where the water goes?"

"Do step away from that," Mr. Bailey urged.

"I won't hurt it. I was just..."

But I didn't hear the end of his sentence because a large hand took hold of my right shoulder. Long, sinewy fingers dug into my flesh.

"What do you think you are doing?"

The voice behind me, the one dripping with venom, belonged to Mr. MacDougall.

CHAPTER THIRTY

IT TOOK EVERY ounce of courage I had not to slip out of Mr. MacDougall's grip and run. "Nothing, sir," I said. It was a lie and he knew it. I faced him. His bony hand fell away. I thought of Mr. Wyck. If I called, would he come?

I shook away the thought. I didn't need his help. I squared myself to the man and stared into his pale blue eyes. "Mrs. Crossey sent me to help." Another lie, but I needed something to get me into that room.

His lips pulled into a razor-straight line. "I see." His thumb and index finger rubbed the bony tip of his chin. "Let's see what Mrs. Crossey has to say about that, shall we?" He moved up beside me, forcing me away from the door and back toward the hall.

I was more than happy to go. Mrs. Crossey would set things right. I'd seen well enough how she could put him in his place.

I followed him down one hall. "This isn't the way to her room."

"No," he said, offering no other explanation.

Had she already left her sick bed? We turned down another corridor then another. We were approaching a part of the castle completely unknown to me. The hallway narrowed, and the walls were bare. No art, no furnishings. Where was he taking me?

I was about to ask when he stopped in front of a simple paneled door. He opened it and stepped aside. His hands swept forward, indicating I should enter.

"She's in there?" But I didn't wait for his response. I hurried over the threshold, eager to see her.

The room was dim except for hazy light filtering through gossamer sheers that covered three tall, narrow windows. If I had a better sense of where we were in the castle, I would know whether they looked north or east, but it could have been either. Or neither, I suppose.

I searched the empty chairs along the wall and the settee in front of a cold, empty fireplace. I searched every shadow for her cheerful grin.

But she wasn't here. Mr. MacDougall had made a mistake.

I turned to tell him so just as the door closed behind me. A lock dropped into place.

I ran to the door and pounded with my fist. "Let me out! You can't do this." I pounded again, harder. "Mr. MacDougall!" There was no response. I leaned my ear to the surface. Not a sound. I bent down to peer through the keyhole. I could see only the wall across the corridor. "Mr. MacDougall!"

There would be no answer. I knew that, but I yelled again. When my voice cracked from the strain, I leaned back and wiped my eyes.

Stop it. Crying wouldn't help anything. It certainly wouldn't get me out of this room.

I scrutinized the wood-paneled walls. In the castle, doors were often disguised as panels. Beginning with the nearest one, I ran my gloved fingers around the trim searching for an edge, then pressed against the places that might release a spring. Nothing gave. I moved to the next panel, then the next.

When I reached a window, I peered out and recognized the Northern Slopes. Below, along the terrace, I searched for someone, anyone to hail for help. Had it been the Quadrangle, there might have been someone. Perhaps a guard making his rounds or a page on an errand. But the northern side was less traveled. I saw only the wall and the woodland beyond with those strange, menacing trees.

That image came roaring back. Red tendrils snaking around my arm, pulling at me. Draining me. Was *he* still there? A shiver shot through me.

Join me. Don't fight.

That was *his* voice. *His* words. Fear filled me all over again. A wave that could crash and drag me down. I pulled back from the window and shook off the thought. It was my own fault. I'd been stupid to follow McDougall. Stupid to believe he'd take me to Mrs. Crossey.

I berated myself as I scoured every panel, and again as I tried each one a second time before sinking—sprawling really—into a heap on the floor.

How could I help the Queen? I couldn't even help myself.

I pulled the Faytling from beneath my blouse and worked it over my head. Stupid, useless thing. Mr. MacDougall must have known I would be helpless here.

I clutched the cold metal and crystal to my chest. I don't know how long I sat there on my knees. It felt like hours, wallowing in my failure, until a distant horn perked my ear. Its strange, sonorous notes breathed deep and long.

The calliope. It had to be. Full-throated gusts of sound that weren't yet a tune. Only a check. A test before the performance. It was enough to send me scrambling from the floor and running to the walls, listening at each. From which direction was it coming? The easternmost wall provided the clearest sound.

Pounding with my fists, I screamed, "Help!" I screamed it again and again, yet there was no movement.

No answer to my call. Panic tangled with my fear and exasperation. I pounded harder. "Let me out!" My voice cracked with the strain of the words and the force of my strikes.

But then something else happened.

In my hand, the Faytling began to glow as it had beside the divining pool and again in the tunnel. But this time, the light was a vibrant purple, and it cast out purple tendrils. They reached away from me, undulating and floating toward the wall. I stared without understanding, with no thought but one single phrase that swelled within me until it spewed forth with volcanic force:

"Let me out!"

Somehow, with the Faytling in my grip, I knew what to do. I closed my eyes and took a step back from the wall. But I was doing more than that, I was stepping out of myself. I opened my eyes to see I was still standing at the wall, caught in an immobile pose, fingers still gripping the now dim Faytling. Only it was no longer me.

I was gazing on that figure from a good two paces behind and in my hand was a specter of a Faytling, still glowing at its brightest.

What madness was this? I could see my hand and my skirts with my boots peeking out beneath, only they were all edged in a soft lavender light. I was glowing like the Faytling.

Was it a hallucination?

Or was it another Faytling power?

I shook my hand, and the glowing hand shook. I shook my foot, and the glowing boot did the same. I stepped forward and my body, if it could be called that, moved though I couldn't feel the floor or anything really. Only a coolness, like the breeze on a late November morning.

I knew nothing of spirits, but I was quite certain that's what I was now. A spirit without bodily form and that meant...

I moved closer to the wall. With the fingers of my right

hand wrapped around the Faytling, I reached out with my left toward the wall. My fingers, my palm, my whole arm passed through the solid wood, which felt like something more than air but less than water and rather like a thousand tiny pinpricks along my limb.

I yanked it back and examined it. Still whole. Still intact. I tried to make sense of it. But there was none. Echoes of Mr. Wyck's words returned to me: "When it comes to the Other Realm, the world plays by different rules."

At the sound of the calliope, I pushed my arm forward again then closed my eyes and moved the rest of me through as well.

When I looked again, I was in the corridor. I was... free!

The calliope howled once more, reminding me there was no time to marvel or muse. I had to act, and I had to be fast.

Quickly, I moved toward the instrument's wail, retracing my steps with Mr. MacDougall. At the anteroom, two footmen stood sentry beside the door.

"Stop that performance!" I cried, flinging propriety and what was left of my good sense to the winds.

Neither man flinched.

With more vigor, I yelled again, "You must do something. The Queen is in danger!"

Still they didn't move, as if I wasn't even there.

I waved my hands wildly in front of their faces.

Not a twitch.

I may be free of that room, but I was apparently invisible and mute. What good was a spirit form if I was still powerless? My mind raced, until it settled on one word. One name.

Marlie.

I needed to find her. Without a second's hesitation, I flew through the corridor and down a staircase. It had to be flying for it was much faster than I could possibly run, but by the time I reached my roommate in the Great

Kitchen, I could feel my energy waning.

"Marlie, I need your help," I whispered over her shoulder as she pulled the tiny leaves off a thyme stem and dropped them into a bowl.

She didn't move.

What was left of my strength was evaporating like steam billowing from the stockpot behind me. "Please, you must help me!"

The Faytling in my hand glowed more brightly.

Curiously, the talisman beneath Marlie's blouse glowed as well. Noticing it, she dropped the thyme stem she was holding and covered the jewel. Her glance darted around, searching for something.

"I'm nearly out of herbs and need a few more sprigs," she said to the cook behind her. "I'll be right back."

Without waiting for permission and her hand still over her chest, she hurried to the pantry. I followed. When she closed the door behind her, she pulled out her Faytling and stared straight at me. "You? What are you... I mean, how—"

"You can see me?"

Relief flooded through me, overriding the lethargy that had taken hold.

"Of course I can. I'm talking to you. But how—"

"There's no time to explain. The performance is starting. You must stop it."

She froze. "The calliope?"

I nodded and gulped for air. "You have to do it."

"But the color is draining from you. You must return to yourself before it's too late."

I didn't like the sound of that.

"Where are you?" she pressed.

"I don't know the room, but I can take you there."

"Hurry then."

The Queen was my paramount concern, but I was too weak to argue with Marlie. Instead I pointed at the door, and when she opened it, I led her back to the room that imprisoned my body.

We were standing in front of the locked door when I realized I still had no way to open it. "The key," I murmured, the lethargy making it almost impossible to form words. In the distance, I could hear someone testing more chords on the calliope. "MacDougall... has... it." I should have been frustrated. Angry even. But I was too tired. Sleep was all I wanted. A nice bit of floor would do just fine.

"Don't you worry about that." Marlie slipped her hand in her pocket and pulled out a hairpin. "Step aside, if you would. I could do this *through* you, I suppose, but I'd rather not."

Somehow I moved away from the door and she went to work at the lock. She poked her pin into the crevice, jiggled it, repositioned it, jiggled it again, and there was a distinct click. She turned the knob and pushed it open. "There we are! Now let's get you together."

Her words seemed so distant now and I didn't even care about the calliope. I was drifting off. I didn't care where. I didn't care about anything.

"Sounds like we don't have much time, so c'mon. Don't give up." She snapped her fingers in my face. "Remember the Queen. Remember who you are." She paused and looked over her shoulder, then turned back and in a lowered voice said, "You are Jane Shackle. You are a Fayte Guardian."

Jane Shackle. A Fayte Guardian. Was that who I was?

Yes, that was it. And the Queen. I had to save her. From the calliope. From the shadow creature.

Somehow, I moved into the room, and I saw myself standing at the wall, paralyzed.

"Squeeze your Faytling and think 'awake,'" Marlie urged.

I mustered my last shred of strength, squeezed the Faytling, and thought the word.

All at once I was spinning and falling until just as

suddenly it stopped. I opened my eyes. The wall stood before me. I looked at my hands. They weren't glowing and they were heavy. My feet, too.

"Everything all right?"

I turned to find Marlie's forehead creased in concern. I wiggled my fingers and moved my feet. "I think so. I feel... better."

"Good, then——"

The start of a calliope tune stopped her short.

"I think that's our cue. Let's go."

She ducked out the door and I followed. Then she stopped and straightened. With her arm behind herself, she waved me back.

"You shouldn't be here." It was a male voice I didn't recognize. I heard hard steps coming our direction.

Marlie moved farther into the corridor, away from the door. "You're right about that. I got myself good and lost. I was trying to find the orangery, if you can believe it. Know how I might get there from here?"

"The orangery? That's clear on the other side. Here, if you'll just take these stairs and then..."

The rest of the conversation was lost as they moved down the corridor.

So, once again I was on my own. I couldn't wait for Marlie to come back. I had to move now.

The calliope had gone silent, which meant the performance must be starting soon. Or had whatever Mr. Bailey—whatever that shadow creature—had in store already been done?

Was I already too late?

That fear drove me forward. I didn't know where, but my feet carried me, fueled by something beyond myself, down one corridor then another and through a drawing room until I was back in familiar territory. I stormed through the anteroom, where I again found the two footmen lingering.

This time, they saw me and pulled back.

I can only imagine how I appeared. Locks of hair worked loose from my usually tidy bun, eyes frenzied and wild.

I didn't care. My only thought was to get through that door, to stop this evil in its tracks.

The door opened, and Mr. MacDougall emerged. His hateful gaze trained on me, his shoulders squared. He shut the door behind himself and drew up to his full, terrifying height. Narrow shoulders sharp and rigid. Lips slashed in a tight, twisting sneer. "Come no farther, Jane."

He looked to both footmen and issued a single, deliberate nod. In unison, they fell in beside him, flanking him, one on either side. Like guards.

"Don't do this," I begged. "We must save her. You won't let him harm the Queen, will you?"

Something shifted in the footmen's gazes. Their blank stares on me darted to Mr. MacDougall.

"She's lying," he said flatly. "She's a trickster. She will lie and steal, anything to achieve her ends. Do not allow her to pass."

My ends? What was he talking about?

"I'm not the threat here."

"Oh no? Then how is it you know exactly when to get underfoot with your mischief? You are playing with things beyond your understanding, girl. Now leave us to our business."

"What business?" I cried. "The death of our Queen? The destruction of our empire?"

The footmen looked to him, new questions in their eyes.

Mr. MacDougall waved them off. "Don't listen to her, men. She's lying. The only thing that will be destroyed is that damnable efficiency campaign. You want your colleagues back, don't you? Our household restored in its entirety? This is the way. When the mayhem ensues, Her Majesty will see for herself that it is people that keep this castle in order, not her Prince's modern ideals."

What nonsense was this? Was it a ruse, or did he truly believe what he said?

The light in his eye gave it away. He didn't know what Mr. Bailey intended. Mr. MacDougall had only been a pawn in this game, not the mastermind.

I could see there was no point in arguing. These men meant to block me. Nothing I said would change that. I balled my hands into fists and pressed them to my temples.

Lady, tell me what to say! Tell me what to do!

No answer came, not that I expected one. Not really. I could traverse the entire castle in spectral form and unlock every secret with a touch, and none of it would help me stop the violence about to unfold behind those doors. Even this stupid Faytling was powerless against that.

I stared at it in my hand. Still glowing its stupid purple light, but who cared? It was useless. Worse than useless because it, more than anything, had given me hope.

Edward Bailey had won. That shadowy creature of a man in my nightmares had won.

Fury welled within me. A swirl of rage that replaced every other thought. The Faytling's glow intensified. The purple brightened to white, pure as starlight in my hand.

I sneered at it. "Worthless." I hurled the thing across the room, striking the door inches above Mr. MacDougall's head. I smirked. It would have hit him square in the forehead if he hadn't ducked.

"Take your stup—"

Purple smoke billowed from the Faytling.

A footman stared at the place where it had landed. "You broke it," he muttered and looked to Mr. MacDougall. "Sir, they never break."

Mr. MacDougall pressed himself against the door as if to block it, but it didn't matter. Smoky tendrils seeped through the space between the door and its frame. It seeped into the room where the calliope now played at full force.

"No, no, no," Mr. MacDougall repeated frantically. He

wheeled around and pulled the door open.

In the confusion, the footmen stepped aside, and I ran into the room behind Mr. MacDougall.

"Stop!" I screamed. "Stop the music! It's a trick! It's dangerous!"

I rushed to the instrument. A monocled man in a waistcoat and tails sat at its piano keys, gaping at me. He opened his mouth, but it was Mr. Bailey's voice I heard rising at the far end of the room.

I turned and was struck dumb, seeing that I was standing not only before the Queen, but Prince Albert, the royal children, the ladies in waiting, a number of grooms, and I don't know how many other officials and members of the household, their chairs all arranged in tidy rows.

Mr. Bailey stood in the center aisle, his face red and eyes bulging with rage. "What have you done?" he wailed.

Yet I hardly noticed him barreling toward me because I was watching a cloud of the purple smoke slip out an open window at the back.

Was that it? Was that all it was going to do? I had hoped for something that would help. Anything.

But it did nothing.

My will to fight drained from me. Nearly.

I spied the Queen. She appeared in good health if not fine spirits, cowering as she was into Prince Albert's shoulder. So it wasn't too late. I approached the man sitting at the calliope. "Don't lay another finger on that instrument."

"Don't listen to her," Mr. Bailey said, gasping and breathless. "She's only a maid for goodness sake. She's mad." He grabbed my elbow and pulled me.

I yanked out of his grip. "Don't touch me."

But then other hands were on me. I turned back. MacDougall's footmen were pulling me, dragging me from the room. I fought them, and fought the onslaught of images, wild and chaotic images, that descended on me.

The Queen hid her face behind a black lace fan and

whispered to the Prince. Then others were whispering, filling the room with low murmurs.

"No!" I yelled. "You're going to be—"

Before I could finish, a violent crash shook the walls and the back window exploded inward in a cloud of shattered glass and gray mist. No, it wasn't mist. It was a mass of tiny wings. Hundreds, thousands of tiny wings. Dragonfly wings. A swarm of silvery-white angels identical to my beloved friend.

CHAPTER THIRTY-ONE

IN PERFECT UNISON, the tiny insects lifted one of the crimson draperies from the window, carried it over the crowd like a canopy, and then, in one smooth and coordinated motion, let it drop over the calliope. I watched it descend with a soft *thump* over the instrument, trapping the steam and the danger beneath it.

"No!"

The scream was Mr. Bailey's. He rushed to tug at the curtain, trying to free the pipes. Each time he exposed a corner, the dragonfly horde moved it again. He batted at them, but they ceded no ground.

Still, as I watched that battle, I could see a small wisp of red smoke emerge from a corner of the fabric and float along the floor. Like the purple cloud, it traveled among the chaos of boots and limbs and chairs to the far edge of the room.

I rubbed my eyes. Was it a trick of the light? No, it was there, a ball of crimson mist fluttering in the afternoon sunlight. All around people screamed and ran. Dragonflies hovered in a massive cloud. But I ignored it all and followed the tiny red trail to the window.

The thing, whatever it was, moved like a breeze beneath chairs, some of them overturned in the occupant's haste to get out of the way.

I hurried after it, winding my way around the legs of people and chairs when I could and anything that got in my way. I followed it to the window, where it climbed the wall to the shattered glass and the splintered sill and traveled out into the open air.

I stood at the broken window and watched. Where was it going?

After a moment, I spied the tuft of smoke again, traveling along the ground toward the castle's northern wall.

Then I knew.

I bolted for the door.

Mr. MacDougall blocked me. "You aren't going anywhere." His furious eyes glared down.

"Leave her alone!" Mr. Wyck yanked Mr. MacDougall's hand away.

The older man's fury collapsed into confusion then alarm. "Stand aside, boy."

Mr. Wyck squared himself to the man. His height was not as great as Mr. MacDougall's, but the breadth of his shoulders and fighting stance made him more formidable. "I will not." The words came from somewhere deep within him, like a growl.

I stepped back.

"Go." Mr. Wyck motioned to me then stared down Mr. MacDougall. "And you need to explain why you've been lying to me."

Mr. MacDougall glared at Mr. Wyck. "You have no idea what you're talking about." He turned to me. "Don't you dare leave this room. You will be held accountable for what you've done."

"As you and Mr. Bailey will be held to account," I snapped back before running to the door. I paused and glanced back. Mr. Wyck's face was as red as I'd ever seen it. He spewed words I couldn't hear over the chaos.

If there was any doubt where his loyalty lay, there was none now. He was on my side, and I could have kissed him for it.

Quickly, I tore through the corridors, past the baffled pages and footmen jogging toward the Rubens Room, alerted by the screams and commotion. I slipped by them all easily until I reached the door to the northern staircase.

A small flutter at my shoulder stopped me. I turned to find my dragonfly perched there, gazing at me with an inscrutable expression.

"Thank you," I said, though those words had never sounded so inadequate.

Still, I could feel her smile even if I couldn't see it.

"I don't know how you did it, but you saved the Queen. Maybe everyone in that room."

My heart was full to bursting with pride and appreciation, but she wasn't interested. She wanted me to follow the crimson trail.

"All right. I'm going." I scanned the garden. I couldn't see the smoky tendril anymore, but I could feel my dragonfly urging me toward the castle gate. "The Slopes?"

Even as I said the words, a prickly sense of dread clawed along my spine. "I'm going."

I moved as quickly as I could. At the gate, I heard someone call my name. It was Mr. Bailey. And it was strange beyond belief to see his portly frame lope across the garden's pathways.

My dragonfly urged me on. She didn't want him catching up.

"Don't worry. I know what to do."

I searched the ground near the door until I spotted it. The rock I used to prop open the door. I grabbed it and held it until we were on the other side. When the gate latched, I wedged the stone into place at the door's base. I tested it again. It barely budged. I hoped it would at least slow him down.

I turned back to my dragonfly. "Where to now?"

She set off, banked a curve, and headed toward the trees.

"We're going back to that place?"

She didn't answer, but she didn't have to. I knew that's where she was taking me. "I hope you know what you're doing," I muttered as I hurried behind her.

When we reached the grove's edge, I nearly lost my nerve. My dragonfly must have sensed it because she darted in front of me, urging me to leave the path for the trees.

Reluctantly I did. Perhaps it was my fear, but the grove seemed different. Was my memory skewed? Was this not the place Mrs. Crossey and I had been before? But that tree wasn't there. That singular tree that had drawn me in.

I trudged deeper searching for something familiar. The temperature dropped and a thin blanket of fog swept across the ground, swallowing my feet and ankles.

That's when I realized we weren't alone.

Something was moving farther on. A shadow that slid among the trees. I knew that shadow. Just as I knew those bloody red eyes.

My dragonfly darted through the trees after the shadow creature, and I followed. When we reached a clearing, she slowed.

"Where did he go?" I lifted my hand, offering a perch.

She ignored the gesture and circled around me instead of answering.

It was hardly necessary, though. I could feel him like a burning ember in the midst of all this cold. He was close.

"Who are you?" I called out to the shadows.

Come to me, and you will see.

It was a voice—his voice—but it didn't come from him. It was part of the forest. It came from the trees and the brambles, from the very air.

"What do you want?" I yelled back.

Come to me.

My dragonfly buzzed the perimeter of the clearing, skirting the darkness. But then she reeled back and flew in a straight line deeper into the grove.

"Wait." But it was too late. She was gone. I didn't want to follow, but I knew I must. I left the clearing and entered the shadows.

A dirt path extended in front of me, but when I took a step, I was falling, endlessly falling, until my foot landed on the ground. Was this a dream? The space I'd occupied a moment before was only inches away, but a wall of liquid light now separated me from that spot.

Instinctively I grabbed for the Faytling around my neck, but it was gone. Shattered and abandoned on the Rubens Room floor.

It wouldn't protect you. A low rumble from the shadows, a figure half hidden behind the trunk of a tree.

I pushed back the fear stealing over me. "What is this place?"

The density of trees, the thick carpet of dead, decaying leaves and twigs, the fog dampening my skirts. It all looked like an ordinary grove, but it was darker. Grayer. Colder.

Despite its strangeness, I knew this place. I had been here before.

Yes, remember. His word trailed off like a whisper in the wind.

Before I could refuse, an image flashed in my mind. A memory. Moonlight pierced the canopy, painting the trees a sharp silver. And he was there, a silhouette beside me. "No!" I grabbed my head, willing the image away. "I've never been here."

Your spirit has come. You remember. It has tried to come home.

Mrs. Crossey had told me he was a trickster, and that's what he was doing now. "No! That's a lie."

They tell you lies. They tell you that you belong to them, but you are mine. You've always been mine.

Mine. The talons of that word dug deep, scratching into a past I had never seen.

The beast's lips stretched into something unmistakably malevolent. *You feel it. You know.*

"I don't." Another flash of recognition hit me. Something vaguely familiar. Like a memory. I was a child.

Do you know me now?

It was coming back. In fragments. "Krol... Your name is Krol."

His burning red eyes glimmered. *You remember.*

"How was I here? I don't understand." Fear swelled within me.

You already know.

"No!" But even as I said it, my panic mellowed into something new. Another kind of knowing. My arms tingled with strange new awareness. I knew him, but how?

You are mine.

His words burned through me again. Not as a threat but a truth. A revelation. I should have been angry or frightened, but I wasn't. Only curious.

"How could I? I belong to no one. I never have."

Laughter like the grinding of rock. *You will remember.*

"Tell me."

He moved in the shadows. I could see more of his form. He wasn't a beast. He was a man. A tall, sinewy man, as tense and watchful as a predator on the prowl. He was watching me as I was watching him.

So very like your mother.

I straightened, my fingers curling into fists. "I never knew my mother, and I don't care to." How many times had I said those words? Every time I wanted them to be true, but they rang false, now more than ever.

And your father?

He was goading me, the bastard.

A father and a daughter. What a wonderful pair, don't you agree? Have you ever considered it?

Something buzzing behind me made me turn. My dragonfly. She flew frantically near my head, darting, circling. "I don't understand." Her message was too confused, too crazed.

I should have known. I could hear the sneer in his voice. But he wasn't speaking to me. He was looking at her.

Try if you must, but you can do nothing in that powerless form.

She flew to my shoulder and perched there.

The move vexed him.

Leave!

That was her message now to me. *Leave while you can.*

But I didn't want to leave. I wanted to know what this man or this creature or whatever he was knew of my parents.

You don't want to know.

I shook off her message, but I turned to her. "Why?"

She only stared at me.

"Tell me."

My sister will never tell you the truth. But I will.

He was moving in the shadows again.

"Then tell me."

Another rumbling laugh. *You already know. You've always known.*

"You're lying." My voice cracked. I did know something, or at least I thought I did.

You belong to me, he repeated, his voice growing more commanding, more vicious. *We can rule together, you and I. You can let me in.*

"I will never help you. I stopped you from taking the Queen."

I meant no harm.

"That's a lie!"

The thought was mine, but the muffled words were not. I turned to find Mrs. Crossey, standing with Marlie and Mr. Wyck at the edge of the grove, behind the liquid wall.

My heart leapt and I wanted to go to her, to embrace her. She was up! She was here!

Stay where you are.

I stared at my dragonfly, not understanding her

hesitation. "But she can help."

If you leave, he still has you.

What did she mean?

Sister, you may have mastered that tiny form, but you will not stop me. I may not be able to claim the Queen, but any host will do, as you well know. Even my daughter.

I spun back. "Your daughter?"

Those red, vengeful eyes held me.

My knees buckled beneath me. Perhaps he answered, I don't know. It didn't matter because I knew the answer. As he'd said before, perhaps I'd always known. The dark parts of my heart. The envy and despair. The detachment. Even the stealing, I was sure. That was him. I was always part of him.

Yes, you feel it now.

My dragonfly lifted from my shoulder and flew at him, her brother, if he was to be believed. She aimed herself like a spear at those hateful eyes, and I rooted for her.

He tried batting her away, but she fell back and attacked again and again.

I knew she couldn't win, but she persisted.

Fight me, sister, but we both know you cannot prevail. Not like this. Remember, it didn't have to be this way, Druansha. You could have given me what was rightfully mine. But you horded this world for yourself.

She circled and dove at him again.

He batted her away, slamming her hard against a tree. *You let them call you Lady of the Fayte, but now you will be Lady of Nothing.*

Had he called my dragonfly the Lady of the Fayte? I whipped around to Mrs. Crossey, the answer to my question plain on my face.

But she couldn't move. None of them could. Their bodies were lost in a tangled wall of tree roots and vines, slithering and wrapping themselves ever more tightly around my friends.

But I didn't need to hear from any of them to know the

truth. My dragonfly was not *my* dragonfly after all. I was not a friend. I was simply a means to an end.

Had it all been a lie?

I closed my eyes and said the word. "Father."

The sound of it filled me. He was my family, all that I had. I truly did belong to him.

When I opened my eyes again, he was in front of me. A towering figure dark as ash and hard as rock.

He extended his hand. *Together, no one can stop us.*

I slipped off my glove and put my hand in his. His touch sent a lightning bolt through my fingers and my limbs. That invisible power held me captive. I was part of him, and he was part of me. This was not a lie. This was blood and bone.

In a riot of sensations, everything flowed into me through that touch: his past, his present, his pain, his heartache, and now this, his victory.

He was telling me the truth. He wanted me beside him. He needed me.

Somewhere in the distance I heard Marlie, Mr. Wyck, and Mrs. Crossey call out. Their voices a cacophony of shrieks and screams that hardly registered.

Krol heard them, too. He stretched his other arm in their direction, and the trees responded to his will like minions, tightening around my friends' throats, making them gasp and choke. He was squeezing away their breath, and they would die if I did nothing. I knew from his touch that was his intent.

"Leave them," I said. "I'll go with you but leave them."

He turned to me, his fiery eyes a question.

I nodded, giving him the assurance he sought.

His hand lowered, and the tree limbs slackened. The gasps subsided. My choice was made.

Then that haunting awareness was there again. His message to me: *We will rule these worlds together.*

"Yes." The word skipped on my lips, so I repeated it with more force. "Yes, I will come with you."

From Krol—from my father—I sensed only… relief? Not joy, but conviction. The certainty that I would do his bidding, that there was no doubt.

I shuffled forward.

Yes, child. Come with me.

Wails again erupted behind me, but they didn't matter. I knew what I had to do.

The Gray Wood is only the beginning of your new world. The world that was stolen from you, as you were stolen from me.

He led me onward, deeper into the forest. Along the shadowy path, past gray gnarled trees and withered bushes. Dead leaves and twigs scattered across the woodland floor. We walked so long, I was sure we should have emerged at the banks of the Thames. But the trees only grew denser, darker.

"That night on the Slopes," I said when I could no longer hold back the question. "The girl who perished. Was that you?"

There was a long pause. I sensed his frustration. Or was it something else?

Your phantom wandered in the Gray Wood that night. I tried to reach you, but you were gone before I could.

My phantom? Had I traveled when I fainted? But what did that have to do with the village girl?

When she appeared, I believed it was you, returning to me. I approached too soon, and the stupid creature made such noise. Such awful cries. She would have ruined our plans. She would have ruined everything.

In his thoughts, I saw him trap her in the tall grasses and drain away her life. I could see her face locked in fear. He wasn't sorry he'd done it, only annoyed that it had to be done.

If he sensed my horror, he didn't show it. His thoughts seemed drawn elsewhere.

It's your power.

Were his words a response to my silent question? I didn't know, but I remained silent to urge him on.

You have remarkable strength, like your mother.

"What happened to her?" The question slipped out before I could stop it.

Choices had to be made. I paid the price, but you... you can change everything.

Perhaps I could. But I had to keep my mind blank. Keep his mind's claws from my thoughts.

I focused on each step as we proceeded in silence until we came to a low hanging branch. He swept it aside, and I could see we'd reached the edge of a meadow. But a meadow unlike any I'd ever seen.

The sky was still wrapped in inky darkness, but each tree, every shrub and flower was imbued with its own glistening, shimmering light. Even the stones and the dirt beneath my feet twinkled with a preternatural glow. Orange, yellow, blue, violet. I saw every color of the rainbow as I gazed across the luminous landscape.

Even my hands and limbs emanated with color.

I have much to show you.

I wanted to see it all. Truly I did. Here, I felt light and limitless. I wanted to explore, but there was something else I wanted more.

"Can you take me to the tree?"

He cocked his head to the side.

Would he feign not to know which one I meant?

How do you know of this tree?

"I've seen it in my dreams."

They were not dreams.

He probed my thoughts, seeking the truth.

I held the image I'd plucked from his own mind.

This stalemate lasted so long I nearly lost my nerve.

Then he nodded. Satisfied. *It is close.*

He led me back toward the woodland and we walked along the border of tall trees until we came to it. Straddling both the Gray Wood and the shimmering meadow, that ancient oak rose to an astonishing height, just as I'd seen it in my vision. When we reached it, I slumped against its trunk. "Allow me to rest a moment."

He watched me, wary. *Why?*

"I'm so tired." I made a show of heaving my breath.

Only for a moment.

I stared at the ground and nodded, as if it was too much to even hold my head upright. The truth was I was searching for something.

Krol circled me and the tree in a beastly manner that unnerved me. When he was far enough away that he couldn't stop me, I dropped to a crevice in the bark and touched the thing I sought with my bare hand.

"*Fosgail*," I said aloud, praying it was an adequate pronunciation of the command I had plucked from the vision.

It must have been because the bark beneath my fingers slithered apart and the slim crevice widened to a gaping hole. I saw the blur of him rush toward me, but it didn't matter.

My fingers wrapped around the smooth cold stone before he could reach me. I grabbed it, and its violet light burst through the space between my fingers like rigid shards of glass. I opened my fingers and let it tumble from my grip.

In an instant, my dragonfly flew into its light and it pulsed with vibrant purple hues. Their lights merged and swirled together, and they wound themselves into a shining column that rose to the clouds above.

In a moment, when the light receded, a woman stood before me. She towered over me as she had towered over Queen Boudica, and her silver-white hair flowed behind her, cascading over a lavender gown girded by a silver cord. Pointed ears protruded from that wild mane, and at her neck sat the egg-sized gem, now wrapped in a golden lattice as delicate as a spider' s web.

This was the Lady of the Fayte.

I dropped to one knee and bowed my head.

She approached and touched my hair.

Rise, Jane.

Like my father's voice, hers came to me as a thought not a sound.

You have released me from my brother's curse.

At the mention of him, I looked past her. There was nothing where he had been.

He is gone. For now.

A tug of sadness pulled at my chest.

He is too weak to face me now. But it doesn't matter. I am free, and I can again pass freely between our worlds.

It took all of my courage to look up into her lavender eyes and ask: "You were my dragonfly?"

The sweetest, softest smile curled her flower petal lips. *I was.*

"But why?"

So many reasons.

I shook my head. I was trying to understand, but the world was closing in around me.

You are tired. It's time for you to rest.

The words were soothing, and I *was* tired. So tired.

A darkness gathered at the periphery. I fought against it, until I no longer could.

CHAPTER THIRTY-TWO

MUFFLED SOUNDS. WORDS? Whatever they were I wished them away. I only wanted to return to the comfort of oblivion.

"She's twitching. I think she's waking up."

"Shhh!"

The voices were clearer now. Familiar.

"There! Did you see her eyelids? She's definitely waking up."

"Move away, Marlie. You're crowding her."

It was Mrs. Crossey, but the concern I heard in her voice jolted me further into awareness.

"I'm all right," I said. Or at least I tried to. What tumbled over my lips sounded more like gurgles and grunts. Did they even hear me?

"Off with you now," Mrs. Crossey said, I assumed to Marlie. "There's work to be done in the kitchen. Go see to it."

"But the white willow bark tea. It will ease the pain."

"Give it here, then close the door behind you. That's a good girl."

I heard another balk from my roommate, but then a

door closed.

Two hands enfolded themselves around one of mine, which lay, I now realized, at my side. I tensed, but the hands were muffled in mittens. Even now she was protecting me.

"It's all right, dear," she whispered. "You're safe. The doctor says you'll be just fine. Don't strain yourself."

Her words poured over me like sun-warmed honey, and I soaked them in. *I was safe.*

But from what? I tried to remember.

Flashes returned to me. The shimmering, otherworldly grove. Those beastly eyes.

My father.

An icy shiver raced up my spine.

"It's all right, dear." Her wool-covered hand patted mine. "Everything will be fine."

I yearned for it to be true. I wanted to forget about the Fayte and the Lady and Krol. I wanted to turn back the clock, before the summons to Mr. MacDougall's office, before everything fell apart. When it was just me and my dragonfly.

I breathed the word aloud. "Dragonfly."

Another pat from Mrs. Crossey's bundled hand. "Oh, yes. That." Her words floated on a wave of amused wonder. "How you kept that secret, I'll never know. But my, what a secret."

My secret friend.

Another flash from the Gray Wood. But my dragonfly was much more than that. The Lady of the Fayte. Krol was my family, but she was, too. My thoughts swirled with this unsettling new notion. "Where...?"

"Where is she?" Mrs. Crossey finished my thought. "I don't know. Back to the Brightlands, I suspect."

The Brightlands. So that place had a name. Of course she would return there. It was her home. Where the leaves had shimmered, and tree branches glowed. Where the air smelled of new blooms and crackled with life. Where she'd shed her insect form and become the Lady once more.

It was all coming back. I opened my eyes.

"She saved me." My voice was stronger now. My memories were, too.

"Yes. She saved us all, but I think you saved her as well. Here, sip this."

The edge of a teacup pressed against my lower lip followed by a steady drip of something warm and soothing. I breathed in the spicy fragrance of cinnamon and clove. When I'd taken enough, Mrs. Crossey pulled the cup away.

"Now, you need to sleep. We'll talk in the morning."

But I didn't want to sleep. I had too many questions. How was I here? What had happened to the Queen? What had happened to Mr. Bailey and Mr. MacDougall?

And Mr. Wyck.

My chest tightened at the memory of him standing beyond the boundary with Mrs. Crossey and Marlie, and of him subduing Mr. Bailey. He had been on our side after all. I should have believed him. I should have known.

It was my last thought before slipping back into oblivion.

~ ~ ~

Another day, maybe two, passed in the hazy space between slumber and wakefulness. Meals were delivered on trays and left on the bedside table. Mrs. Crossey or Marlie sat at my bedside and talked as I sipped at broth and nibbled buttered biscuits, which was all I could manage because I had no appetite. Not even Dr. Holland, who stopped in several times a day, seemed to know why.

At no time was there a mention of what ailed me, and my questions about what had happened were outright ignored.

By the third day, I was too restless to remain in bed, so I rose and was happy to discover my limbs were up to the task. As a precaution, I moved slowly and kept hold of the side table.

The room shifted and tilted at first, but it steadied soon enough. I counted it a victory when I released the table, lifted my chin, and squared my shoulders. Up and out of bed for the first time in days. A victory, indeed.

The longer I stood, the stronger I felt.

I made my way to the vanity table and lowered myself onto the tufted velvet cushion in front of it. I hardly recognized the reflection in the mirror. Tendrils had worked themselves out of the long braid that fell down my back and curled into frizzy coils at my cheeks and forehead. My face was so pale it might actually be gray, and there were shadows beneath my eyes and the hollows in my cheek that hadn't been there before. I looked like someone had wrung me like a wet dish towel, and I felt as limp as one, too.

That had to change.

I pulled my braid forward and untied the ribbon keeping it in place. I loosened the curls with my fingers then went to work with a silver hairbrush that sat beside the mirror. I hoped its owner wouldn't mind.

A knock at the door stopped me.

It was too early for Mrs. Crossey or Marlie, so it must be Dr. Holland. "Yes. Come in."

The door opened and when I turned to greet the good doctor, I was stunned into silence at the sight of the wide and dark wool skirt of a diminutive woman. I scrambled to my feet and lowered into a clumsy curtsy. "Your Majesty."

My mind raced with reasons why she might enter this room. Was my stay unauthorized? Was I trespassing? I chided myself for getting so comfortable in a place where I certainly didn't belong.

"I'm so sorry," I added hastily.

She guided the door closed and waited for it to latch before saying, "What on earth do you have to be sorry about, child?"

For being here, for not being in the kitchen, for the calamity in the Rubens Room. A thousand answers tumbled through my mind, but nothing passed my lips.

She moved to the window and pulled back the curtains, then muscled the lever that pivoted the glass so the afternoon breeze flowed in. "That's better. You cannot recover in stale air."

A chill filled the room. I pulled the sleeves of my sleeping chemise down to my wrists and peeked up between my brows to see she was standing at the end of the bed, taking stock of the food tray on the table and the pillows pushed haphazardly around the bed. She frowned. "Are they keeping you fed and comfortable?"

"Yes, ma'am." My head still tilted downward but I tried to gauge her expression.

"And Dr. Holland? Has he kept an eye on you?"

Again I nodded and replied yes.

"Is there anything else you require?"

The way her fingers laced and unlaced at her waist, I was quite sure she was as uncomfortable as I.

"No, ma'am. I'm quite well."

"Good," she said. "Then I was rather hoping you could answer a few questions for me. I'm having some difficulty understanding certain events."

Her gaze probed mine.

I held my blankest look. If no one else had told her the truth, I surely shouldn't be the one. Who was I, after all?

But all the lies and secrecy had put her in danger. They had put all of us in danger. Something had to be said. "What do you wish to know, Your Majesty?"

For the next half hour, I told her what I knew of the Fayte Guardians who protected her from the shadows and the monster who had come after her—leaving out the fact he had called himself my father. I half expected her to dismiss my words as the ravings of a fevered mind.

She didn't.

She merely settled herself on the edge of the bed,

folded her hands gently in her lap, and took in every word.

It was cathartic, in a way, to share these burdens, even if it didn't lighten them.

When I finished, the Queen rose and moved to the window again. She stared out over the eastern view, the early afternoon sun making a halo over the smooth sweep of her sandy-brown hair, ornamented with a simple square of lace pinned above her chignon.

I shifted on the stool as the silence between us lengthened. "Perhaps I said more than I should have," I muttered, wishing I had been more judicious in my telling.

"No." She turned back, and the light from the window silhouetted her features. "I appreciate your candor, however much it may strain one's understanding. And rest assured, the Prince and I will be discussing this efficiency campaign of his."

A sound at the door stopped her. When the physician opened it and saw her, he stepped back.

"Pardon me, Your Majesty. I shall come back."

"No, Doctor. Your timing is fine. I was just leaving." She turned to me. "I am pleased to know you are recovering well. If there is anything you require, do let it be known, and it shall be provided."

"Thank you," I muttered. I rose and curtsied again.

The doctor watched the Queen until she disappeared through the door that he held for her. He closed it, and his weighty gaze returned to me. "So, Miss Shackle, how are you feeling?"

The Queen had come to see me. Me! I was at once elated and panicked. "Honestly, I'm not sure."

The man smoothed the few strands of hair he had left at the freckled top of his head and scrutinized me for a long moment. "I see you're out of bed."

I stared at the vanity table. Recounting what I knew to the Queen was like reliving the ordeal all over again, but there was still so much I didn't know.

"If you would, Doctor, would you tell me what's wrong

with me? Why am I here?"

He fished around in his satchel and pulled on the pair of black leather gloves he'd taken to wearing during his visits. I'd never said anything to him, so I could only imagine what he'd been told. "Just a precaution after your swoon," he said. "Nothing more. Are you in any pain?"

Not that I could pinpoint. Just the same familiar ache where my heart should be. "No, I feel fine."

He bent over me and took a long look into my eyes. Asked me to follow his finger. Asked me to lift my arms, bend my elbow, extend each leg and bend it. Then he held his chin and sucked in his lips. "I would say I'm looking at a perfectly healthy young woman."

Healthy? Maybe. But perfect? Not even close.

CHAPTER THIRTY-THREE

THE NEXT MORNING, I arrived early to our familiar corner of the kitchen, hoping to avoid any commotion or questions about my absence. Mrs. Crossey was already at the stove, stirring a batch of what smelled like porridge.

A line of freshly baked loaves lined the worktable. I took up a knife and went to work slicing them for the Servants' Hall breakfast table.

"Welcome back," she said when she noticed me behind her. "You're in quite fine order this morning."

"I tidied up before I left the room. Stripped the bed and left the linens for the chamber maid. I can collect them, though, if you think I should. I didn't know what was appropriate."

"Calm yourself, dear. It's all right. You needed the rest. Everyone agreed."

Who agreed? I wanted to know but the morning cooks and kitchen maids were drifting in now, so I focused on the loaves and then, when they were done, moved on to a mound of potatoes that needed peeling for the servants' evening stew.

When I reached the bottom of the pile and set the pot

259

of water and potatoes on the stove for Mrs. Crossey, she frowned at me. "Perhaps this is a bit too much too soon. Why don't you take a break?"

"I feel fine." The truth was, I didn't feel fine. Not at all. I was going through the motions, but nothing felt right. It was as if I were moving underwater. Sounds were muted. My thinking was muddled. "Maybe a bit of fresh air would feel good."

"Of course it would. Take as long as you need."

I removed my apron and hung it from a handle on the worktable before making my way out to the terrace.

The outside air was crisp, and the sun was beginning to break through the gray blanket of clouds. I settled on the bench and looked out over the field and wished for my dragonfly.

I missed her.

I knew she was so much more than my dragonfly now, and I knew I should be happy that she'd been freed from her curse. She was back where she belonged.

But would I ever see her again?

At the creak of the door, I wiped away the tears that had invaded my eyes and tried to breathe.

"Mrs. Crossey said I might find you here."

It was Marlie.

"Yes, I'm here." I coughed away what was left of that stray emotion.

"It's good to see you up and about. It's been lonely in the room without you, though I'm sure it'll seem quite humdrum to you now that you're accustomed to such luxurious accommodations."

"Honestly, I'll be happy to be back in my own bed."

It was true. I'd even missed Marlie's company, and no one was more surprised by that fact than I.

"Is something wrong?" She looked at me like I was keeping a secret, and perhaps I was.

A month ago, I wouldn't have considered asking her the question that was nagging at me. A month ago, I never would have breathed a word about anything to anyone but my dragonfly, and on this topic I probably wouldn't have breathed a word even to her.

But there was a smile and an understanding in Marlie's eyes that somehow made it all right. And she knew so many of my secrets now. Nearly as many as Mrs. Crossey. Still I couldn't quite meet her gaze when I asked, "Have you seen Mr. Wyck?"

The look that came over her told me she knew it was not the casual question I was pretending it to be.

"He's made himself quite scarce. Even Abigail hasn't seen him since... and, well, you know she tends to follow his whereabouts quite closely."

Actually, I didn't know that. And now that I did, I regretted saying anything about him.

"You should probably try the mews, though, if you need to speak with him. *Do* you need to speak with him?"

She eyed me with that funny look of hers.

"No," I said quickly. "I was only thinking I hadn't seen him since... I wanted to thank him is all. He was a great help. To all of us."

She sucked her lips against her teeth, trying to hold back a grin. "Just thank him? Are you sure that was it?"

"What are you implying?"

She shrugged without conviction. "I'm not implying anything."

"I should get back." I stood and brushed imaginary dust from my skirt. "Mrs. Crossey will be wondering where I am."

Marlie scoffed. "That's one way to change the subject."

I ignored her and grabbed the door handle. "It doesn't matter, I suppose. I don't think we'll be seeing much of Mr. Wyck anymore anyway."

"Who knows what the future will bring?"

The friendly glimmer in her eyes eased my consternation. "You're right. Thank you."

"It's what friends do," she said.

Friends, indeed. Perhaps for the first time I truly believed it.

I went back to my table to find a bowl of white onions waiting, and I got to work.

The afternoon passed in the blur of dinner preparations. Then later, as I wiped the table, cleaning away the accumulated residue of another day, Mrs. Crossey pulled up close.

In a whisper, she said, "Meet me in Fayte Hall at our usual time, if you would."

I looked up, not without disappointment. It had been such a long day, and I was eager to slip into my own bed. Our mission was done, after all. The threat was gone. Couldn't training take a night off? "I'm not sure what use I'll be to you or anyone. It's all I can do to stay on my feet."

The regret on her face looked sincere. Still she shook her head. "It's necessary. I can't say more, but I'll explain tonight. I promise."

A promise? From Mrs. Crossey's own lips. Well, that was something.

~ ~ ~

I slept soundly that night, so soundly I nearly slept through my meeting with Mrs. Crossey. Marlie jostled me awake.

"C'mon, sleepyhead. We have to get you-know-where."

"You're coming, too?" I asked, half-awake.

She answered by handing me my coat and putting her own around her shoulders before ushering me out the door.

When we neared Fayte Hall door, I could hear voices within. A lot of voices.

Marlie pulled it open, revealing robed figures everywhere. Twenty? Thirty? I tried to tally them all, but there were too many.

Marlie removed her coat, grabbed a robe, and pulled it around herself. "Have you guessed why we're here yet?"

I shook my head dumbly.

"C'mon." She urged me toward the divining pool.

"Wait."

We both turned. It was Abigail.

I froze.

"She's going to need this." Abigail took a robe from a hook and handed it to me.

I looked at Marlie.

She nodded as if she knew my thoughts. *Yes, she's a Fayte Guardian, too.*

I took the robe and tried to meet her gaze but only managed to stare at her hand. "Thank you."

"You're welcome."

I expected sarcasm, but there was none. And no bitterness. She turned and strode away.

I hurried to catch up with Marlie.

"Why didn't you tell me about her?"

"I couldn't. I couldn't tell her about you, either."

I glanced around. How many other faces did I know?

Mrs. Crossey stood behind the pool in her purple robe. Beside her was a towering lanky man with his hood pulled low, but I knew him instantly. Rage burned inside me. "Why is Mr. MacDougall here?"

"I know what you must think," she said quickly. "But he was deceived along with the rest of us, perhaps even more so. There was a gathering while you were away, and it was decided he should become High Councilor, the position Mr. Bailey abandoned. People make mistakes, and they should be allowed the opportunity to atone for them."

I could hardly believe it, but who was I to question? "So Mr. Bailey is gone? What happened to him?" The last I'd seen of that man, he'd been chasing me down to the castle wall. "Was he forgiven, too?"

Her expression clouded. "He fled that day. No one has

seen him since, and it's probably just as well. What he did—what he meant to do—could never be forgiven."

I took solace in that, but instead of saying so, I occupied myself by searching for other familiar faces. I recognized Pierre, the night cook, along with a few maids and footmen. And standing at the very edge of the temple room—watching me intently—was Mr. Wyck.

I nearly stumbled over my own feet.

"Ah, there you are," Mrs. Crossey called over the pool. "Our guest of honor."

"I told you I'd get her here on time," Marlie said.

I leaned closer to Marlie. "Did she say, 'guest of honor'?"

"Yes, Jane, that's exactly what I said."

My cheeks burned.

"Come closer. Let me tell you why you're here."

I looked again at Mr. Wyck, but he'd moved. I searched the room, but all the hoods were now pulled low.

I gave up and moved to the pool.

Mrs. Crossey clapped her hands loudly three times and the dozen or so people milling about straightened and, in near unison, formed a wide circle around the pool. Others quickly joined, filling in the empty spaces.

Marlie left my side and took a place in the circle as well.

"Come here, Jane," Mrs. Crossey said.

It was like being summoned to Mr. MacDougall's office, only tenfold. My palms moistened beneath my gloves.

I moved beside her. "What is this?" I tried to steady my voice, but I could hear it quaver. I was sure others could as well.

"Haven't you guessed?" Mrs. Crossey said. Her sly smile confused me.

"Should I have?" I glanced at Marlie. Her eyes were obscured by her hood like the rest, but I could see her nibbling her bottom lip. She knew.

"This is your initiation," Mrs. Crossey said.

I could say nothing, only stare dumbly at my mentor.

"With your eighteenth birthday nearly upon us, I believe it's time you had this." She raised a Faytling in her hand. Was it the one I had thrown at the calliope? No, I could see that one—somehow repaired or duplicated—hanging from her neck.

The one in her hand was a golden cylinder like her own, but its metal braided and swirled differently around the rose-colored crystal it encased.

Mrs. Crossey lifted the talisman over her head and spoke words I didn't understand, intoning them like prayer.

Suddenly, a lavender mist rose from the pool and cascaded over the side to the floor. Mrs. Crossey dipped the Faytling into the mist then lifted it again above her head.

"Through the pure wellspring's touch, may the Lady grace the stone with guidance and wisdom, and allow it to protect our new Fayte sister in her..." A shimmer at her left stopped her and from that shimmer a form resolved. It was the Lady of the Fayte herself. Her long, white hair and the edges of her diaphanous gown floated weightlessly like smoky tendrils.

Every Fayte Guardian dropped to one knee and bent their heads, including Mrs. Crossey.

I did the same.

I heard no movement, but I soon saw the swaying hem of her luminous gown in front of me.

"Stand, Jane Shackle." Her voice brushed over me like a feather.

I glanced up and a corner of her rose petal lips quirked. "Do not be shy. You know me, remember?"

The image of my dragonfly flashed through my mind. That steadfast, though sometimes exasperating friend who accompanied me on walks. The one who cheered me and consoled me and even chastised me at times.

My cheeks and neck burned with shame as I thought

back to how I'd treated her. "I don't know what to say, but I should probably start by apologizing... I had no idea—"

She raised her pale white palm. "There is no need for that. I kept this secret from you. But tell me, have you missed me?"

There was that familiar twinkle of amused mischief.

"Of course. You were my friend."

She dipped her chin. "I am still your friend."

I grinned despite myself.

She straightened to her full height. "Rise, Jane Shackle, and let us look to the future now."

I looked at the slender white hand she extended to me.

With her nod of approval, I slid my fingers over hers. They felt like silk. Her fingers wrapped around mine, and there was surprising strength in them. Beyond that, I felt nothing but peace. No vision, no tugging, no swirling.

Simple peace.

"Now," she said. "Take your place among the Fayte, where you belong."

Her words resonated within me. *Where you belong.* I looked around. I had never belonged anywhere. But now, in this unlikely place, I finally felt like I was home.

"I don't know what to say." It was the truth.

"There is no need to say anything." She held my Faytling between both of her hands and a burst of violet light emanated between her fingers. She closed her eyes and her forehead creased in concentration. When her brow smoothed again, she opened her hands, revealing the Faytling resting there. The purple glow was gone, but the gold seemed to shine even more brightly.

"Rise, everyone," the Lady said.

All around us, the Fayte Guardians stood.

The Lady turned to Mrs. Crossey and placed her hand on the woman's shoulder. "I owe you my gratitude as well, Master Scryer. You believed in me when you had no reason to believe. You believed in our purpose, even when it put your life at risk. I commend you, and I am grateful to you, Supreme Elder of the Windsor Fayte."

Behind her Mr. MacDougall cleared his throat.

Mrs. Crossey seemed to blush and in a timid voice, said, "Thank you, my lady, but I am not the Supreme Elder here."

The Lady turned to Mr. MacDougall and gave him a withering look before turning back to Mrs. Crossey. "Yes, Sylvia Crossey of the Windsor Fayte, you have earned the title and my admiration." She turned then to gaze on each robed figure. "And I am grateful to all of you who have remained steady and true in your service as Fayte Guardians. My brother is no longer a threat to this world. And while I must leave for a time, I will return soon and often. You may again rely on me."

She reached out to me then and touched my forehead. A tingling sensation passed through me, from that spot down to the tips of my toes. I felt lighter, happier.

I looked at her in surprise. "What was that?"

"A parting gift."

My chest tightened. I didn't want to say it, I didn't want to have to, but I did. "Goodbye, my lady." The words cracked in my throat.

She tilted her head to me as streaks of violet light wrapped around her. "Not goodbye, dear one. We shall see each other soon enough."

I thought I could see that look of amused mischief again as she faded into the violet light.

CHAPTER THIRTY-FOUR

AFTER THE CEREMONY, the Fayte Guardians made their way back to the castle. I hung back, lingering at the edge of the crystal pool, trying to absorb all that had happened and marveling at my new Faytling—my *own* Faytling. I suppose I was one of them now. Truly one of them.

"I thought you'd be off to bed by now."

It was Mrs. Crossey, returning from the Library, where the last stragglers were saying their goodbyes.

"I suppose I should. It's just so much to take in."

"I suppose it is. I'm glad you're here, however." She clutched her fingers and stared into the misty pool, still imbued with the Lady's lavender glow. "Since you have fulfilled your part of our bargain, it's time for me to fulfill mine. That is, if you still wish to learn about your parents."

That promise seemed so long ago. Before the Gray Wood. Before Krol...

"I've inquired with the Elders at Balmoral," she continued. "They safeguard the old records, and a visit may render more useful information."

"A visit?"

One of her thin eyebrows notched higher. "I have

spoken to a cook there, a Fayte. She's in need of a temporary assistant, and I've recommended you."

"Me?"

"It might help you in your search. That is what you want, isn't it?"

But it wasn't. Not now. What would I do without Mrs. Crossey or Marlie? I belonged here. I didn't want to leave.

"Aren't you pleased?" The crease between her eyebrows deepened.

"I've never traveled so far," I said.

She flipped her wrist as if to bat away such a frivolous concern. "It won't be so difficult, and you won't be alone."

"You would come with me?"

"No, not me. Our Balmoral visitor plans to return home tomorrow."

"Mr. Wyck?"

A sheepishness came over her. "Yes, Mr. Wyck, if that's what we're still calling him. I always knew something was off with that young man, but I rather thought he was here to spy on me, not you. Well, hindsight makes fools of us all." A mischievous glint flashed in her eye. "You don't object to the companion, do you?"

Was she serious? "I can't travel with a man."

She rolled her eyes. "Such silly notions. But yes, I suppose you're right. Perhaps if…"

My heart leapt. "If what?"

She walked to the door. "I'll think of something. Just be at the kitchen gate at the first bell."

"Six in the morning?" Even I could hear the irritating whine in my voice.

She faced me again. "I remember a time not so long ago when you packed your things on much shorter notice."

I opened my mouth to argue but snapped it closed again. She was right, and she knew it. And I knew I had to go. Not because I wanted to—I didn't. But there were questions that needed answers, now more than ever.

About Krol. About my mother. How many secrets were hiding in my past?

That Mr. Wyck would be my companion on this journey, well, maybe that wouldn't be the worst thing that could happen.

~ ~ ~

Early the next morning I slipped out of my room with every one of my belongings stuffed into my carpet bag save one.

The golden locket I'd stolen from Abigail I held tightly in my gloved hand as I made my way to her door. I meant to hang it from the knob, knowing she would find it and surmise the link between its reappearance and my departure.

But I couldn't bring myself to do it. That wasn't who I was anymore, at least it wasn't who I wanted to be. I tapped on the wood.

After some rustling, a sleepy Abigail cracked open the door. "Jane, for Pete's sake. It's so early."

I held up the locket, its chain draped over a finger. "I want to return this. You were right, Abigail. I took it, and I'm sorry."

She stared at it for a moment before taking it. "I don't know what to say."

"You don't need to say anything. You were right to accuse me. I was…" Stupid? Jealous? I was both of those things, but instead I said, "I regret it. Perhaps one day you'll forgive me."

I left then. It might have been the wind outside or my own wishful thinking, but I thought I caught the soft whisper of "I forgive you" just before I turned the corner.

That hope carried me through the corridors and past the kitchen. Having little practice with goodbyes, I decided it was better to avoid Mrs. Crossey, and Marlie, too, for that matter. It wasn't truly goodbye, after all. Mrs. Crossey had said I could return when I wanted. I just needed to say the word.

I made my way with my carpet bag to the bench outside the kitchen gate and watched the early sun warm the fog rolling off the Thames and clinging to the Slopes and the castle wall.

Even now, after everything, the place still reminded me of my dragonfly.

My dragonfly who was the Lady of the Fayte.

I was almost ashamed to admit that it comforted me to remember her as she'd been. That brazen insect. That charming friend.

The kitchen door creaked a warning that I was no longer alone. I braced and hoped the interloper would hurry and leave me in peace.

"We're to be traveling companions, then?"

It was Mr. Wyck. He tugged on the wrists of a stiff tweed jacket that would have looked right at home on High Street.

I watched his eyes scan the horizon and tried to discern whether he found the prospect agreeable. Or not. "Yes, Mr. Wyck," I said cautiously. "That is my understanding."

He plunged his fists into his front pockets and rocked on his toes. "So, it's still to be Mr. Wyck, then?"

"Yes, I believe so." I gnawed my lower lip. Had I misinterpreted those tender moments between us? Did he even remember them?

"Well, look at you two!"

The burst of Marlie's voice snapped me back from my thoughts.

She dropped a bag beside mine. "It's going to be quite a trip. Are you ready for it?"

"I'm not sure. Are you going somewhere, too?"

"I'm going with you! I told Mrs. Crossey not to tell you. I wanted it to be a surprise. Are you surprised?"

I could only nod. It was a shock, but not unwelcome. Having her with me would make leaving easier, but still not easy.

For the first time, I belonged somewhere, yet I had to go. I knew that. I had to know why there were years—and a family—I couldn't remember and why I had talents I didn't understand.

At least this time, it would be my choice to be an outsider.

"You won't be an outsider," Mr. Wyck said plainly, still looking off into the distance.

His words jolted me. "What did you say?"

"You won't be an outsider. That's what you were thinking, wasn't it?"

"But how did you know?"

He shrugged.

"Have you always...?" The possibility sent my mind reeling but I couldn't focus on that now. The carriage was approaching.

"C'mon." Marlie grabbed her bag and ran off to meet it.

I took up my own bag and looked back at the castle. I would be back. I could feel it deep in my bones. And when I did, I hoped I would have some answers.

I hurried to catch up with Mr. Wyck and Marlie.

And I wasn't the only one. Lagging behind, just out of view, a twinkle of light followed, a fluttering spark in the distinct shape of a dragonfly.

The End

If you'd like to continue Jane's magical journey, the story continues in *Slivering Curse: The Queen's Fayte Book Two*. Learn more at www.DDCroix.com/Slivering-Curse.

DEAR READER

Thank you for taking time to read *Dragonfly Maid: The Queen's Fayte Book One*. If you enjoyed the book, please consider leaving a review at Amazon or Goodreads.com. Good reviews and positive word of mouth are immensely helpful and always deeply appreciated.

FREE BOOK

To get a free copy of *Memory Thief*, a prequel story set in days before Jane lands at Windsor Castle, and to be notified by email of new releases, join the Readers Brigade at www.DDCroix.com/Readers-Brigade.

ABOUT THE AUTHOR

D.D. Croix is an award-winning author who writes delightfully dark fantasy with hopeful and bright ever afters. Under another name, she also writes award-winning romance and historical novels. When she isn't plotting new adventures for her characters, she oversees Orange County Writers, a network of published and aspiring authors based in Southern California.

If you'd like to be notified of new releases and have access to exclusive content, giveaways, and other fun stuff, please join the Readers Brigade: www.DDCroix.com/Readers-Brigade.

If you'd like to send her a message, please contact her at dd@ddcroix.com.

To connect on social media, you can find her at the following:

Facebook: www.facebook.com/DDCroix
Twitter: www.twitter.com/DDCroixWrites
Instagram: www.instagram.com/DDCroixWrites
Pinterest: www.pinterest.com/DDCroixWrites
Goodreads: www.goodreads.com/user/show/77702468-d-d-croix

ACKNOWLEDGMENTS

These characters and this story have been living with me for a long time, and I'm thrilled to bits to finally let them loose in the world. So many times Jane and her friends had to take a back seat to Other Things, and more than once they were put off for Someday But Not Now.

Although I almost gave up on them, their voices stayed with me, and their antics grew into scenes that eventually grew into this novel (with at least two more to follow!). I'm so thankful they never gave up on me, and the fact that you're reading these words now is a testament to their grit and tenacity.

So, see, Mom? Hearing voices can have its perks. And speaking of Mom, I must thank her as well, because I can always count on her support and encouragement, and it means the world to me. The same can be said for my Other Mom, too, as well as my Dad and Other Dad. Yes, less might be more in some things, but not when it comes to parental love. More is always better, and I'm lucky enough to enjoy it in abundance.

I'd also like to thank some special people who have helped in a number of ways. Greta Boris and Megan Haskell ran O.C. Writers, our local writing organization, while I was doing Other Things. They not only kept it going but made it better while I was away. My critique group colleagues at O.C. Fictionaires read a portion of an early draft and their encouragement and feedback was invaluable. I'm also deeply grateful to Shannon Cramer for her enthusiasm for early chapters and her eagle eye on the final draft.

Katrina Roets' editorial prowess made the manuscript better, and Karri Klawiter's artistic talent is responsible for the gorgeous book cover. Both are true professionals, and I was fortunate to have worked with them.

Finally, the people who deserve my deepest thanks and gratitude are my two favorite people in the world: my wonderful husband and daughter. They are tolerant beyond measure about the piles of research and writing notebooks that accumulate in any room I inhabit, the dinners that are late when I get lost in a story, and the ridiculous amount of time I spend tapping away on my laptop computer. In case you haven't figured it out yet, writers aren't like normal people, and I'm blessed that my family loves me anyway.

Printed in Great Britain
by Amazon

15042639R00164